CW01082110

The Bird and the Buddha –

A 'Before Watson' Novel - Book Two

By A. S. Croyle

Further Reminiscences of P.S.T.

(Based upon my own recollections, notes, newspaper

clippings

and correspondence received from Sherlock Holmes)

© Copyright 2016

A.S. Croyle

The right of A.S. Croyle to be identified as the author of this work has been asserted by her in accordance with the Copyright, Designs and Patents Act 1998.

All rights reserved. No reproduction, copy or transmission of this publication may be made without express prior written permission. No paragraph of this publication may be reproduced, copied or transmitted except with express prior written permission or in accordance with the provisions of the Copyright Act 1956 (as amended). Any person who commits any unauthorised act in relation to this publication may be liable to criminal prosecution and civil claims for damage.

All characters appearing in this work are fictitious or used fictitiously. Except for certain historical personages, any resemblance to real persons, living or dead, is purely coincidental. The opinions expressed herein are those of the authors and not of MX Publishing.

Paperback ISBN 9781780929361
ePub ISBN 978-1-78092-937-8
PDF ISBN 978-1-78092-938-5

Published in the UK by MX Publishing
335 Princess Park Manor, Royal Drive,
London, N11 3GX
www.mxpublishing.co.uk
Cover design by www.staunch.com

For Ruth

Reviews

Thomas A. Turley, author of "Sherlock Holmes and the Adventure of the Tainted Canister" - A.S. Croyle returns with her second "Before Watson" story, based on the memoirs of Poppy Stamford, Sherlock Holmes' first love. Four years after their adventures in Ms. Croyle's wonderful first novel (*When the Song of the Angels is Stilled*), Poppy and Sherlock reunite to investigate a series of ritualistic murders outside the British Museum. Like its predecessor, The Bird and the Buddha is set against the background of an actual Victorian disaster: the sinking of the Princess Alice in the Thames with seven hundred souls aboard. Populating the story are well-drawn secondary characters: some real (Oscar Wilde); some Canonical (Mycroft and Lestrade); and some original, like Poppy's uncle, Dr. Ormond Sacker, who wrestles with an ethical dilemma central to the case. Croyle demonstrates her mastery of the period's historical detail; and various intriguing elements, such as the Four Noble Truths of Buddhism, are woven skillfully into the plot. Meanwhile, Poppy and Sherlock struggle to redefine their own relationship, after his disavowal of her love for the sake of his vocation. A progressive new physician, seeking acceptance in Victorian Britain's unwelcoming milieu, Poppy must also face the frustrations of loving a young man who wants to turn himself into a reasoning machine. Even cast adrift emotionally, she remains the most appealing heroine since Irene Adler. While their romantic future remains uncertain at the novel's end, the good news is that Ms. Croyle has more cases for Poppy and Sherlock in the works.

Book One – When the Song of the Angels is Stilled:

Kirkus - This fast-paced tale will appeal to those who like to ponder what made Sherlock Holmes the great detective he was. An engaging addition to Sherlock Holmes legendry.

Foreword - Five-Star Review - For anyone in love with Sherlock Holmes, this story must be savored, not merely read.

Chris Redmond (Author of 'Lives Beyond Baker Street)

One involves the "angels" referred to in the title — infants being done to death by baby-farmers, a real enough social evil in mid-Victorian times. Holmes, Poppy and other characters in the novel are drawn into a crusade against this form of murder at the behest of (naturally) Mycroft Holmes, who has no scruples about risking others' lives to do what the government needs done. Holmes makes some deductions, Poppy takes the lead in a sting operation, and arrests are made, though the plague as a whole is not yet ended.

Second, Sherlock Holmes witnesses and investigates not one but two train crashes — again, a common enough phenomenon in that era. It is a trifle odd to see Holmes using his powers as a transportation safety investigator rather than a detective, but Croyle plausibly portrays the young man not yet sure what career will enable him to make use of his intellectual powers, so the experiment is interesting and satisfying.

And third, the novel retells the events of "The 'Gloria Scott'," which have always been considered a little odd anyway. Holmes on his way to chapel? Holmes with a friend, Victor Trevor? In Croyle's version of things, Poppy is on a path toward marriage with Victor when her (not his) dog bites Holmes's ankle and an acquaintance naturally begins. Then the arrival of Hudson and the terror and eventual death of "old" Trevor, the Justice of the Peace, unfold as Poppy watches and Holmes tries to understand. To a Sherlockian these are of course the most relevant pages of the book.

Croyle writes interestingly and articulately, and her picture of Victorian society is convincing with only a few exceptions. The title page indicates that When the Song of the Angels Is Stilled (the title, incidentally, is taken from a contemporary Epiphany hymn) is "A 'Before Watson' Novel, Book One." So there will be more, and that is good news.

Acknowledgements

Once again, I must take off my hat to Sir Arthur Conan Doyle for creating one of the most enduring characters in literature – Sherlock Holmes.

Deepest gratitude to Steve Emecz and everyone at MX Publishing for this opportunity. I appreciate the encouragement of fellow MX authors and would especially like to note David Marcum for giving me more insight into how many Sherlockians feel about chronologies, other pastiches, and The Great Holmes Tapestry. I think we can agree to disagree on some of the fine points but share love and admiration for the Great Detective.

Thanks also to Pam Turner for her publicity expertise, and to my first readers – Nancy Schmock, Tim James, Scott Britton, Susan Wenz, Cindie Green, Thomas Turley, and Phillip Turner, who kindly edited portions of and made invaluable suggestions for this novel (see his blog The Great Gray Bridge) . . . I am deeply grateful to Debbie Clark, a fellow Sherlockian, and Rae Griffin, my BFF, whose careful proofreading, suggestions and comments were immensely helpful in polishing the novel.

Very special thanks to my friend, mentor, advisor and editor, Ruth E. Friend, who spent so many hours proofreading, editing and making suggestions for improvements, and without whom not a single word would have made it to the page.

Last but not least, hugs to Michael, also a First Reader and the love of my life, who is patient and understanding, who puts up with my need to escape to my writing cave, and who has promised to spend the rest of his life bringing me coffee when I do.

Author's Note

This novel takes place in 1878, four years after the events of the first book in the series, *When the Song of the Angels is Stilled.* Once again, the narrator is Poppy Stamford, a new fictional character and the sister of Dr. Michael Stamford, the man who would introduce Sherlock Holmes to Dr. John Watson. I was very pleased to read a review by Thomas Turley of the first book, in which he said that Poppy is "the most appealing heroine since Irene Adler." [Tom, I am glad you still liked like her in Book Two!]

Though I, like many other authors of Holmes pastiches rely heavily upon Baring-Gould's 'biography,' it is nonetheless a fictional chronology and account of Sherlock's life. There are many gaps in Doyle's stories, and little is actually known about Sherlock's family or his background. Doyle never revealed whether he attended Cambridge or Oxford or both (as Baring-Gould asserts). Doyle gives few dates certain in his tales and only a handful of events and landmarks to which we can point as real.

This novel is in part a re-imagining of *The Musgrave Ritual,* one of Sherlock's early cases. Some may take umbrage with them being alumni of Oxford and in placing the Musgrave case in 1878 rather than 1879, the year noted by William S. Baring-Gould, the noted Sherlock Holmes scholar, best known as the author of the influential fictional biography, *Sherlock Holmes of Baker Street: A life of the world's first consulting* detective. According to Baring-Gould (see *Sherlock Holmes of Baker Street*, published in 1962, at page 41), Reginald Musgrave walked into Holmes' rooms on Montague Street on October 2, 1879 to ask his former college acquaintance for assistance with a case. It had been several years since they had been undergraduates at Caius College, Cambridge. Baring-Gould quotes Sherlock (at page 28) as stating to Watson, "You never heard me talk of Victor Trevor? . . . He was one of the only friends I made during the two years I was at Christ Church." But then Baring-Gould admits in a footnote ((3)) "In his published account of the first case in which Holmes was ever engaged, Watson saw fit to tender this line: 'He was the only friend I made during the two years I was at college.'" Thus, Baring-Gould speculates where Sherlock Holmes went to college and met Trevor. Doyle never says. I set Sherlock Holmes' death in the early 1940's. But Baring-Gould estimates Sherlock's death occurred on his 103rd birthday. (January 6, 1957). Many other dates have been suggested by other authors.

I do not take Baring-Gould or any other author as gospel (though Baring-Gould is certainly a great jumping-off point), nor do I consider any 'facts' in the vast array of pastiches to be 'cumulative evidence.' If it is not in a Sherlock Holmes tale scripted by Doyle or in his notes or scribbles or insights into what inspired him in writing the Holmes stories (i.e. *Dangerous Work: Diary of an Arctic Adventure*—a truly wonderful account of Doyle's time as a ship's surgeon), then I do not consider it sacred, untouchable, or carved in granite. Hence, for purposes of this novel, I place the events, including Sherlock's case with Musgrave, a year earlier than Baring-Gould, and I proffer that Poppy Stamford, who narrates the story, was his only love.

St. Bart's is, of course, a landmark hospital in London, and I have attempted to depict it as it was in the late nineteenth century. Many of the characters in this book were real people. Oscar Wilde, poet, author and dramatist, lived. Dr. Robert Bridges was a physician at St. Bart's before he became the poet laureate of England. Charles Bradlaugh served in Parliament. The executioner, some of the employees at the British Museum, Richard Assheton

Cross, the Home Secretary, and Sir Charles Edward Howard Vincent, the Director of the new Criminal Investigation Department, all lived. Rabindranath Tagore, poet, activist, musician and author, lived. Tagore enrolled at a public school in Brighton, East Sussex, England, in 1878, and briefly read law at the University College, London, but left school, opting instead for independent study. In 1880, he returned to Bengal degree-less, resolving to reconcile European novelty with Brahmo traditions.

I like to pepper real people, places and events (such as railway disasters in Book One and the Thames collision in this novel) with fiction. I hope readers will enjoy the mix.

Once again, the action in this novel takes place before Sherlock Holmes meets Watson, while he is still a novice consulting detective. Sherlock is still finding his way, and he is more committed than ever to shunning romantic entanglements. As Thomas A. Turley, author of *"Sherlock Holmes and the Adventure of the Tainted Canister*, stated in his review of my first novel in this series, Holmes might have been a less lonely man had he allowed himself to love.

Hopefully, you will enjoy the journey and begin to understand why Sherlock Holmes became the man he was.

*If only I could stir him once again to joy, light a flame, make him quiver as he once did, and split his stone heart,
I would trade castles for dungeons and mansions for huts.*

PROLOGUE

27 December 1941

Pearl Harbour is no more.

As my daughter and I sit in her parlour, listening to BBC on the radio and watching the snow silently lace the trees outside the window, more updates dribble in about the bombing of the ships and the air strip and the horrible loss of life. The clouds that gather overhead make it easy to imagine the smoke hovering like black crows with wings spread wide over the Pacific Ocean and the beautiful island.

The war is not new to those of us who live in England, of course. Hitler has been bombing England for many months. Last fall and again in May, the blitz destroyed or damaged over a million homes in London and left more than forty thousand people dead. Stately buildings and cathedrals that I admired have collapsed to rubble. The church at my beloved St. Bart's Hospital was damaged as well. Now Germany has declared war on America and Mr. Churchill, who just addressed the Joint Session of Congress to win support for the war, has suffered a heart attack. As a physician I am worried about Mr. Churchill. As a grandmother, I am concerned about my grandson, who is in the RAF, I fear that he may not return unscathed.

Panicked, our community has drawn together, trying to find a voice of reason in the madness. We all try to believe, as my old friend, the poet Rabindranath Tagore, counseled, that when clouds float in our lives, they will not carry rain nor usher in a storm, but add colour to the sunset sky. It is hard to believe this when the clouds of war gather like a pack of grey wolves.

If Sherlock Holmes were still here, surely he would be racing like a wild hare to Germany to ferret out the evil and wickedness that has caused such devastation, though this time there would be little he could do.

Sherlock Holmes . . . I don't think I ever stopped loving him. I had never met anyone like him.

We met on the grounds of Oxford University. Seeking to protect me from the strange young man with the fencing foil who approached, my bull terrier sunk its teeth into Sherlock's calf. Sherlock sustained a deep wound and twisted his ankle. From that day forward, I was drawn to him.

I came to respect the many talents and qualities he shared with my Uncle Ormond. Because my family home was in the Broads in Norfolk, I had resided with my uncle and aunt in London for many years while attending a private girls' school and nursing school and, later, medical school. I adored my uncle, so perhaps I saw in Sherlock what I so admired in Uncle . . . his focus, his brilliant mind, his wry sense of humour, his tenacity, the uncanny ability to observe and deduce, the appreciation of logic, the fierce dedication to his work above all else. Before I met him, my life was like a deep, deliberate breath, measured, purposeful. My uncle said that from childhood I seemed to have an innate and obdurate insistence on carefully calculating each step of my life's journey, anticipating every solution without an aquifer of emotion and barely a tincture of eros. Even as an adolescent girl blossoming into adulthood, I refused to let my dreams be blighted by societal limitations and expected no moments of ecstasy. I was content to soldier on and to numb my emotions if necessary.

My personality, up until then at least, was a million kilometers away from one of Chekhov's romantic heroines. But like Madame Ranevskaya in *The Cherry Orchard*, when I met Sherlock I suddenly felt the same foolish yearnings. At times I seemed to suffer from some mysterious infestation, luminescent though it might be, which could have spread, which could have robbed me of my own ambitions, so entwined did I become with his. Without judgment, without blinking, and completely unaware of the spectre of loss or humiliation, I plunged into a kiln of emotional tar from which I could not break free. I was propelled toward that sparkling beauty that seemed to glide over Sherlock's disturbing darkness, savagery and loneliness. I was thrown off balance by my response to him. It seemed so undignified and immature.

We were very different, Sherlock and I. I held to a Dickensian view of the lives of the poor. I often felt a moral urgency when presented with poverty, tragedy or cruelty; sometimes he saw these as merely didactic hypotheticals for someone else to deal with, and often the poor and homeless children who ran errands for him seemed to be mere secondhand casualties. I gave in to my emotions, more often than I like to admit. He could be warm but rarely intimate. He let few people get close.

As I fell in love with him, my feelings for him collided in a kind of slurry that lay somewhere between bewitching and bewildering. But he seemed astonished that someone could love him and alarmed by the idea that he could be capable of having his heart broken.

When it fell apart, I was crushed. His withdrawal from me was sudden and laced with logic, but that made it no less brutal. It was as unexpected as the sting of a hornet—swift and sharp—but such pain can linger the longest. It was the most terrible hurt of my life, and when we parted, I tried to shed Sherlock Holmes like a snake sheds its skin—because he had outraged and frustrated me. But he had also stimulated, inspired, even humbled and moved me. I had been lost in it all, in quests for justice, in him, and felt shaken and overwhelmed. So, for several years, while Sherlock completed his education at Oxford and I finished medical school, I managed to put distance between us. Snippets of information about what he was doing and how he was faring were ferried to me now and then by my brother Michael Stamford, a physician at St. Bart's where Sherlock conducted many chemistry experiments. I tried not to pay attention.

But when I ran into him again at an Oxford event, I was like a bride unveiled as she enters her new world. After all the years of practiced isolation from Sherlock Holmes and great efforts to keep my distance from him and his hold on me, I met him again at Oscar Wilde's poetry recital in June of 1878. Determined as I was to eschew the pursuit of the elusive vulnerability Sherlock kept beneath his exterior reserve, and though I believed I'd finally slipped from the surly bonds of Sherlock Holmes, my self-imposed exile was an imperfect refuge. I realized that I could no more deny my feelings for the quiet, sheathed watcher who would, with one glimpse, absorb everything beneath my skin, than I could will myself to stop breathing.

They say that a new star shines its brightest, burning like a fiery cauldron, but eventually evaporates into space. They say that after eons, the core will cool and the star will vanish. I waited for that to happen to my feelings for Sherlock. I tried to recapture my life, my logic and objectivity, traits I had honed for years and upon which I prided myself. I thought the layers of time would help. I suppose I did not realize that an imploding star is a very dangerous place to be . . . and so, we continued our adventures.

18 August 1878
1

I could not believe that I was about to witness another hanging.

A few weeks after Oscar's recital at Oxford, Sherlock invited me to watch an execution. The invitation shocked me. Since the recital, we had taken long walks, enjoyed a few lunches, and he'd visited my medical office once or twice to pick my brain about anatomical things in relation to his experiments at St. Bart's. All very mundane and socially acceptable.

I did not want to let myself become involved with Sherlock again. I certainly did not want to see another death sentence carried out.

True, I had watched two other human beings swing from the rope: Margaret and Millicent Hardy. But I had attended the Hardy executions only because it was so personal. In 1874, Sherlock and I had worked together for months to find these baby farmers and have them arrested for willful murder. In the time that had passed since their executions, I had too often tossed and turned as I remembered their faces, remembered the sound of the trap falling.

But Sherlock insisted that I see the fruits of our labour, the continuance of the fight to purge England of baby and child farmers who abused and murdered helpless children for profit. I had involved him in that mission shortly after we met and he continued on his own, though he had told me long ago that he was done with it.

And so, there I was, looking up at a gallows again.

The hanging was at Wandsworth Prison. Executions took place on the third Sunday after sentencing at precisely 9 a.m. in a shed constructed in one of the yards. They called it the Cold Meat Shed.

The condemned man, Alan Horton, stood on the scaffold. He was a plump, middle-aged man with ruddy cheeks, a bulbous nose and flabby arms. The only witnesses present were Sherlock, a prosecutor, Under Sheriff Captain Colville, the prison governor, the prison doctor, two male warders, and two reporters. Actually, that would be three counting me, for Sherlock had lied about my profession, telling them I wrote for a women's magazine, so that I would be permitted to attend.

Horton drooped his head at first, but then he lifted it to stare with wide eyes at the sound of the rumbling laughter of the warders and the cheers of a small crowd of people that had gathered just outside the gates. The assembly would see and hear nothing, but apparently they could not help themselves.

Alan Horton had been convicted of murdering dozens of children. He was a child-farmer, much like the baby farmers who Sherlock and I had investigated and brought to justice four years earlier. They profited by pretending to take in and care for illegitimate babies for a fee and then murdering them to make room for more. Now the time for Horton to meet his maker had come as well.

At precisely 8.45 a.m., the prison bell began to toll. I shifted nervously and, knowing what was about to come to pass, I could not take my eyes off the gallows. I whispered to Sherlock, "I think I am going to leave."

"Why? You were with me at the Hardy executions."

"That was . . . different somehow. We worked on that case together and Millicent Hardy nearly killed me. And I have changed, Sherlock. I do not think I believe in the death sentence anymore."

"Not even for murder? Rubbish. This man murdered several hundred children over the years. I should think your love of children would make you glad he is to get the rope. Don't you remember anything from your religious classes? 'He that diggeth a pit shall fall into it; and whoso breaketh an hedge, a serpent shall bite him.' Or Psalms, if you wish. 'His mischief shall return upon his own head, and his violent dealing shall come down upon his own pate,'" he added, touching his head.

"I am glad for justice being done, yes," I said. "But I don't think I want to watch. I became a physician because I value life. All life. I don't think it is up to us to take a life."

He took my hand and clenched it. Such a simple gesture, the warmth of his skin against mine, usually diminished any uneasiness I felt. I stayed, but I stepped behind Sherlock and fixed my eyes on the curly, dark hair at the nape of his neck. I felt myself perspiring. I meant what I said. I'd become a doctor because I wanted to *save* lives.

At 9 a.m., when the doors to the shed were closed, I glanced up and stared at the white painted gallows, the rope dangling and the noose lying on the trapdoors. The executioner, William Marwood, stopped Horton at the chalk mark on the double trapdoors, placed a leather body belt round his waist, and secured his wrists while a warder encircled his ankles with leather straps. Horton's knees buckled. The warders, who were standing on the planks next to the trap, supported him while Marwood placed the white hood over Horton's head and adjusted the noose, leaving the free rope running down his back.

I raised my eyes to the gallows and winced when he said, "Lord, have mercy upon me."

His last words were, "I helped those children. I helped them."

Marwood stepped to the side and pulled the lever. I dragged my gaze from the gallows and closed my eyes, but I heard Horton plummet down some eight feet into the brick-lined pit below. The whole process took less than two minutes, but his body would be left to hang for an hour before being taken down. When we exited the prison, we saw that a black flag had been hoisted on the flag pole above the main gate.

Sherlock dragged me through the crowd in silence, keeping me close. It reminded me of when we'd gone looking for Oscar in an opium den near Limehouse Beach. He had said, "Do not leave my side. Do not speak to anyone. Keep hold of my hand."

And I had answered, "Yes. I will." That was perhaps the first time—and one of the few—that I had obeyed him without question.

When we reached Heathfield Road, Sherlock finally said, "His body will be buried in an unmarked grave in one of the exercise yards."

I did not respond.

"I heard the Governor say that Marwood was compensated in the sum of twelve pounds. That's more than any fee I pocket."

"Perhaps you should change your career path then. Become an executioner."

He did not reply.

"Sherlock, what if an innocent person is condemned to death? What if you and the police are wrong and execute a—"

"I never guess, Poppy," he interrupted. "It flies in the face of logic to do so. Horton was guilty. You are succumbing to an emotional response. And you know that I believe emotions are antagonistic to clear thinking."

I wrapped my arms around myself and leaned against the building, feeling my heart sink further into the darkness. "I want to go to Victoria Park to feed the swans," I blurted.

His mouth pulled down, he grimaced. "Why?"

"Because they are beautiful and I need something beautiful to erase the images in my mind."

He thought for a moment, as did I. Sherlock had mentioned something about accompanying him to St. Bart's to discuss another murder case, so I used that as leverage. "I shall not go with you to the hospital if you do not take me to Victoria Park first."

I touched his hand, feeling the fire lick my skin as it always did when I touched him. "Will you do this for me, please?"

He did not answer immediately, so I stared into his eyes, longing to see desire, longing for him to show the affection that I knew he felt for me. Longing to let the words spill out of my mouth, the ones I continued to hold back as I had for years, and desperate for him to remember what he had said to me once before:

"Poppy, my nerves are like fireflies. I cannot think because my feelings for you get in the way. It suddenly seems more logical to allow them to flourish and keep you close so that I can teach them to live side by side with logic and deduction."

In the short time since we had rekindled our still tenuous relationship, there had been a few occasions that, for one breathless moment, he seemed to teeter on the edge of something more. Sometimes I felt we were but a fraction of a second from fanning the dying embers. We would dance like two swans in a courting ritual. I attributed the demise of our prior romantic interlude during the summer of 1874 to Sherlock's terrible guilt over betraying Victor Trevor, Sherlock's only friend and the man who wanted to marry me, and to Sherlock's need to immolate any emotional attachments in favour of his passion for objectivity and logic. Nevertheless, I kept the fires of hope burning. I was willing to be patient. I tried to comfort myself with an illusion; after all, the swans' courtship ritual is relatively long and drawn out because the displays they make to each other are so significant in forging the special bond that exists between them, the kind I had once imagined Sherlock and I would have.

But Sherlock was no swan. He dedicated every waking hour to being the detective who looks—and finds—that one thing that nobody else has found, and his *froideur* had grown exponentially. It was terrifying at times. Logic and deduction always seemed to trump fondness and love and physical intimacy.

"Will you take me to Victoria Park or not?" I asked.

Finally, Sherlock sighed and muttered, "Fair enough," and hailed a hansom.

2

As we travelled to the park, I listened to the clip-clop of the carriage horses and watched Sherlock closely. I was still shaking and I tried desperately to banish the sights and sounds of Horton's final moments from my mind. But Sherlock was calm, completely unruffled. No trace of regret or doubt or horror such that I was feeling was apparent on his countenance.

And then I pondered how such a man could still have such a hold on me. I had managed to get along without him for several years while I finished medical school and opened my practice near the British Museum. I'd even travelled a bit. But, then when he abruptly came back into my life, once again it seemed so natural to walk with him or dine with him or talk about everything under the sun with him. When he'd sent the page to my office inviting me to join him at Horton's private execution, I simply could not refuse him.

"Sherlock, tell me more about the man who . . . about Mr. Horton. Why did you involve yourself? You told me that you were done with chasing down baby farmers."

"I was between cases and it was interesting. It served to distract me from the monochromatic tedium of life," he added with a sigh.

"From the beginning I was certain it was a copy-cat crime. A few months ago, I went to visit my brother Sherrinford. He urged me to come and take away some of the things I'd left at home when I went off to Oxford and had no room for them. Essentially, he advised that if I did not cart them away, he would discard them. And he gave me some of our father's things, a lovely roll-top desk, for example.

"At dinner one evening, Sherrinford said that he had an odd feeling about a neighbour, Mr. Horton. His farm was nearby and Sherrinford passed it almost daily. He noticed that there usually children playing near the road, but it dawned on him one day that he hardly ever saw the same children. There always seemed to be new arrivals. As I'd told him about the Hardy case, Sherrinford was concerned that it was a similar child abduction scheme. I proceeded to check at the workhouse from which these children were taken. Hundreds had been placed with Horton. According to the employees at the workhouse, Horton's arrangement seemed noble at first. For a fee, he agreed to take the children to his farm. He would teach the boys trades, and his wife would instruct the girls in needlework, laundry, washing, and general household work. The children ranged in age from ten to fourteen.

"I also learned that authorities were planning to see the children to determine if they had been vaccinated. A wise decision, given that in London—the best-vaccinated city in England—some five to ten thousand people have died of smallpox in the last five years. So I accompanied the doctors to Horton's farm. It turned out that he used the children as slaves. They plowed, they cleaned. He worked them to the bone.

"When we started taking account of them," he continued, "we realized that many of the children were missing. Some of the children had been there only a few months and they were but ten or twelve years of age. Of course, Horton argued that many had left on their own, but they were not there long enough to learn a trade or mature enough to go off on their own to make a living."

"You're right. His scheme was similar to that of Margaret and Millicent Hardy."

He nodded. "We found hundreds of graves. It became quite clear that when Horton acquired too many to feed and when they became too ill and malnourished to work, he got rid of them. He simply made room for new ones."

I felt sick to my stomach.

"You said you saw it as a copy-cat crime, Sherlock. What do you mean?"

"I use the term to describe someone who imitates another person's crime."

Almost twelve years later, I realized that perhaps Sherlock coined the term, for it was not until I purchased Sarah Orne Jewett's novel, *Betty Leicester: A Story for Girls*, for my daughter that I saw the term 'copy-cat' in literature for the first time.

"You, see, back in the late 1840's," he explained, "a man named Bartholomew Peter Drouet was tried for the murder of several children. He also was a child farmer who neglected and abused poor children he took from an overcrowded workhouse. But what Bartholomew Drouet had not counted on was an outbreak of cholera that brought doctors to his farm to treat the pauper children. Drouet's immensely profitable business came quickly to a halt. Likewise, Horton had not counted on his farm being investigated as to whether the children had received smallpox vaccinations. So now his sordid business and greed and the deaths at his hand of these children led him to the Cold Meat Shed."

I simply nodded and turned my head to stare out the window, wondering how such cruelty and heartlessness could exist in the world. Yet I still questioned the right to execute anyone, even for such vile crimes as Horton committed.

Clearly, Sherlock felt it was a suitable end. More than once he'd told me that when one commits a heinous crime, when one does something very bad, it needs must end on a gallows. Just now, all I wanted to do was banish the sights and sounds of Horton's final moments out of my mind, but I could not.

I was thankful that public hangings had finally ceased. For years, hangings were a public spectacle. In fact, the proceedings were so popular that not very long ago, twenty-eight people died in a crush after a crowd of up to twenty thousand would-be spectators rampaged out of control. Things had changed a little. Horsemonger Gaol and other prisons had closed. The death penalty was now reserved for heinous crimes like wilful murder, malicious assault, and treason. To hasten death and cause less pain, Executioner Marwood had made some improvements to the process of execution. He had introduced the 'long drop' method, designed to break the person's neck and cause near-instantaneous unconsciousness.

But efforts to repeal capital punishment altogether had failed. Charles Dickens opposed it vehemently and wrote many letters trying to stop executions, to no avail. He was appalled at the swelling crowds, the people clustered together to watch a hanging of a criminal, to applaud as his head dangled, to clap as the body was cut down.

So was I.

I had considered the moral arguments and come to the conclusion that though it might seem right to punish the vicious and reward the virtuous, such renderings were not up to us, to Man. Indeed, if there is an immortal soul, should not its Creator be the one who decides when the soul comes into the world and when it leaves it? I'd come to the conclusion that the death penalty should be abolished.

Finally, I said to Sherlock, "It surprises me, Mr. Holmes, that you have become an avenging angel. And obviously because retribution for certain crimes is sanctioned, you have no problem with the death penalty."

He scoffed. "No, I do not. But you are mistaken if you think me an avenging angel. That, Dr. Stamford, is a moniker that *you* should wear. I do not make the laws nor do I enforce them. And if I am adept at capturing a very cruel person, it does not mean I am any kind of an angel, as you put it, and I leave dispensation of punishment to others. Working a case is simply a cathartic release, a way to defeat the mundane frustration of living." Then he asked, "The hanging really bothered you, didn't it?"

I heaved a sigh and turned away. Then he turned to stare out the window.

Cases were the nerve-centre of Sherlock's existence, but I felt sad for the soul for whom crimes and misery brings a smile. His brain could readily shut out the noise in the wind tunnel at such an event, so how could I make him see that while everyday mishaps might generate a mere dust-up in my brain, witnessing a hanging invited a tornado?

3

When we arrived at Victoria Park, many children were gathered near the bank of the river to feed the swans. A crowd had also assembled nearby, on the big central lawn. It had become a tradition for political and social activists to gather there to preach their ideas and dispute everything from the value of slavery to atheism, euthanasia, Darwinism, socialism and the like. I'd heard that one man exalted his own ability to make prophecies, saying the Holy Ghost inspired him. He'd been locked up in an asylum. I was glad that my late, psychic friend Effie had never chosen to reveal her gift on this lawn.

Sherlock was not one to fritter time away and almost at once, he seemed anxious. He immediately wandered off to listen to someone who was speaking about the deterioration of religion because of medical advances. Often he eschewed any philosophical or political discussions. Sometimes he seemed ignorant of both subjects, but he was not. He could quote Hafez, a fourteenth-century poet, and he frequently recited lines from Shakespeare's *Twelfth Night* and other plays and framed them into politically relevant discussions about English government.

I was uncertain of Sherlock's stand on religion. Perhaps because the existence of God could be neither proved nor disproved, he leaned toward agnosticism. How often he had said, "If all the possible hypotheses are eliminated except for one, then that hypothesis, no matter how unlikely, is the correct hypothesis." Though he often lamented that life was pathetic and futile, he also referenced Biblical passages, if not citing them and then paraphrasing them, as he had that morning at the execution.

A few minutes later, Sherlock crossed the lawn and stood in front of the soapbox of another gentleman, and I followed. We listened to him for a moment. He had a round face, a high forehead, and thinning hair. He looked to be about my uncle's age, mid-forties. He was speaking about atheism. The climate was ripe for controversial subjects. Though Charles Darwin had published *The Origin of Species* twenty years ago, the debates about evolution raged on.

"Who is that, Sherlock?"

"Charles Bradlaugh," Sherlock replied. "He is a courageous and stirring orator, Poppy. His skills will serve him well in Parliament."

"Parliament?"

"He's going to run for Parliament soon. I'm not sure he will get elected but if he does, it will be quite entertaining."

"Why?"

"Because Bradlaugh is a passionate non-believer. He would be required to take a religious oath to take his seat. I don't believe he will do it. He scoffs at those who claim to have particular knowledge of what a Creator wants us to think. He is a progressive who disagrees with the sentiments of those in government who insist that one must take a religious oath. He has no reverence for the little words they would force him to say and does not see why they are necessary. He's been pressing the government to permit non-religious affirmations for years. If he can pull it off, he will be Britain's first atheist MP."

"Mother says that atheists are immoral. It was the one concern she had about my residing with Uncle and Aunt Susan."

"Rubbish!" Sherlock yelled. "That is the battle cry of those who would preserve the myth that godless people are immoral. But those like Bradlaugh say that the answer to that canard is the promotion of science and logic. I must loan you my books by Auguste Comte, the French philosopher."

"I have not read any of his works."

"I am not convinced in the innate goodness of humanity, but Comte makes a good argument in his *In Système de politique positive.* He posits that the restoration of order and progress are the pillars of morality."

He glanced in Bradlaugh's direction again and said, "You should learn more about him, Poppy. Last year he published a pamphlet called "A Plea for Atheism," and founded an influential magazine called *The National Reformer*. And he favours rights for women. Just last year, Bradlaugh was tried, with his friend Annie Besant, for publishing a pamphlet supporting birth control. He wants birth control methods to be available to the masses. He was sentenced to six months imprisonment and a large fine, but the verdict was overturned on appeal."

I pondered this for a moment. It was another issue with which I wrestled. As a doctor sworn to save lives, did it contradict that duty if I supported the position that a woman could choose whether or not to conceive a child? Without artificial contraception, women frequently bore five or six or a dozen children. I'd seen the tragedy that lived in their haunted eyes. I'd seen how the children languished in miserable poverty and squalor, or were forever cursed with the imprint of violence when they were 'rescued' by degenerates like the man I'd just seen swing from the rope.

Most churches, not only the Roman Catholic Church, opposed artificial contraception. But I wondered . . . would it be better that these children were not born at all? Or should we just increase our efforts to feed and clothe and house them and put to death those who harmed them, as Sherlock advocated?

Sherlock waved his hand to the west. "That man over there is countering with all sorts of religious reasons why Bradlaugh should be arrested. He thinks Bradlaugh is a stealer of souls because he proffers that religious beliefs undermine modern medicine and because he renounces God, and, in particular, some religious rituals. He openly scoffs at priests who insist on telling their flocks that wine can turn into Christ's blood."

"Some people do believe that happens, Sherlock."

He laughed and said, "Ah, yes, because nothing says rational thinker like transubstantiation."

I did my best to hide a smile. I was used to Sherlock's veiled swipes at the Holy Trinity. He thought of preachers as talking heads behind which there was always a ravishing candlelight, as if to emphasize their imagined halos. The perfect *chiaroscuro* to separate them from the less worthy.

I walked down to the bank of the river and gazed at the herd of swans, the silvery edges of their delicate feathers shimmering in the sunlight as they glided across the water, which shone like polished glass. One shook and trembled and undulated, and its long neck stretched high out of the water. Its feathers spread wide, casting a shadow that muted the rays of sunlight bouncing off the surface of the river, but as it slid away, the golden beams that sparkled on the water returned and glowed like an aurora or a rainbow. The water was glazed in violet-blue and gold and red, like the luster of an exotic bird's glossy, iridescent plumage.

I watched wistfully as two swans came clearly into focus and met in the middle of the river, wings lifted like angels. They had drifted away from the others and gently rubbed each other's beaks, then bobbed and dunked their heads below the surface, blowing bubbles in the water and wrapping their necks around each other in foreplay. Fascinated, I saw them dance their way toward bliss, like two exquisite performers in a ballet. They were so graceful, so beautiful.

First, they swam side by side, their wings lowered close to their bodies. They dipped their heads below the water surface and then pulled them back out and preened themselves. Again and again they did this, faster and faster, occasionally stopping to raise their necks, angle their heads down and look at each other. Then they moved almost as one, synchronizing their actions, united in the dance. They pressed their breasts to one another and raised and lowered their necks, staring into one another's eyes. Their necks intertwined, one bird draped his neck over his partner's and then the other did the same. Up and down, up and down, they lifted and lowered their heads and gently caressed each other's long necks.

The male climbed on top of his mate in a swift move and the sounds of pleasure exploded in whistles and snorts. The episode was brief but magnificent. Afterward, in a synchronous movement, they circled one another, touching cheek to cheek, like newlyweds, in a charming exhibition of after-glow.

I found myself drowning in the serenity of it and in the warmth of the slanting sunlight. My sadness disappearing into a chimerical daydream, I rose from that dark vault and breathed in the soft tapestry surrounding me. The children laughing, a woman's momentary smile, the flaxen flowers on the bank, the canopy of trees across the river hanging low, the swans' wings striking the water, causing it to spout like a sputtering geyser in their wake. I felt transformed. The dismal gloom of the execution and Sherlock's science and deduction and logic were the furthest things from my mind, and I felt compelled to keep them at bay.

I found Sherlock and tugged at his sleeve.

"I'm going to Covent Gardens Market."

"But what about St. Bart's?"

"Later. Come. Walk with me."

It was about five miles from Victoria Park to the market, but at Sherlock's brisk pace, we were there in less than an hour.

The market was teeming with chatter. I wandered from the flower women selling bouquets to women shelling walnuts. A cyclist riding a penny farthing beeped as he flew by, an Italian harpist entertained on one corner, and a shellfish stall holder sold oysters and whelks on another. Across the road stood a locksmith mending locks at his stall on the spot. Mush-Fakers—vendors who repaired umbrellas and collected discarded ones beyond repair in order to combine the good bits of two or more for sale—and ginger beer makers hurried back and forth with their carts. Sherlock bought some nuts and I also bought a bag for Uncle. Then I purchased some daisies for Aunt Susan and a ginger beer for myself, and hailed a cab to go home.

"Poppy, what are you doing?"

"I can't go to Bart's just now. I simply cannot. It's . . . I'm done with death for today."

He gave me an odd look. He had, after all, been with me when I attended to dozens of the dead and dying at the horrible train wreck in Norfolk a few years before. I'm sure he thought that I handled death quite well.

He was wrong.

I gave his arm a squeeze and said, "I'm going home."

I looked around the market one more time. *This* was life, and not even Sherlock Holmes could convince me to abandon my belief in the infrangible human right to live.

4

A few weeks later, in early September, Sherlock sent a would-be page, one of his homeless helpers, to my medical office. The young boy was dressed in ragged clothes and tattered shoes. He looked sweaty and parched. Out of breath, he said, "Me name's Rattle, Miss. Mr. 'olmes sent me t' fetch yer." Then he asked, "Kin I 'ave a drin' a wa'er, Miss?"

"Of course." I poured some water from a carafe into a glass and he drank it down in one gulp. "So Mr. Holmes is summoning me to St. Bart's?"

He nodded. "T' meet with 'imself and Detective Inspector Lestrade."

"He is with Detective Inspector Lestrade? You are certain?"

If Lestrade was involved, some serious game was afoot.

"I'd sooner starve than lie, I would," the boy said.

Glancing around my empty office and staring down at the page of my daily, which displayed nothing except a luncheon date with my friend Oscar Wilde, I mumbled with a sigh, "I certainly have nothing more pressing."

"Wha's tha', Miss?"

I slammed the appointment book closed. I could not refuse Sherlock, but I wanted to show him that I did not have to drop everything at his beck and call. "I have some appointments and a luncheon engagement. Advise Mr. Holmes that I shall be there by three half. Tell him I shall meet him at the fountain."

"The wha', Miss?"

"The fountain at St. Bart's. He shall know the place."

"Bu' 'e wans yer t' come *now*. And 'e wans yer t' read somefink in fis newspaper." He shoved a copy of *The London Daily News* into my hands.

"Oh, he does, does he?" I snarled.

The boy nodded.

I glanced at the front page of the paper. There was a follow-up article to one I'd read in the spring that had reported Mr. Thomas Edison's presentation to the Academy of Sciences about his new carbon telephone. Graham Bell had displayed his version of the device, which could transmit speech, a few years earlier at the U.S. Centennial Exposition in Philadelphia. The exhibition judges, Emperor Dom Pedro II of the Empire of Brazil and Sir William Thompson, an eminent British physicist, took part in the experiments, and the voices of each were recognized by their accents and peculiarities of speech. They recommended Bell's device to the Committee of Electrical Awards and he won the Gold Medal, but Mr. Edison's new carbon telephone was a complete novelty. He had made changes in its design after he discovered that certain kinds of carbon are enormously susceptible to changes in conductivity when subjected to different pressures.

When I'd read that article, I thought it was just the kind of thing Sherlock would be keenly interested in, given his experiments with chemicals and different properties of ash, wood, blood and so on. I would have loved to get his opinion. But Sherlock and I were not on speaking terms at that time.

"Does Mr. Holmes want me to read this front page article about Mr. Edison?" I asked.

"Why is yer askin' sich a 'eap of questions fer?"

"Which one, Rattle?"

"Th'one on page twenty and one, 'e says."

I put the newspaper on my desk and said, "Do apologize to Mr. Holmes for the delay, but I have things to attend to."

"Yer sure, Miss?"

"Quite sure."

The boy grimaced and groaned, "Mr. 'olmes won' be 'appy, Miss." Then he said, "Good day to yer," turned and left.

5

I busied myself for a while, cleaning instruments, and then reading an update in one of Uncle's medical journals about risk management and surgical intervention in railway and industrial accidents. Railway surgeons had long been regarded with contempt by most physicians. After reading a disparaging article about them, Uncle Ormond said to me, "The level of discourtesy on the part of my colleagues is extremely unkind and entirely uncalled for. We know, Poppy, don't we, what it is like to treat the victims of a railway accident?"

Oh, yes, I remembered. I still heard their voices in the night.

Uncle and I had been, by default, railway physicians for one horrible night in 1874, a night I would forever remember, one that had spurred in me a deep desire to promote and foster specialties in trauma and emergency medicine. We had treated dozens of injured passengers and railway employees scattered on the tracks that rainy, foggy night after the head-on collision near my home in Norfolk.

Like physicians who worked exclusively for the railway, we were faced with impossible conditions. One brakeman's hand was crushed between a link-and-pin coupler. He had wrapped an oily rag around his severed hand. Unconscious, he was not found until the next day, his hand dangling, and his shoes and clothing awash in a pool of blood. By the time he was transferred to the nearest hospital, he was unconscious. Though Uncle amputed the hand, the poor soul had contracted gangrene and died a few days later.

But even without a crash, it was not unusual for a railway employee to sustain an injury during the scope of his

20

employment—to have an arm or leg crushed—and he could not expect proper treatment. Such casualties, like the poor boy we could not save, were treated with old rags, oily handkerchiefs, or whatever was lying about, and transported for hours and miles in a chilly, dirty car. Too often, by the time a victim arrived at a hospital, he was grey and unconscious, or without a pulse at all, having bled to death, and his crushed limb was tossed into the rubbish. Sometimes, the patient did not even get to a hospital. More often, operations were performed out in the woods, on the backporch of some filthy house on the wayside, or occasionally in a nearby hotel room. But the rooms were rarely suitably equipped, and the railway were billed outrageously for room charges as well as replacement of bloodstained furnishings.

Railway doctors had no special training; they learned on the job, as they went. No major surgery textbooks would include the unique techniques involved in railway surgery until many years later, and the specialty would not appear in *Index Medicus*, the major index of medical literature, until 1903. Worse, railway surgeons were socially and professionally isolated, and they often lived a very difficult and austere life compared to their metropolitan counterparts. But, oh, they were innovative. They had to be, for railway and manufacturing facilities presented unique hazards and created new types of injuries to which most doctors, even brilliant surgeons like Uncle, were unaccustomed.

England's railway surgeons were just starting to learn techniques and methods from America's Civil War doctors, for both the Union and Confederate armies had made extensive use of freight cars and bunk cars to transport injured soldiers to regional hospitals. Such locomotive ambulances were virtually non-existent in England when I started my practice. But railway surgery was finally being recognized as a specialty with its primary goal to study accident and trauma surgery, and in America, the railway surgeons had already introduced their concepts to civilian medicine.

My country's railway doctors were finally creaing emergency packs with medicines and sterile dressings for the trains, the forerunners of the first aid kit. They trained the railway workers as well. But 'normal' British physicians objected to this, feeling that laypersons could not administer medical care correctly.

"What they really fear," Uncle said, "is that their own lofty importance might be diminished."

He and I found this ridiculous; where urban surgeons operated was a far cry from the make-shift and filthy conditions under which we had worked at the Norfolk crash. We were ecstatic that these railway trauma surgeons were starting to be recognized for their revolutionary concepts in patient care. Uncle had recently read about a railway employee, a flagman, who broke his leg when it caught in a running gear. The conductor, who had received emergency training from the railway doctor, wrapped the jagged bone in sterile gauze, stabilized the leg with a splint, and gave him pain medication. A telegraph was sent to a nearby depot where a railway surgeon awaited the patient's arrival. In a special car fitted with operating equipment, the boy was anesthesized; the doctor sterilized his hands with carbolic acid before setting the bones and stitching the wound. After a few weeks in the railway's own hospital, the boy went home. He survived.

I had thought about closing up my faltering practice in London to become a railway doctor. The specialty was growing, and with the number of accidents and railway-employed doctors beginning to swell, I thought perhaps even a female doctor might be welcomed into the budding medical specialty.

I was wrong, of course. Such musings were hopelessly optimistic.

Even though railway surgeons were far more progressive than their typical colleagues, it would not be until the late 1890's that a female surgeon would be hired by a railway. The appointment of Dr. Carrie Lieberg as a division surgeon for the

Northern Pacific would send tidal waves across the medical community. It would not be until 1907, by which time I was in my fifties, that a railway hired a woman as chief surgeon.

I was considering my options and day-dreaming about what kind of life I might lead in the frontier if I mustered up the courage to travel to America just as the clock on the fireplace mantel rang out, reminding me that I was due to meet Oscar Wilde in a few minutes. I put away the journal and locked up my office.

As I hurried to meet Oscar at the restaurant, I thought back again to that horrible September night when the two trains collided near my home in the Broads. Sherlock had refused to help us tend to the injured; all he could think about was unearthing the details of the crash. It was the first time I had really witnessed how cold and calculating, how unfeeling he could force himself to be, but it was not the last. For that reason, and many others, soon after we parted on uneasy terms, but he had finally sought me out at Oscar's poetry recital to try to make amends. And, for reasons that escape me, I sought *him* out a few weeks later.

6

On that hot afternoon in early July, just a few weeks after I'd run into Sherlock at Oscar's recital, I went to the lab after having had lunch with my brother Michael. When I entered, Sherlock had spread before him an assortment of coloured plates, pipes and tobaccos. Of course, I had asked him what he was up to.

"I have recently revisited Friedrich Tiedmann's *Geschichte des Tabaks*, published in the year of my birth, 1854. It spurred me on to take all the more seriously my research into the distinctive characteristics of ash."

"And why is that relevant to your avocation as a consulting detective?"

"*Vocation*," he said deliberately. "It is not a hobby, Dr. Stamford. And it is important because a person's habits are part of his or her identity. For example, if the perpetrator of a crime left a note, I would compare handwriting. Or let's say you were arrested and the only evidence against you was a footprint left at the scene. I would compare the size of your boots to the footprints left behind. Or what if you were accused of a crime and an eyewitness had described the criminal as a delicate flower, slender as a sapling, tiny in stature, with blonde hair, and as colourful as an Easter bonnet? I would immediately point out that *you* could not be the suspect."

His words precisely painted an image of Effie, Oscar Wilde's cousin, my best friend and my brother's young wife, now deceased. I missed her terribly and for a moment, I looked down at the hat I held in my hands, the one she had made for me. It was made of bright blue fabric with a black lace ruffle around the narrow brim. It had a black feather plume and a short train of black tulle. I remembered she laughed and asked, "Doesn't this have high society written all over it?"

"Poppy, are you listening?" Sherlock asked, bringing me sharply back into focus.

I blinked and looked at him. "I'm sorry. You were saying something about a witness identifying someone."

"And that someone could not be you because you are tall and athletically built. You have dark hair, not blonde. And," he added, "It is only on the rare occasion that your attire exceeds the bounds of dark blue, grey or beige. Unless, of course, your mother insists that you wear some new fashion she forces upon you."

Unsure of how to take his apt description of me, I asked, "But what has that to do with ashes?"

"Oh, Poppy, use your brain—it's slightly less ordinary than the average person's! It's about observation! One can identify the kind of cigar by the ash or butt left behind. For example, do you know what the ash of a bird's eye looks like?"

"I don't know what a bird's eye is, Sherlock."

He sighed. "Of course, you don't. Because you have a limited knowledge of the habits of men. Victor did not smoke, did he?"

I winced at the reference to Victor Trevor. That was still—and I feared always would be—a wedge between us. Sherlock would always feel that he had betrayed Victor, his only friend, by caring for me, and I think he also felt he could not trust me because I had once been very close to Victor but turned my affection to Sherlock almost the instant I met him. No matter how many times I explained that Victor and I were not betrothed, that he had not asked my father for my hand, and there was no marriage contract, Sherlock felt he had come between us.

"No," I said. "Victor does not smoke. Well, he may now that he is in India. I don't know."

"So, well, bird's eye," Sherlock continued, "is a tobacco in which the mid-rib, which is slightly woody, is fermented along with the lamina, whereas in most tobaccos the mid-rib is removed before fermentation. When you smoke it, it produces a pattern of circular dots and its ash is like a white fluff."

He showed me another ash. "This one is called honeydew."

"Surely it is not made from honey."

"No, but honey, like rum or whiskey, can be added to tobacco after it is cured. Perhaps in my twilight years, I shall oversee a tobacco farm and raise bees and experiment with adding fresh honey to various tobaccos." His eyes were a vacant stare, as if at the age of twenty-four, he was actually pondering retirement.

"Honeydew. Sherlock you were saying—"

"Oh, yes, quite. Honey gives tobacco a different flavor and prevents it from drying out. Now, our friend Oscar was kind enough to give me this opium ash," he said, pointing to one of the coloured plates. "I also have some opium for smoking in a water pipe. It looks like chopped spinach. And this is a true opium pipe," he added, taking some odd-looking implements from beneath the counter. "It is designed for vaporization and inhalation. In other words, it allows the opium to be vaporized while being heated over a special oil lamp. Like this one," he said, pointing.

I picked up the pipe. It had a long stem, a ceramic bowl and a metal fitting called, Sherlock told me, a 'saddle' through which the pipe bowl plugs into the pipe stem.

"Why is the bowl detached from the stem?"

"One must scrape the insides clean of opium ash after several smoking episodes."

"Is it made of bamboo, the stem?"

"Good eye, Dr. Stamford. Yes, it is. But they often come in ivory, silver and jade. Generally, however, bowls are fashioned by combining yixing clay and blue and white porcelain."

"Yixing?"

"A type of clay found only in certain areas of China. Mr. Brown has an interest in Chinese artefacts and I've seen him smoking a pipe very similar to this one."

I was slightly acquainted with Mr. Brown, one of St. Bart's apothecaries, because he was often deep in conversation with my uncle when I visited Uncle Ormond at the hospital. He was an odd little man who kept an array of trinkets in his little pharmaceutical area. He had completed medical school, but he had never passed his examinations. He seemed more interested in studying birds than in mixing medicines, and Uncle often said he was surprised the man hadn't been sacked.

I put the pipe down. "I do not like to think of poppies this way," I said. "I like flowers, particularly those given to me on special occasions."

Our eyes met, both of us remembering the early morning hours after we'd spent the night together; Sherlock had gathered wildflowers and left them for me to wake up to the scent and the dizzying colours.

"And I don't like my nickname linked to a drug."

"It's a harmless substance, Poppy."

"I disagree."

"It simply opens the mind a bit and lets one escape from the dull routine of living," he insisted.

"That's not how you felt that time when we went looking for Oscar in that opium den, Sherlock. And living isn't dull. It needn't be."

He thought a moment. "You are too harsh. After all, opium, cocaine, morphine, laudanum . . . they are all legal."

"They have side effects. We have seen them. People use them as a panacea for everything from toothaches to labour pains, I know, but it can lead to a kind of drug mania, a narcotic addiction. Promise me you will not indulge."

"I am a practical man, Poppy. I would indulge in nothing that would interfere with my work or cloud by judgment. Nothing," he said again for emphasis.

"Now, here," he said, stepping to the end of the counter. "We have a collection of pipes."

"You will have quite the abundance of choices when you encounter a three-pipe problem, won't you?"

"Quite so. This one is rather old. A clay pipe. Here is one made of brier and this one is made of cherry wood. The type of pipe that one smokes has some effect on the remaining ash, I believe."

That lesson in ashes and pipes continued for most of the afternoon, but still, I could not tear myself away from him. I never could.

7

I put memories of that lesson in ashes and thoughts of Sherlock aside as I entered the Café Restaurant Nicols, later known as the Café Royal, on Regent Street. This was a favourite of Oscar Wilde's when he was in London. I looked forward to a nice meal with my unorthodox and jovial friend. I went inside and saw him waiting for me at a table in the corner, reading the newspaper. He wore emerald green silk stockings and breeches, a braided coat with a sunflower in the lapel, and a large, green tie. Eccentric attire was his way of telling the world he was an artist and 'not like other men.' He had told me once that revolutionizing dress was far more important than religious reformation and that "Luther's neckties must have been deplorable."

I gave him a peck on the cheek and sat down next to him. Clutching his hand, I asked, "How is my famous friend?"

"Not very famous yet, but I am working on notorious," he laughed.

I squeezed his hand. "You will be famous, Oscar. As a poet or a writer or both."

He smiled. "Or a dramatist. I am going to write a play in which Sarah Bernhardt shall be the star."

"The actress who sleeps in a coffin?"

"The same. She is wonderful. I've met her, you know."

"Really? Where?"

"I was there when she stepped ashore. I threw lilies to her feet."

"As only you could do. You've ingratiated yourself to her already then?"

"I believe I have. And I've just seen her at the Comédie Française. They performed the fifth act of *Othello*. Monsieur Mounet-Sully was Othello and she was Desdemona. It was . . . inspiring. I do fear, however, that idiotic censorship may destroy the play I am working on, or at the very least spoil it," he added.

He took my hand in his again. "It's good to see you."

"You as well. So what were you reading? You looked intensely interested. Was it about a new play or something?"

"A murder actually. One that occurred far too close to home. Your home, in a manner of speaking."

"Pardon?"

"The account in the newspaper recounted a death, possibly—no, probably a murder—near the British Museum, just around the corner from your office."

"Really? I have heard nothing about it."

"Nor had I. But a reporter from *The Times* happened to be on his way into the museum to cover some new exhibit when the police arrived. A crime had been reported. They found the corpse of a young man behind the museum and the circumstances of his death seem quite suspicious. A small Buddha statue and a dead bird were left at the scene. I understand it is not the first time."

I shuddered. I'd forgotten to read the article as Sherlock requested, but instinct told me it was the same one of which Oscar spoke and that it was, perhaps, related to the reason he'd asked me to come to Bart's after witnessing the hanging.

"Do you remember the essay I wrote for the *Irish Monthly* last year?" Oscar asked. "The one about the tomb of Keats? Do you remember the rhyme contained within the article?"

I nodded.

Oscar put the paper aside and closed his eyes. "Rid of the world's injustice and its pain, He rests at last beneath God's veil of blue; Taken from life while life and love were new." He sighed. "Perhaps it is not such a tragedy to leave this world of pain and sorrow behind."

"You also said that Keats died before his time, Oscar," I reminded him. "As did, I am sure, the young man who was murdered."

"And as did my dear cousin Effie," he said. He froze for a moment, as if he had just heard a voice from the past. Though his silence filled the air like the crisp stillness of a winter night, a film of perspiration glazed his forehead. His eyes became hard, like agates. The expression on his face reminded me of an animal pinned against a wall in fear, terrified of some invidious predator.

Then he slapped his palm on the table with a great thump and twisted his lips into a smile. He drank some water and said, "I like to think of our Effie in Tir-năn-Og, where age and death shall never find her. But I have been thinking about spirits lately, of ghosts and saints who live in a state intermediary between this world and the next. I think something holds them here. Some earthly longing or affection, a duty unfulfilled, or anger against the living. Perhaps they gather all around us in hurt silence, and it is that which casts off the sudden chill in a room that people say they feel when a ghostly presence is nigh.

"I think some shades take the form of insects," he added. "Butterflies. I can see our beloved Effie as a butterfly, can't you?"

I felt a tear stinging at my eye. "Yes. The most beautiful of butterflies."

"Yes. And she would be unique."

"Like a Swallowtail."

"A what?" he asked.

"Swallowtail. It's a kind of butterfly found in the wetlands near my parents' home in the Norfolk Broads. They have large creamy yellow wings with black stripes near the edges. The hindwings have two long black extensions, which look similar to the tail of a swallow's, and they also have two large red dots which are known as 'false red eyes.'"

He laughed. "Perfect. Effie would definitely be a Swallowtail. Certainly she had those false eyes . . . another set of them at least . . . the ones that saw into the future. I have never known anyone like her who could make predictions with such accuracy."

I looked down. I missed her so much and her death had shattered my brother.

"And how is her darling little boy, Poppy? I have not seen him in months."

"Alexander is wonderful. He looks more like Effie every day."

We sipped wine and finally ordered a meal. We were quiet a long time.

"I've been making new friends here in London, Poppy. I've even cultivated a friendship with Lillie Langtry."

Like Miss Bernhardt, Lillie was the toast of the stage.

"I do have some competition, though," Oscar said.

"I don't understand."

"Surely you have heard. Lillie is involved with Bertie."

I stared at him, puzzled.

"The Prince of Wales? Albert Edward."

I had certainly heard the rumours. "But the prince is married with children."

"Such a state has never stopped a man from longing for a woman like Lillie. She is beautiful, bold, and intelligent. The Prince likes to show off Miss Langtry, but he also is building a place where they can be alone. The house is not finished—the masons' strike, you know—so they apparently use rooms at Lord Derby's mansion nearby. But he has purchased land near Bournemouth's East Cliff and told Miss Langtry she can design the home for them. A romantic love nest. Lillie told me that Bertie's chamber will be filled with original paintings and the fireplace is to be made of carved oak and hand-painted tiles with scenes from Shakespeare in blue and white enamel and gold leaf. She says in the minstrel's gallery, she will place a statement, one that says 'What say they? Let them say.' There will be stained glass windows that depict swans in a loving embrace. Lillie has even had special curtain tie-back hooks made which reflect the prince's own emblem. It sounds marvelous; I wish I could avail myself of it."

I almost laughed. Oscar could be wonderfully malicious and exuberant in repeating gossip, while looking down at gossipers. But in this particular venture, I feared for him.

"Oscar, do take care. If she is the prince's mistress and he is building her such a home, he must be deeply infatuated with her. Surely you do not wish to incur the wrath of the future King of England! Besides, what about Florence?"

His face clouded over in such a way as I had not seen since Effie's funeral.

"Oscar? I asked what about Florence, the young lady to whom you were going to propose?"

"That is another matter," he said sharply.

I sighed. "All right, then. Aside from Florence, how was your recent trip to Ireland after your classes ended?"

"Well, I visited relatives, of course. I went riding and hunting. I attended a shooting party at Ashford Castle in County Mayo, which was quite grand."

I had never been to County Mayo, but just before I'd entered nursing school, I'd joined Effie and her family on a short excursion to Ireland to visit their relatives there. It was a lovely country. Before returning to England from Dublin, Effie, her father and I had travelled north to see other relations in Crossmaglen. I would never forget the sun beating down on the undulating hill and dale, the small, oblong berries of scarlet on the haw shrubs, the turquoise turnip fields, the showy purple irises that flagged in the breeze, and the thick, white mist of the bogs, like clouds hovering low to the ground. The streams of sunlight fell through branches that hung over the road, turning the trees into Gothic windows, like those in a great cathedral, with traceries through which golden beams and rose rays danced.

Oscar prattled on about his new associations with other celebrities and a collection of poems he was working on. When we finished lunch, I asked him if he wanted to walk with me to St. Bart's.

"Walk?" he scoffed.

I laughed. Oscar would rather hail a hansom cab to cross the street than walk.

When I was ready to leave, I kissed his cheek, and he touched my arm. "Wait, Poppy. I have something to tell you before you go," he said quietly. I sat back down.

"What is it, Oscar?"

"My Florence is engaged to marry someone else."

"Oh, my God, Oscar, I am so sorry. Who?"

"Abraham Stoker. Well, he calls himself 'Bram' now. His father died two years ago, and I think it was a way of freeing himself from his father's shadow. I knew him at Trinity. We were friends, or so I thought." His tone was bitter and it was obvious that this turn of events had thrown him into a melancholy.

"I'm so sorry," I said again.

"He lives at St. Stephen's Green now, but they are to be married this December, and they are moving to London. He's travelled quite a bit and published short stories and a non-fiction work about the duties of clerks of Petty Sessions—that's his occupation, some civil servant position. A year or so ago, he started doing theatre critiques, and he gave a favourable review of a production of *Hamlet* at the Theatre Royal in Dublin. Henry Irving was the star. Bram and Irving struck up a friendship and apparently, Irving has convinced Bram to move to London and become acting manager and business manager at Irving's Lyceum Theatre here. Florence told me that he is a gentleman with a permanent job and a steady income, whereas life with me would be filled with uncertainty.

"So, Poppy, now I know how Victor felt when you tossed him aside for Sherlock. I understand why he sailed off to India."

As my face grew hot, I glanced sideways. "Oscar, I did not toss—"

But he cut me off.

"Of course, I did not move to London to get away from the pain—and that would have been an irony, wouldn't it, considering *they* are moving here. But I understand Victor's need to extricate himself from the situation. India is a bit far for an escape but . . . ." He heaved a sigh. "At least Stoker is marrying Florence."

He paused and threaded his fingers through my hair as if he were admiring a ribbon of fine, black silk. "But Sherlock will never marry, Poppy. Not even you. So do not stay under his shadow."

I pulled back and looked away. I need not be reminded of Sherlock's brick barrier to emotions.

He clasped his hands over mine. "Poppy, look at me."

Reluctantly, I turned to face him.

"You know I am the last person on Earth to criticize nonconformity. I am endeavouring to master the art of nonconformity and the unconventional. To set my own rules and live the life I want. Sherlock annoys me at times, but I also respect him because he, too, sets his own rules. And your independent streak . . . I applaud it. But you should be cautious. Send him out of your life."

Suddenly the room felt grey and grizzled, covered in fog. I felt as if I were spiraling and tumbling down a slippery slope of slimy mud.

He withdrew his hands from mine and reached into a rucksack. He retrieved a leather-bound journal.

"I have been waiting for the right time to give you this. Effie gave it to me just before she died and told me to give it to you only when I felt sure you had the strength to read it. I'm still reluctant. I know that it has been well over a year, but you were devastated by her untimely death and still mourn her. But you need to have it. It is her journal and contains happy memories . . . and predictions, of course."

I took the journal from him and ran my thumb over the beautiful tan leather binding. It had the O'Flahertie coat of arms emblazoned on the cover, marbled edges, five raised bands and gilt lettering on the spine. I looked up but Oscar's face had disappeared into the fog my mind created. Instead I saw a translucent figure, buried in shadow, like a nymph who lives in the fairy wood. A beautiful woman with golden hair and billowing sleeves slipping down her soft shoulders and acres of fabric drifting behind her. I blinked and she was gone.

I thanked Oscar, then rose to leave. He touched my hand and repeated, "Poppy, be wise. Get out of Sherlock's shadow."

I hurried away as my eyes welled up, and I kept trying not to lose control, trying to act as if my grief belonged to someone else.

As I made my way to St. Bart's, I was reminded of the many long walks I'd taken recently with Sherlock since that tutorial in ash. He was determined to build a mental grid of every inch of London.

Occasionally, during these long walks, he would take hold of my hand. When he did this, my heart would abruptly beat so fast I feared he could actually see it swelling in my chest.

I would find myself day-dreaming about how wonderful it would be if I were truly a part of Sherlock's life, not just an assistant, not just the woman he almost gave his heart to. I was reminded again that "almost" is harder and that I should take Oscar's advice . . . simply

36

walk away, not allow myself to settle for this. But I still wanted to be with Sherlock, to make sure he ate properly, to fill those voids when he had no urgent problem to solve and feared stagnation, so was tempted to resort to cocaine and chain smoking and too much claret or port. I truly was not greedy for the kind of happiness my parents or my aunt and uncle shared. At least, I told myself that I would gladly ask no more from life than those moments when Sherlock acknowledged me as something more than a colleague, for no more than days and nights by his side. Each of our afternoon promenades was a succession of victories for me as I attempted to plant the seeds of a lasting relationship, the kind to which he had alluded just before Victor found us in an embrace.

The region of sadness I entered after these walks was distinct from that in which I had lived constantly in my long absence from his presence. Now the episodes were sporadic, and I hurled myself with great joy into the walks, the visits to the lab when he would display ashes, some black as soot, some green ones, some brown . . . and the occasions when he joined me, my uncle and aunt for dinner. The desires and goals and dreams I had nurtured—to be a medical doctor, to be a wife and mother—seemed very far behind me whenever I was in Sherlock's company. I believe I would have given it all up in order to be able to fall asleep each night in his arms. But his control over his emotions was not just an exterior layer of granite; it was embedded deeply now, necessary to his existence. He could be charming and reserved in the space of a breath. He could be happy as a young bird taking flight one moment and crabby as a hansom coachman the next, sensitive and antisocial in the space of a heartbeat.

Yet there were tender moments between us. One afternoon—it was late and the pink ribbons of sunlight danced off the glass plate windows like the moon bouncing off the ripples of a river in The Broads—I stumbled on the cobblestone and fell into him. I saw our silhouette in a window, the two of us pressed against each other. I wanted to stay that way, clamped in his embrace until the sun slipped beneath the horizon, until twilight faded into night, until the globe rose again and the lark's song heralded morning. In such moments, I saw not the Sherlock that other people knew but the one I wished he would return to someday, the one that had surfaced in the idle hours we had spent by the river in The Broads, the one who tutored me in vintage wines, the one who asked me to dance in Victor's ballroom, a memory now so brief and vague yet so sweet a residue.

Sherlock needed to make only one concession—to be what he wanted to be with everyone except me. But I feared that moment would never arrive. And to see him vexed would destroy all the calm he had brought me the moment before. But those times, however short, when he brought me into the game, into the riddle, were still sweet compared to those when, because he was resolute in never again succumbing to his emotions or physical needs, he—seemingly effortlessly—withdrew from me completely for days on end.

One afternoon, sitting near the fountain at St. Bart's, I'd tried to broach the subject with him. I told him we could do much good if we worked together, hinting that I meant as a 'couple' and he responded, "Oh, Poppy, you can be far too idealistic . . . and altruistic."

I said, "Perhaps, and I know neither are always rewarded. But what you do is so grim and relentless."

"Ah, but immensely satisfying."

"Sherlock, together we—"

"Oh, come now, Poppy, one cannot tie up life neatly with a shiny bow and glitter. I swear you would try to wave a magic wand across the belly of this beast we call London and give every day a happy ending. As if *we* could have a happy ending."

"But you need not go it alone. Life is—"

"Life is monotonous," he interrupted. "Predictable. Melancholy."

"Sherlock, this is what I mean. You must keep who you are at the centre. Do not let boredom affect you so, or be so permeated with a sense of dread that you lose yourself in cocaine or worse. Please do not let the evil you crave to extinguish seep into your own soul. It's important that you do not stare so long into the abyss that you become what you have beheld."

He simply stared at me as if he thought I'd lost my mind.

At such times, after such exchanges, when night descended, came with it involuntary tears that fell more quickly than I could wipe them away. For always, I was alone in my bed, engulfed in the solitude, and my only consolation was the memory of our night in the cottage. That was when I would hear our soft murmuring, our gentle laughter, the chords and melodies of that ancient dance. I wished so much that the memory of that one lovely night would transform into my life's most painful moment, so that I could close the door to it forever. But it never did.

To what state of mind had he brought me? To what level of anguish would my affections take me? I could no longer picture myself out of Sherlock's life. I could no longer comprehend a life without him in it. Sometimes he made me tremble. He was like a fever.

8

It was not yet three o'clock when I entered St. Bart's quadrangle. It held the same awe and wonder it always had, despite the fact that I knew I would never be hired as a surgeon by the hospital. In operation since medieval times, it was the oldest hospital in all of England—though those at St Thomas, where I'd attended nursing school before I became a physician, would beg to differ. My uncle said that the inscription and date over the old surgery at the corner of Duke Street, 'Liber Fundacionis,' was conclusive evidence that 1123 was the true year of St. Bart's foundation. But St. Thomas had also provided healthcare since the twelfth century. As early as 1215, it was already described as 'ancient,' but it was named for St. Thomas Becket, suggesting that it was founded after Becket was canonized in 1173. Supporters of St. Thomas Hospital's claim to being England's oldest hospital said it was only *renamed* in 1173 and that there was an infirmary at the Priory as early as 1106, pre-dating St. Bart's. The debate continues.

By the mid-seventeen hundreds, St. Bart's consisted of four buildings: the church of Little St. Bartholomew, the outpatient department, the residential quarters of the medical school, and the medical school. In 1859, the pump in the centre of the square that had provided clean water to the hospital was replaced with the fountain. Sherlock and I both loved the fountain, and often we would meet there before meandering to wherever it was he needed to go.

I took a seat on the bench near the fountain, intending to read some of Effie's journal, but the welcoming breeze from the well-grown trees that adorned the quadrangle made me close my eyes, remembering the way the change of seasons affected The Square, as it was called by the locals. I always looked forward to the changes in the seasons, especially autumn when the turning leaves added so much colour to The Square. The hum of the wind gave way to murmurations of starlings and house sparrows.

Sometimes there were pigeons and rooks and jackdaws in the branches. When Uncle told my father that someone on the roof of the hospital had sighted peregrine falcons on the weathercock of the church of St. Michael Queenhite, Papa, an avid birdwatcher, took the train to London at a moment's notice. Poor Papa, he stayed three days at Uncle's house, walking each day to the hospital in hopes of spotting a falcon, but never caught even a glimpse.

I let my mind drift back to memories of this place, this almost-hallowed place that I'd started visiting in my childhood and that, with my uncle's assistance, I now knew like the back of my hand. While I appreciated having had the opportunity to attend the Florence Nightingale School of Nursing at St. Thomas, it was St. Bart's that felt like home.

My first memory was when I was just a little girl, perhaps four or five, and Uncle Ormond would take me by the hand or put me on his shoulders and point out various things of historical significance at the hospital. We had stopped at the great gate in the middle of the Smithfield front, and he had pointed to an inscription. "This front was rebuilt anno 1702 in the first year of Queen Anne–Sir William Pritchard Knight and Alderman President; John Nicou, Esq. Treasurer." On the course above the inscription are the words, "Founded by Rahere," who built the priory and associated hospital in fulfillment of a vow to the apostle and in thanks for his miraculous recovery from malaria. Rahere believed that Bartholomew had come to him in a vision and promised that prayers for healing made in his church would always be heard and answered.

And thus was the beginning of St. Bart's, a place that has given solace to the poor and dispossessed of London since its establishment in the twelfth century.

Unlike most physicians during the time he was a young aspirant, Uncle Ormond had first dedicated himself to his studies to become a physician and later turned to surgery. In times past, physicians tended to attain a medical degree while surgeons apprenticed, like trades people. He had done both, and then briefly served as a ship's surgeon before becoming a house physician and surgeon at the hospital. Since his first day, he'd taken an intense interest in St. Bart's history and his study contained stacks of journals with notes about the inscriptions, renovations and the hundreds of physicians who had practiced here for centuries.

Uncle's journals documented most everything. There is a statue of King Henry VIII in the niche of the archway, with two pillars on each side and the figures of patients. In between the figurines is a window with an ornate canopy which contains a clock. On that first trip to the hospital, Uncle pointed out a map of the reign of James I and an engraving executed after the building of the Smithfield gate but before the reconstruction of the hospital in 1728. We went into the church and then walked the pathway leading to the hospital and the Great Hall. I saw where the cloisters had been and we visited the garden of the hospital, called the Garden *dorter,* to the right of what once was the monks' sleeping area.

Uncle particularly liked discovering little facts about his predecessors and had compiled long lists of their names and accomplishments. But my study of his journals focused on the architecture, artwork and engravings scattered throughout St. Bart's, like the windows in the church and the panels dedicated to famous people.

My reverie was interrupted when a young man tapped me on the shoulder and asked, "May I join you?"

He had a beard, close-set eyes, a long, hawk-like nose that reminded me of Sherlock, dark wavy hair, parted in the middle, and long side-burns on both sides of his thin face. I guessed him to be about thirty years of age.

I shrugged and said, "If you wish."

"I shan't disturb you," he said as he sat down and opened a journal. Then he proceeded to do so by asking, "Do you come here often?"

"Yes, I find the fountain soothing."

"As do I. I like to sit on the edge in summer evenings and read Theocritus. Even on busy days, it seems none of the noise of the city penetrates The Square. On Saturday and Sunday afternoons, it is so wonderfully quiet."

Years later, I would ponder that observation for the roar of war disturbed the lovely stillness of The Square in World War I. A bomb was dropped on Bartholomew Close and struck stone posts of the Little Britain gate, leaving its mark and passing through two wooden doors into the matron's office. Again, during the London Blitz of 1940, bombs severely damaged the chapel.

For a few minutes, we sat in silence but then my curiosity compelled me to speak. I closed Effie's journal and asked, "What are you writing there, if I may ask?"

He looked up and smiled at me. "A hospital report about the events of this morning." He sighed. "Quite the morning it's been. Nearly driven to madness."

Driven to madness? I thought. *Perhaps he has made Sherlock's acquaintance.*

"Is it not always a bit maddening? My uncle works here."

He gave my face closer scrutiny. "Of course. You are Dr. Sacker's niece. I've seen you when you visit him here. And you also know Mr. Sherlock Holmes."

"I do."

"He's a bit . . . odd."

I sucked in a breath. "A bit. But he is brilliant."

Sherlock was a polarizing force, but while weary of him at times, I also felt a need to protect him, for to preserve something— someone—so original, so invested in erudition and the science of deduction, someone who could so effortlessly invert the rules, seemed to come naturally to me.

The man shuffled through a sheaf of papers and began writing again.

"So, you were telling me about your mad morning. How went it, sir? You look tired."

He closed his journal. "At twenty minutes past nine, there were over a hundred persons in the hall and perhaps another four hundred on the range. Now, it must be conceded that they were quite orderly, trying not to push, the women engaged in conversation, the men generally silent. But the staff," he added proudly, "made short work of it. By eleven the room was nearly empty."

I understood his gratification at this feat. Clearing the hall was accomplished by a junior assistant physician, three casualty physicians, of which this man likely was in concert, an assistant surgeon and four house surgeons and their dressers. Uncle said it was not unusual for over thirty thousand patients to be processed through the hall in a year, and he said all of it was done with a glitter of wit and the greatest dignity and virtue.

"But," he said, "my fatigue is not due solely to my morning duties. I was cajoled into a race in the wee hours last night."

"A race, sir?"

"Which I lost miserably," he said laughing. "I had just finished treating a battery of votaries of Bacchus who were unable to reach their homes or even say where they lived. So, we let them stay to restore themselves to consciousness. And then there I was at two in the morning, running from Oxford Circus to Holburn Circus, though I had to be on duty before eight this morning. But I ran anyway, against Dr. Willoughby Furner and Dr. Ormerod, both alumni of the Rugby School." He shook his head and added, "What was I thinking?" he laughed.

I did not know Dr. Furner, but I was acquainted with Dr. Joseph Ardene Ormerod. He and his family lived on Wimpole Street; Uncle and Aunt Susan knew him well. He'd recently written an article about diseases of the spinal cord, and Uncle was co-authoring an abstract regarding tumors of the cerebellum for a medical journal, *Brain—A Journal of Neurology*. Uncle and Dr. Ormerod shared a keen interest in the workings of the brain and neurological diseases, especially ataxia.

I laughed and asked, "Are you sure you were not in the company of these votaries of Bacchus yourself to so indulge in such a marathon?"

"No, I was not. I was coaxed from writing poetry."

"Poetry?"

"Yes," he said, his chest puffing. "I published my first book of poems just last year."

"How on earth do you find the time?"

"We find the time to pursue those endeavours which interest us most."

"And that is not medicine?"

He smiled again. "I believe the muse and St. Luke are a bit at odds with each other where I am concerned."

I was about to ask him if I could read some of his poetry when Sherlock came dashing across the courtyard.

I glanced at the little silver watch pinned to my lapel.

"Yes, I know," Sherlock said through heavy breaths. "I am a bit tardy. But Poppy, I've just discovered that Dr. Haviland keeps bees here! They obtain nectar from the sunflowers growing on the banks of the river. I must make a list of the equipment I need to start studying hives in earnest."

"And why the sudden fascination with bees?" I asked.

45

"Not sudden. Bees have always intrigued me because they are logical and orderly," Sherlock said.

"Pardon me?"

He sat down on the bench next to me. "Bees are highly evolved insects that engage in a variety of complex tasks not practiced by the multitude of solitary insects."

"Ah," I said, smiling. "So they are social creatures. They see the value of living in an organized family group."

He all but rolled his eyes. "Even highly developed creatures generally have a flaw or two," he quipped. "But, yes, their behaviours indicate they communicate, they have a complex manner of nest construction, monitor environmental controls and defences, and have an established division of the labour within their colonies. They might be the most fascinating creatures on earth. According to Dr. Haviland—you know Dr. Haviland, don't you, Poppy?"

I shook my head and the young poet/physician piped up and said, "He is a house physician. We are all indebted for his work regarding a tedious case of empyema and evacuation of the pleural sac."

"Why, yes!" Sherlock said. "It was written up in *The Lancet*. In January of 1873, I believe."

"Quite," said the young man.

"Now, a honey bee colony consists of three kinds of adult bees," Sherlock continued. "Workers, drones, and a queen. Several thousand worker bees cooperate in nest building, food collection, and so on. Each bee has a definite task to perform, related to its adult age, although survival and reproduction take the combined efforts of the entire colony."

"Generally, reproduction does take a combined effort, Sherlock," I said with a smile.

He ignored my inference.

"In addition to thousands of worker adults, a colony normally has a single queen and several hundred drones during late spring and summer. The social structure of the colony is maintained by the presence of the queen."

"Oh, I quite like that. A queen in charge."

Ignoring my comment yet again, he said, "According to Dr. Haviland, the presence of bees is very important to the future of humanity."

"How so?"

"They pollinate, Poppy. Harvests depend upon them. Almond orchards, for example. Oh!" he exclaimed, jumping up as he uttered the word almond. "Poppy, we must get going."

Finally, the poet stood and extended his hand to Sherlock. "Sir, my name is Dr. Robert Bridges. You are—"

"Sherlock Holmes. A pleasure to make your acquaintance. What are you writing there?" he added, nodding toward Bridges' journal.

"Oh, just a hospital report."

"But he also writes poetry," I interjected.

Sherlock gave his head a little shake.

When Dr. Bridges took his leave of us and wished us a good day, Sherlock stared after him and said, "Another poet," he mumbled, referring obviously to Oscar Wilde. "You do attract them like—"

"Bees to honey?" I asked.

"Exactly."

"A doctor who writes poetry. A waste of a scientific mind," he added. "Nothing shall come of it."

We did not know then, of course, that the young physician we had just met would be England's Poet Laureate from 1913-1930.

"Come, Poppy," Sherlock urged. "I have much to show you."

A few minutes later, I was once again standing in the pathology lab of St. Bart's, staring at the thin, lanky, mopey, impossible man who was well on his way to becoming the world's most famous detective.

9

As I entered the lab, I stared at him, assessing him. *He never changes*, I thought. But then I realized that though he looked the same, he had matured tremendously in the four years since we met. No longer the odd Oxford fellow, his expression revealed a new confidence. He had set out to become the world's first and only consulting detective . . . or if not the only one, then the *best*. If at the tender age of twenty-four he was not there yet, he was certainly getting close. His dark hair tousled and unkempt, Sherlock quickly tossed his morning frock over the counter, took his place behind the microscope, and focused on whatever was on the slide beneath it.

An English gentleman, rarely did he abandon his cat-like tidiness, but in the privacy of his room back at Oxford, while he was playing melancholy tunes on his violin, he often donned one of his many dressing gowns. These days, in the lab, he gave precious little thought to his appearance or anything but that upon which he was working . . . solving the problem, the case, was all that mattered at those times, and he forgot about the current standards of fashion, as well as about eating or sleeping.

"You look thin, Sherlock. Are you eating? Are you—?"

His head shot up and he said, "Oh, Poppy, come in!" It was as if he had forgotten completely that I had just followed him into the lab.

"Do come in! I need your assistance."

"My assistance?" I was incredulous. "What is it?"

"In a moment. But first, a gift for you," he said, reaching down to the floor to pick up a package.

"A gift? What is the occasion?"

"Is this not the first anniversary of the Grand Opening of your medical practice?"

I nodded but the reminder almost made me cringe. My practice had not been much of a success.

"Congratulations," Sherlock said.

"I am not at all sure congratulations are in order. This year has been neither profitable nor satisfying."

"Times will change, Poppy," he urged. "Just a few years ago, a medical school in England which allowed women to attend and obtain a medical degree was pure fantasy. Now, look at you. You have graduated. You are a medical doctor. You treat patients as a physician, not as a nurse or an apothecary."

"A few patients, Sherlock," I agreed, "but put emphasis on the word 'few.'"

I untied the red ribbon and opened the box. I removed the trumpet-shaped wooden tube.

"A stethoscope?"

"When I visited your office last week, I noticed that yours was quite bent and worn."

"It was second-hand."

"Well, that," he said, "is because you stubbornly refused to accept anything beyond the small loan you obtained from your uncle to commence your practice. However," he added, pointing to the new one, "that should remedy one need. Will it suffice?"

"Yes, it's perfect. Thank you so much."

"Good. Did you know that a French physician invented the instrument so he could examine a very fat woman whose heart he could not hear when he pressed his ear to her chest? Necessity is the mother of invention. And I have just learned that a British scientist has used a galvanometer to measure electric impulses from the brains of animals."

"Yes, Richard Caton," I said.

"Quite right. Astounding. I think remarkable inventions are on the horizon, Poppy. I do wish I would live to see all the medical tools and scientific and forensic advancements that the next hundred years will bring."

"Why, Mr. Holmes, don't you plan to live forever?" I quipped.

"I do, of course. I should like to attain immortality. *That* would be quite the invention, wouldn't it? At least my monographs will succeed me."

He placed the stethoscope around my neck, took me by the arm, and without further conversation, he guided me to St. Bart's mortuary.

As we walked, I stared at his gift, pondering how few times I had actually used any of the equipment in my medical office.

Female doctors were still not trusted or visited by most of the general public. Bart's had a casualty ward, but I had not been able to convince anyone there to hire me to work in it nor had any of the other hospitals in London opened a triage department, a goal I had set for myself after Uncle Ormond and I had treated the injured at the site of the horrible train collision.

I was not the only female doctor who had been unsuccessful. Of the twenty-five young women who entered the freshman class at the London School of Medicine for Women, the first in Britain to open its door to women, only a handful graduated. It was not until the year I matriculated, in 1877, that an agreement was finally reached with the Royal Free Hospital to allow our students to complete their clinical studies there, so I thanked God every day for the experience I garnered under my uncle's tutelage. Some of my classmates dropped out and became apothecaries. Some obtained a midwife's degree from the Obstetrical Society. One woman, Alice Vickery, passed the Royal Pharmaceutical Society's examination. She became the first qualified female chemist and druggist. But there were only five women who were practicing medicine in the whole Kingdom, and we were not well received by the public.

Eventually things began to change, just as Sherlock said they would. Women in medicine and other professions earned respect. The roles of women began to move away from the stereotypes of the sad Lily Bart of *The House of Mirth* and most of the females portrayed in *Little Women* . . . we started to see as many 'Jo's as 'Amy's.' The restlessness of even the most well-born of women was exposed by Nobel Prize winner Edith Wharton and other writers. But at the time, I was certain that Britain's orthodoxy regarding gender was unyielding.

When we entered the morgue, Sherlock threw back the sheet that covered a man in his early forties. A dead man, of course.

"It's a corpse."

"Elementary, my dear Dr. Stamford."

"You haven't robbed any graves, have you?"

Knowing his propensity toward scientific methods and how studying the dead might impact solving crimes among the living, I put nothing past him.

"Fresh corpses are useful, to be sure, but I leave grave robbing to those still seeking profit as Resurrectionists."

"I am glad to hear you have not resorted to that," I said.

The so-called Resurrectionists—grave robbers with a fancy name—capitalized on the fact that dead bodies were much sought after by scientists and physicians for the study of human anatomy, so they commanded a premium price; seven to ten pounds each had once been the going rate. The best sources were mass graves or pits in which paupers were buried. Until the laws changed in 1820, it was an easy way to make money, almost as easy as the heinous baby-farming industry that still plagued the British Empire.

These most monstrous practices had endured, but fortunately, public outcry and new regulations had diminished both.

Though bodies were certainly useful in the study of anatomy and physiology, particularly in medical schools, the law provided for cheap, legal cadavers by turning over to medical schools the bodies of those who died in caretaker institutions and prisons, thus discouraging grave robbers.

"This, Poppy," Sherlock said, "is one of several men who have recently died under similar and suspicious circumstances. He died just twenty-four hours after the one who was reported in the newspaper today."

"And . . . why have you called upon me, Sherlock?"

"Your uncle is out of town, lecturing in Scotland, is he not?"

Uncle Ormond was indeed in Edinburgh, lecturing to first-year medical students on the subject of toxicology and its usefulness in determining the cause of death and how that knowledge could be useful in criminal investigations. The faculty there had been courting him for some time, hoping to convince him to take a permanent position as a professor in pathology.

"Yes, he is, but there is a coroner here in London, and if there are suspicious circumstances surrounding this man's death, he will summon a jury and investigate how the deceased died. He will interview members of the family and there will be an inquest and—"

"Oh, but you know how the people of this city are; they love a spectacle."

I had to admit that was true. Coroner's inquests were frequently held in public houses or in the open air; rumours quickly spread through the excited crowds who clamoured for a verdict, even if it was not substantiated by any evidence.

"Lestrade wants to keep this quiet. But soon it will be public knowledge. Did you read the article in the newspaper as I requested?"

"No, but Oscar told me about it when we had lunch today."

"How is Oscar?" he asked, but his attention was fixed upon the corpse. He held a magnifying glass over the men's fingernails and studied them.

"He seems well. He's trying hard to rid himself of his Irish accent. He seems desperate to be a true Londoner."

"Hmm," he responded. Sherlock cared little for trivial facts that might clutter his brain.

"I'm a bit worried about him. He seems enamoured with Lillie Langtry."

"The actress?"

"Yes, who also happens to be the mistress to our Prince."

He murmured, "Hmm" again.

"It could do Oscar harm, Sherlock."

"I agree Oscar should not interfere with the Prince's affairs. Mr. Brown, the apothecary here, was saying the other day that Bertie is building a retreat for their trysts."

"Yes, Oscar mentioned that."

"Now where did I put my notes?" he asked himself. Picking up a notebook near the foot of the gurney, he said, "Here they are." He clearly was disinterested in gossip and wished to proceed with his investigation. "It could be a serial killer, Poppy."

"A what?"

"The person who killed this young man. This is not the first victim near the museum. It is the *fifth* such corpse in as many weeks. I think we have a serial killer on the loose."

"A what?"

"A serial killer. A situation where several murders can be tied together."

"I've never heard of such a thing. Would you count the baby farmers as a series?"

"I would not. They were committed as separate events by many so-called Angel Makers with no specific time between them. Only the motivation to murder the children was the same—to make room for more out of greed. That is really the common denominator—the desire for profit."

I looked down. "Yes, that's true, of course. So these victims are not chosen at random?"

"No, Poppy, this was not some random spree. This is a series of murders and I believe they are linked, for several reasons, the first being that a small statue of Buddha and a dead bird were found next to each corpse, and the bodies were arranged in precisely the same manner. A murderer who chooses victims in a deliberate series or sequence, generally engaging in the same rituals or mode, is nothing new, of course. When I was investigating our prior case, I read about a French nobleman named Gilles de Rais in the fifteenth century who attacked children. He raped, tortured and killed them very methodically."

"How many?"

"The estimate is over eight hundred."

"Did you say eight *hundred*?"

Sherlock nodded. "And this murderer who is on the loose is likely not London's first nor will he be our fair city's last. Some of the boroughs breed crime, Poppy. Cheapside, Whitechapel, for example, where some of my young sleuths hail from. They are filled with prostitutes, the destitute, and demented individuals. Who knows what fate might befall them if someone takes it into his mind to rid the city of those he considers wicked or immoral or useless, a drain on society? I fear such places are ripe hunting grounds for someone who seeks out his prey where the lawful do not venture and a criminal may go unseen and slip away in the fog."

All at once, the air felt heavy. It was almost like Sherlock had acquired Effie's psychic gift. There would come a day in the not-so-distant future when I would recall those prescient remarks because just such a serial killer would roam the eerie streets of Whitechapel and become known to the world as Jack the Ripper.

55

Exasperated, Sherlock stomped around the room. "I am baffled and I do not like it. So, who is able to find these men and who has the power to overcome without striking a blow? I have checked this man's hands and fingernails. There is no sign of a struggle or defensive wounds. And it is a ritual of sorts." He paused a moment, then said, "I suspect our killer is a man, of course."

"Why is that? Do you not consider a woman capable of such cunning?"

"*You* would be intelligent enough. But most women I know would not be and women are by nature nurturers. They grasp at hope when none exists. Men do not.

"Now, most men in this city are Caucasian so the balance of probabilities suggests that is the race of our killer, yet the Buddha is intriguing."

His face turned, as if shaded by a darkened sun.

"Transient or geographically stable?" he asked himself.

"Stable," I answered, "given they were all found here."

"Yes, London is his fertile hunting ground. For now, at least. But motive," he muttered. "Does he enjoy killing? There is no sign of torture," he added, his voice drifting to a whisper. "Is he delusional? Playing out some fantasy? Or have the men wronged him or his religion in some way and he seeks revenge?"

"The ultimate revenge," I added.

"The murders follow a regular pattern, a very specific pattern, and the bird and the statue are part of the ritual. I've read of cases in Africa called Voodoo Death. People chanting and humming like zombies as some tribal leader dressed up in witch doctor regalia points a bone at the victim." He thought for a moment, then said, "The victims were not robbed. It does not appear to be larceny or blackmail, but I will check their financial records further." He paused a moment. "No gun. No knife or other edged weapon. No blunt objects. And not a single witness or accuser, according to Lestrade. I spoke to employees at the bank where this victim worked and none acknowledge any sort of grudge against him."

"So what is your plan, Sherlock?"

He stared at me blankly, as if he were surprised I needed to ask the question. He said, "Has your brain turned to dust like a crumbled building? I will examine the crime scene again. I will determine the cause of death. An autopsy will illuminate many things. I will evaluate the finest details. Then I can begin to build my case file."

"And?"

"And then I will invade the killer's mind to determine his vulnerabilities. A killer reveals himself through his victims. How they are killed, where and when. In the end, I will have a portrait of the killer's mind—a good part of it, at least. A profile of his personality, if you will. I will keep an open and non-judgmental mind, unlike those idiots at the Yard. And I will find the truth."

10

"So, here it is, Poppy. The coroner has thus far ruled them all natural deaths. He is a buffoon. In fact, in County Kent, he was investigated for neglect of his duties. Besides, the coroner only obtained his position through Mycroft, and so he answers to Mycroft, who wishes even more than Lestrade to keep this quiet. Lestrade is sometimes out of his depth, I'll grant you, but his motives are pure. He does not wish to start a panic; Mycroft simply wants to be in charge of it all."

There it was again, the rivalry between Sherlock and his brother Mycroft. Sherlock was the youngest of three brothers. The eldest, Sherrinford, had managed the family estate since their father passed away. Mycroft was seven years Sherlock's senior and he held some mysterious position in the British government. Sherlock insisted he was the right hand of Her Majesty and ran the whole institution. He had told me that Mycroft had created his position, his own destiny, as it were, just as Sherlock insisted he had shaped his own position of Consulting Detective. He said that Mycroft frequently decided national policy and that his great brain could hold so much minutiae that he was now indispensable to Her Majesty.

"Lestrade has a great deal of faith in your uncle," he said, "particularly since he undertook to be a part-time pathologist here at St. Bart's. When Lestrade heard of your uncle's implementation of the advanced protocol of the German doctor, he realized that Dr. Sacker was ahead of most of the physicians in Great Britain."

I couldn't disagree with the assessment of Uncle. He was an incredibly skilled and talented physician. And when Virchow developed the first step-by-step procedure for conducting autopsies a few years ago, Uncle Ormond had devoured the English translation that was published later that year.

"So, since Dr. Sacker is not here, I told Lestrade that you might assist us."

"I am not my Uncle Ormond," I confessed sadly. "I've only been a doctor for a year and—"

"Oh, do not be modest, Poppy. It does not become brilliant people. It is so transparent. Didn't you tell me that you are thinking seriously about seeking a position as a railway surgeon? Must they not be open to new and creative medical practices?"

"What has that got to do with this?"

"Logic dictates that the more experience you have with body trauma and forensic medicine, the better internal guide you will have in the treatment of wounds and injuries. You have freely admitted that your practice has gone wanting. Surely it's best to garner your knowledge of wounds and injuries and disease by examining and cutting into corpses rather than living patients, is it not? Particularly, when living specimens are so few and far between."

"Sherlock, I don't know. I—"

"Don't you need to know about which injuries may cause death within hours?" he interrupted. "Lung bruising or heart bruising, a torn diaphragm or windpipe, a ripped gullet, hollow organ damage, solid organ damage . . . not all body parts are created equal. This body is fresh. It has been just hours since the man's demise. It would seem to me the more you learn, the more you—"

Sighing, I said, "All right. What do you want me to look for, Sherlock?"

"I am hoping you can confirm my suspicions. All five bodies were found in the vicinity of the British Museum. I believe I shall soon know the 'who,' the identity of all of them, and the 'where'—if the bodies were not moved, and the 'when' is obvious. I believe that I have the 'how' as well, which is what I need you to confirm. I have yet to ascertain the 'why.'"

I took off my hat, removed my cape and draped it over a chair in a corner of the necropsy suite. "You said you think you know how this man died. Do you wish to share your opinion?"

He took a small box from a table near the body. He donned gloves—he had been studying both sanitation and preservation of evidence for some time—and removed from the box a small statue of Buddha. It was perhaps fifteen centimeters tall and closely resembled a larger one I had seen on display at the British Museum. Then he removed from the box something covered with white linen. He unwrapped it to reveal a bird—dead and stiff.

"The Buddha is hollow and the bird was next to it. I believe the bird was poisoned. I will draw some blood to examine it microscopically, and I shall do the same with the dead man, for I believe they were murdered with the same poison. I have also asked Lestrade to have the bodies of the other four men exhumed so they can be examined as well."

"They will be in various stages of decomposition."

"Yes, that is true. All the more reason to have at this chap. He is fresh."

I cringed. Only Sherlock Holmes would describe a recently departed soul in such a way, yet I knew that he meant not to degrade and likely had no recognition of the fact that he had.

"I will do the toxicological work, but I want you to examine the body. For some reason, Lestrade refuses to rely upon the conclusions I reached upon my examination of it."

For some reason, I thought. Of course, Sherlock would be incredulous. Why should anyone question deductive reasoning powers that were as sharp and sure as a surgeon's scalpel? Despite his lack of medical degree, despite his lack of any medical or scientific background other than some chemistry and biology courses, he would find it hard to understand how anyone could doubt him.

I started to say, "But I am just a woman. Lestrade will doubt me as well." Refusing, however, to lend any credence to inequality of gender so far as intelligence, competence and medical background were concerned, I said instead, "I doubt that Detective Inspector Lestrade will trust a physician like me with so little experience in this arena."

Sherlock put his hands on my shoulders, which sent the familiar shiver down my back, followed by a rush of warmth through my veins that made my entire body simmer. At these times, I barely recognized myself.

"Poppy, how can you belittle yourself when I have supreme confidence in you and your abilities? Now, put on these gloves and cover that elegant dress with this apron and get on with it."

I opened the curtains, as I knew such an examination required daylight. Colour changes can be invisible in artificial light. I pulled on the gloves, then slid the apron over my head. He slipped behind me and tied it. I turned around to face Sherlock and our eyes met for a moment. Suddenly awash with memories of our one romantic evening in a cottage at Holme-Next-The-Sea—an emotional experience that he generally attributed to both of us having consumed too much wine—I felt my cheeks flush.

How right Sherlock was . . . not all body parts were created equal. The human heart was boundless, infinitely, and sometimes cruelly, inventive. A wound to the human heart could send madness and a bubble of rage to the brain. It could drape you in an aura of anger that darkened and eclipsed everything else. Forced into quietness and stillness, swathed in a bog, it could beat in a dull thump, nothing more than a feeble tremor, barely able to dispatch blood to your vessels. Or it could struggle against your breast, fight to smooth each recalcitrant nerve, make you feel drunk and giddy and littered with hope. When I thought of that night I'd spent with Sherlock, my heart flitted in a powerful frenzy, glittered with light, as though I had come out of a dull, grey shadow and stepped

61

through a gateway to a meadow of rosy warmth and refreshing raindrops. I remembered how he had cupped my face with his palms. I remembered his touch, the scent of the sea, and the fragrance of the flowers he had left for me in the morning. I deliberately averted my gaze, walked toward the body and asked in what position it had been found.

"On the ground, face up," he said. "Hands folded across his chest with the Buddha and the dead bird next to his head on the right."

"Sherlock, is Detective Inspector Lestrade coming? Should we wait?"

"He was here earlier, but since you decided you had more important things to do, he left. He shall return soon; a page came with a message just moments before you arrived," he said. "Lestrade told me to proceed without him."

"Did you remove the man's clothing?"

Sherlock nodded. "And before you ask, no, it was not soiled or stained with blood, there were no signs of a struggle, no torn fragments. There were no objects of any kind in the area except for the statue. I noted the absence of cadaveric rigidity and putrefactive changes."

"Good," I whispered as I examined the body for moles, tattoo-marks, abnormalities, and cicatrices, like keloid scarring or calluses.

"His hands were soft," Sherlock said. "As I said, he worked in a bank so he earned his living in a profession that requires no manual labour. I took the liberty of taking measurements as well." He looked at his notebook. "He is approximately 175 cm. and weighs 70 kg. Not very muscular. No violence to the genital organ, no foreign substances detected," he added.

Sometimes I wondered if he said such things to get a reaction or if he simply forgot I was a woman. Despite the rude manner in which he sometimes addressed people, he was generally respectful of and genteel with women, so I thought this was his way of acknowledging my intellect and medical expertise despite my gender.

As I started to make my observations out loud, Sherlock took up pen and paper and began to scribble down everything I said, as if I were dictating a monograph. Then again, I felt certain that was exactly what he intended to do with his notes.

I had never done an autopsy *per se*, just some dissections in medical school, so I tried to channel the order and procedures I remembered from watching my uncle and reading the treatises of Virchow and others. "Male, Caucasian, appearing to be approximately forty years of age." I lifted his limbs and manipulated his fingers. "Stage of lividity puts the time of death at approximately six to eight hours ago."

I examined the body and saw no stab wounds, no evidence of a gunshot. I considered strangulation by some means that would not show marks—a silk tie or handkerchief—so I looked closer at the neck, but the teguments and the skin over the windpipe showed no sign of an attempt at asphyxiation; there were no contusions or bruising. I checked the palms for some evidence of wounds he might have sustained had he tried to protect himself. Sherlock was right; there were none. Nothing about the gentleman's body gave rise to a suspicion of violence.

"He could have died of a disease. We should—"

"No, Poppy. As I told you, he is the fifth victim in a series of murders and the killer has left his calling card. The bird and the statue itself. He is sending us a message. This man, and the other four men, did not die of natural causes."

I leaned over the man's face—he had a very pleasing countenance—and found no discolouration. I knew that if a man were strangled with a cord or silk or anything at all, it would affect his colouring, but this man's skin was not black as it would have been instantaneously after death in such a manner.

I palpated his neck. The tissue was soft. I examined round his chest and sides. There were no marks at all. "The face is pale, the eyes staring, the jaw firmly closed."

"Open his mouth, Poppy."

I pressed between the man's lips with my fingers to pry open his mouth. I leaned down. "There is a very distinct odor."

Sherlock jumped from his chair and threw his hands into the air. "Yes! Precisely. Poppy, when hydrocyanic acid is present, there is a peculiar odor. But it is very volatile and readily decomposes. In very little time, the odor that would be present when you open the stomach and the thoracic cavity will dissipate."

I whirled around. "You are not suggesting that I perform a full autopsy on this man, are you? Without a jury? Without . . . without any experience in the field?"

"That is precisely what I am proposing. I am certain you will find the vessels of the brain, the liver, the lungs and other organs engorged with blood, and the mucous membrane of the stomach reddened. Oh, and the blood will be a bluish or violet colour. As one would expect in one who ingests hydrocyanic acid."

"Sherlock, truly, your faith in me is most gracious, but I am simply not qualified to undertake an autopsy without supervision."

Sherlock and I both turned as we heard the door swing open.

"No, Dr. Stamford, indeed you are not," a man bellowed.

It was Detective Inspector Lestrade, and he did not look pleased at all.

11

I gave my head a sharp turn and stared at Sherlock. "You didn't tell him I was coming here, did you? You lied to me? You got me here with a ruse? Again?"

Indeed, he had done it before, summoning me to the Diogenes Club under the pretence of a request for my presence by his brother Mycroft. I was assisting Mycroft Holmes with the dreadful baby farming investigation. My involvement with that case commenced when I overheard suspicious rumblings about a possible perpetrator at St. Thomas Hospital where I was a nursing student, prior to attending medical school and prior to meeting Sherlock.

"Sherlock, really, how could you?"

"He might have disapproved," he replied, nodding toward Lestrade.

"I would have!" Lestrade yelled.

"Time is of the essence!" Sherlock exclaimed. "Listen, both of you, it's important that we gather as much information as quickly as possible. If I am right, if it is the poison I think it is, much of the evidence could quickly disappear."

"The coroner is on his way, Sherlock," Lestrade said.

Again, Sherlock threw up his hands. Lestrade crossed his arms over his chest. For the next few moments, it was a bit like watching a long volley during a tennis match.

"Oh, brilliant, just brilliant," Sherlock whined. "Now we'll have a parade outside and a hundred minions voicing their opinions and—"

"No, Holmes," Lestrade interrupted. "No jury. I have spoken at length with the coroner, and he has agreed to do this quietly so that we can confer about it before there is any inquest. But we are all on a very tight rope now, you know, with Director Vincent breathing down all our necks. There can be no more scandals, and the idea that some lunatic is on a murderous rampage and getting away with it . . . we could all be tossed out on the street at a moment's notice."

Sherlock and I exchanged a look. We both knew what concerned Lestrade. The previous year, the Metropolitan Police Detective Branch had been hit by a terrible corruption scandal that ended in a protracted trial and dismissal of several senior offices. It was in all the newspapers from London to Brighton. Richard Assheton Cross, the Home Secretary, a very conservative politician, appointed Sir Charles Edward Howard Vincent as the Director of the new Criminal Investigation Department.

Vincent had an impressive biography. He'd served with the Royal Berkshire Militia and the Central London Rangers. He had travelled extensively and spoke several languages. He'd also studied the French system of a centralized detective force while he was a student at the University of Paris. So now, instead of reporting to the police commissioner, Lestrade, Hopkins, Gregson and other detectives with whom Sherlock worked, all reported to Vincent, who reported directly to the Home Secretary instead of the police commissioner.

I could see the wheels turning in Sherlock's mind.

"So you're doing what you're told. Afraid of your own shadow," Sherlock said. "Just because the Home Secretary is monitoring Vincent, and Vincent is monitoring you. Oh, the spider webs of bureaucracy."

"Well, yes, there's that," Lestrade said. "And now there's this article in the *Times.*"

"Lestrade, all the more reason to get on with it. And for God's sake, the coroner ruled the other deaths by natural causes. You are the one who consulted with me because you thought otherwise. And don't forget that business in Kent-"

"Mr.Holmes, that was seventeen years ago. He is going to do the autopsy. That is all there is to it."

I had not spoken a word nor even tried to get one in edgewise. But Lestrade turned to me and said, "You are to assist."

"I am?"

"Yes, Miss . . . Dr. Stamford. In light of the coroner's background, I would like a *disinterested*—" he put great emphasis on this word while staring down Sherlock— "and genuinely unbiased person to observe Coroner Carttar. Mr. Holmes has a penchant, if you will, for seeing things only his way."

"The correct way," Sherlock said in a caustic tone through gritted teeth. "You know well my philosophy, Detective Inspector Lestrade. Once you eliminate the impossible, whatever remains, no matter how improbable, must be the truth. I seek only the truth, the facts."

"Well, go find them down the street at the museum. I tried to get in to see the curator to talk to him about this Buddha statue that is being replicated, but I kept being told he wasn't available."

As Lestrade explained that the statues left at each scene were exact replicas of an ancient Buddha that had been on display at the museum since 1859, Sherlock scribbled something in his notepad. Then he looked up and said, "But I need to be here!" His eyes pleaded with me to support him.

"I think that it's best to do as Detective Inspector Lestrade says, Sherlock. I shall assist the medical examiner in the necropsy and you should investigate the source of these replicas."

"Very well," he said with a sigh. "I shall be at the British Museum to see what I can learn there."

"Sherlock, I'm sure you are right," I said, touching his hand. "A message is being sent by the killer and when you discover what it is, you will have your 'why.'"

12

An older man, with grey hair and weary eyes, entered the mortuary as Sherlock left. "Good morning, Miss Stamford, Detective Inspector."

Lestrade nodded to him and I was unsure whether to correct the use of 'Miss' instead of 'Doctor,' though it occurred to me that it might not have been meant as a deliberate slight; it could have been that the older gentleman was simply unaccustomed to addressing physicians with that title. Until very recently, medical practitioners, even highly trained surgeons like my uncle, were addressed as 'Mister.' The title 'Doctor' was generally reserved for college professors and Doctors of Divinity. Even on my degree, I was granted an 'M.B.'—Bachelor of Medicine—rather than the 'M.D." for 'medical doctor' that some medical schools now issued.

However, I felt certain that the way Mr. Carttar addressed me, as 'Miss' rather than as 'Doctor,' was meant as an insult. I responded in kind.

"You are the coroner, *Mr.* Carttar?" I asked.

A grimace, then a smug smile. Finally, a nod.

Lestrade said, "Keep me informed," and departed.

Carttar turned to me. "Miss Stamford, would you—"

"Dr. Stamford," I finally corrected. "I am only able to assist you because I am a physician."

Jaw set, he replied, "Dr. Stamford, would you be kind enough to gather several large jars? Preferably new . . . but very clean will do. With stoppers if possible."

I looked on the shelves and found four such jars and set them on the table next to the body.

"And now a large dish, preferably porcelain, in which to place the stomach."

"Yes, right," I said. I found what he was looking for and placed it on the table as well.

Carttar examined the mouth and lips "for injuries or some evidence of corrosive," then said, "Peculiar odor given off from the deceased's mouth."

"Yes, Mr. Holmes and I noted it as well and—"

"Miss Stamford, if you are to assist, it would be helpful if you took notes."

I nodded and grabbed the pen and the notebook in which Sherlock had been writing. When I turned to what should have been the next blank page, I saw a caricature that, prior to being dismissed by Lestrade, Sherlock had quickly drawn of Carttar. In it, Carttar was depicted in a woman's bathing suit, floundering in the water. A woman on the shore, dressed in surgeon's garb, shook a pointed finger at him. I ripped out the page and tossed it away. I could barely suppress laughter and while Carttar conducted the rest of the autopsy, I took the rest of his insults as a grain of salt.

13

Carttar made the primary incision through the abdominal parietes, and again the peculiar odor emanated from the body and intensified when he opened the stomach and intestines. He looked for signs of inflammation. Then he asked me to place a ligature round the lower end of the oesaphaugus and a double one at the beginning of the duodenum between the two. He removed the stomach and placed it in the porcelain dish. He opened the stomach along the lesser curvature and removed its contents. He poured them into one of the jars.

He separated the intestines and put them aside. He asked me to use a lens to look for crystals or berries and other evidence of plants. "Sometimes arsenic and strychnine are mixed with indigo," he said.

But we saw no fragments or evidence of pigments that might be mixed with a poison.

We noted the appearance of the oesaphagus for corrosives or irritant poisons. These could be traced from the mouth down the digestive tract. He uttered, "Hmmm," and placed the oesaphagus in another jar.

The blood was violet in colour, just as Sherlock had predicted. Carttar was surprised. I was not.

I recorded all of the results and labeled the jars. After the autopsy was completed, I made two lists of the jars and their contents. One would be sent to an analyst—in this case, I felt certain it would be Sherlock—and the other was retained by the coroner with the jars which were stored in a cool place. I handed my record to Carttar for his perusal. When he finished reading it, we both affixed our signatures as was required by law.

Carttar looked up at me and said, "I believe your young man—"

My young man?

"—is correct. We must test the blood, but I do believe this man was poisoned."

"And the prior victims?"

"I shall give an exhumation order to the authorities."

I untied the apron and disposed of the gloves. "Thank you for allowing me to assist you," I told him as I put on my black cape, the one I had been issued when I was a nursing student at St. Thomas Hospital, which I still wore. It was practical on a chilly, foggy morning . . . and it made me feel mysterious.

"You will need to be at the inquest," he said. "I do not anticipate that my findings will be in dispute, so I shall not depute you to represent me, but I would like you to attend."

"Of course, sir, if you wish."

I walked toward the door, and he called out, "Dr. Stamford."

I turned around. "Yes?"

To my utter amazement, he swallowed his arrogance and said, "Well done."

No longer able to complain of low spirits, and my feet swift and light as if they were negotiating a skipping rope, I flew down the stairs. I paused for a moment in the Great Hall of the oldest hospital in Britain . . . a hospital that now boasted over six hundred beds. A hospital that treated over a hundred thousand patients each year. A hospital that employed four resident surgeons, one of whom was my uncle, two resident apothecaries, including Mr. Brown, who were always on duty, day and night, a college within itself and a first-class medical school.

I turned to face the Grand Staircase and looked up at paintings that had hung there for over a hundred years: one of "The Good Samaritan," the second, "The Pool of Bethesda," one of Rayer, the jester of Henry I, laying the first stone of the hospital, and a fourth of a sick man being carried on a bier by monks. In this hospital, I had just conducted—well, assisted in—an autopsy.

I set out across the vast courtyard, dipped my hand gleefully in the fountain and took a seat on a bench. Then I opened Effie's journal.

14

I let my fingertips glide over the leather and circle the crest of Effie's journal. I thought of the many lovely books that I cherished back at home in my parents' library, ones with which I had whiled away many afternoons in the sunny window seat. Now they were probably as covered with dust as the bottom of my long, sweeping skirts had been when I went to the stables until Effie made me pantaloons for riding.

I opened the journal to the first page. I recognized the handwriting, of course; the handwriting was small and delicate, just like the author. A shock of grief jolted me as my eyes focused on a tear stain at the silver-edged length of the page, just over the "d," the final letter in her name.

Last Diary of Euphemia O'Flahertie Stamford

I turned the page and found a poem. I had never known Effie to write a poem, but nothing could surprise me where she was concerned.

You must not linger at my grave and cry
For in your memories I cannot pass away
In memories of the small things not forgotten
In diamond tree limbs and scraping blades on ice
In stars that shine and fairy myths and sunny summer days by rivers
In the autumn rush of blowing winds and secrets hushed
Softly tucked away
In trees still green and sky still blue
In wicker rockers on the porch and hope chests
Like ancient stories or antique timepieces that march on
In these I shall remain
So listen just before you wake, not just for tree frogs and the
howling wind

But for the gentlest breeze, and for murmurs, whispers low
in the sweet dreams in your sleep
Do not weep
Something may lay buried there beneath the ground, beneath the
grass
But I am not there beneath the petals and the sprays
For now I scry beyond the rods of sunlight
In the mists, in the haze
So do not linger at my grave and cry

Of course, Effie was as luminous in death as she was in life, and I immediately felt the tears begin to fall. I took out my hankie, wiped my face and continued reading.

August 1876
    "I am not frightened by what I know is coming. I have enough memories for a lifetime," she wrote.
    "A wonderful childhood. A loving family. The truest friend anyone could have—you, Poppy.
    "Do you remember, Poppy, that day we were cycling the grounds of Oxford and I stopped so abruptly that you very nearly ran into me? I was blunt with you—about your complaining nature—because I could be candid with you. We were the truest of friends."

I did remember. Tired of my chronic lamentations about the barriers to women seeking a higher education, she hopped from her bicycle and lashed out at me. "You will find a way, Poppy," she'd said. "Just as I will find a way to create beautiful hats and sell them in London. We will have what we want. Certainly, you will."

Indeed she had. She'd opened her little millinery shop, despite the protestations of her mother and her future husband, my brother Michael.

"And then I found the truest love with Michael. I remember every word he has said to me. Always filled with love. Especially our wedding vows.

"Oh, my wedding day . . . it was everything I had hoped for though Mother insisted that I wear the current fashion instead of something more adventurous. She would have none of my wild sketches, even though I had already seen my visions coming true, especially on the Continent. I know you don't care for such things, Poppy, but heed my words, what we wear now will be completely out of fashion in less than five years."

She was right, of course. Within a few years, women had a very different look. The bustles had diminished, the poufs in skirts had dropped to behind the knees and the bodices were long and smooth in a style known as the *cuirasse.* The cuirasse bodice was corset-like, and *that* is the type of dress Effie made for me to wear as her maid-of-honour. My dress was pale lavender, a lovely satin, but it looked and felt like I was encased in armour!

I closed my eyes, remembering her wedding day.

Though she was not particularly happy with her mother's fashion choice, Effie gave her fairly free reign over the wedding preparations and bowed to her mother's wishes regarding the dress. After all, to Mrs. O'Flahertie, this was the day a girl prepared for from the moment she was born. Despite Effie's fledgling millinery business, her mother still felt down deep that her daughter should have no other ambition than to marry and marry well. We all felt she had, of course, since she was marrying my brother Michael.

In the end, Effie's wedding dress was breathtaking. Wedding gowns fashioned by Worth in Paris were the ultimate status symbol, but they were too dear for a professor to afford for his daughter, so Effie copied one. Her dress was made of cream silk gauze, trimmed with silk embroidered net lace, flared sleeves and an attached draped silk polonaise overskirt, also bordered with lace. She wore a floor-length veil.

My brother had never looked more handsome. Michael wore a frock coat with a vest of black cloth, dark grey trousers, and a folded cravat of dark lavender with matching gloves stitched in black. Effie's sister Marinthe was the ring bearer and their little cousin Geoffrey had the important role of holding the bride's train. He dressed like a court page. Our mothers were dressed in elegant gowns, of course, Effie's in lilac and my mother in a darker shade of orchid.

The ceremony took place at a chapel at Oxford. It was a small, intimate wedding and Oscar was the sole usher in charge of seating guests. He made the most of this occasion, dressing in a frock coat similar to Michael's, but it was impossible for him to be completely traditional. He wore purple stockings and a matching cravat. When he saw me just before the ceremony, however, he was aghast. "You look like you cannot breathe," he said.

"I can't," I choked out.

We walked back and forth on the green just outside the chapel, waiting for the guests to arrive. "Well," he said, "do not be dismayed, Poppy. The beauty of a dress depends entirely on the loveliness it shields, and on the freedom and motion that it does not impede." Laughing, he added, "In your case, today you have a monumental impediment."

"But you love extravagant clothes."

"Indeed, Poppy, I do. But one can have simple, charming garments in excellent colours and beautiful fabrics, like oriental material. I think I prefer a dress that hangs from the shoulders and allows freedom of movement. Beauty is organic. It comes from within, not without. And yours shines through even that medieval cage of armour in which you are imprisoned!"

He paused again, put out his cigarette in a flower pot near the church entrance and asked, "Do you remember, Poppy, when I told you about working with Professor Ruskin on the bridge over the swamp that made it difficult for the two villages to travel back and forth?"

"Yes, you told me a little bit about it."

"I learned many lessons that winter," he said. "It came to me that if there was enough spirit in me and my colleagues, we diggers, to go out and try to build a road simply for the sake of a noble ideal of life, then I could create a movement that might change the face of England. A movement to show the rich what beautiful things they can enjoy and the poor what beautiful things they can create."

"To change the face of England?" I asked.

He nodded. "I simply mean to tell you, Poppy, that you are noble. You have noble ideals. Fashion changes every six months, after all. But you are timeless. I have always thought of you as the perfection of your own being, and when a woman is dressed rationally, she is treated rationally. She certainly deserves to be. You certainly deserve to be." He conjured a wry smile. "And by the way, is Sherlock coming to the wedding?"

Of course, Sherlock was not coming. Marriage vows and celebrations meant little to him. I shook my head.

Effie arrived just then, brimming with vitality and energy. She stepped from the carriage, which, like the horses, was trimmed with flowers. The carriage to the ceremony was drawn by grey horses for luck. The ones that would take them back to the house

77

after the ceremony would be white to symbolize the new and fresh beginning of their new life together.

She came up to us, a basket hooked over one arm. "Oscar, this is for you," she said as she pinned a favour of white ribbon, flowers, lace and silver leaves on his shoulder. The house servants tossed blossoms of purple, white and lavender along the path to the front door of the church, making a carpet to assure the bride and groom a happy life. I felt dizzy, recalling the morning after Sherlock and I had finally expressed our feelings to one another. It was as if I were there, in the bedroom, waking to the sound of screeching seagulls in the distance, the marvelous sound of waves crashing to shore, the sunlight streaming through the windows. I could still see the incredible display of jewels on the fainting couch near the window, wild flowers of every kind strewn the length of it, blooms in gold and violet and blue and red, which Sherlock had gathered at dawn. Just thinking of it, I felt the same jolt of my heart as I had that morning.

When the servants had finished laying their carpet of blooms, Effie gathered them into a circle and handed out gifts she had made herself. She had known most of them since childhood because many moved with the family to Oxfordshire from The Broads when Effie's father took the teaching position at Oxford. Each gentleman received a tie she had sewn, and each lady received a hat she had fashioned.

Her younger sister Marinthe, lavender sash untied and dragging on the ground, ran up to us and pulled at my skirt. "These are the rings," she beamed. They were plain gold bands with Effie's and Michael's initials and the date of the wedding engraved inside of each. As I tied her sash in a bow, she said, "Mama says I have to let the ring drop during the ceremony so evil spirits are shaken out."

Oscar leaned in close and whispered, "I wonder what our friend Sherlock would think of *that* superstition."

I wished he would stop bringing Sherlock up. I simply shrugged.

Elabourate arrangements of flowers decorated the church: potted palms and festoons of evergreens and blossoms of every colour. Once all the guests were seated, the ceremony began. I listened as Michael and Effie exchanged vows, holding hands and smiling so wide, I thought they would burst. It was only when the minister asked them to keep their vows "for so long as ye both shall live" that Effie hesitated. Her face turned dark, frighteningly dark, and she mumbled, "So long as ye both shall live." Then she stuttered in a small voice, "I will. Yes. I will. As long as we both shall live."

The expression on her face scared me.

As the minister recited psalms, I just stared at my brother and my best friend through a haze of tears. But Oscar made me laugh when the minister instructed Effie to be in subjection to her husband "even as Sarah obeyed Abraham, calling him lord." I glanced at Oscar, who rolled his eyes. We had talked about this portion of the ceremony the day before. Oscar had said, "Michael better not expect Effie to obey and be submissive in all things. It's simply not within her ken."

After the ceremony, we went to Effie's parents' home. It came as no surprise that the house was also filled with a profusion of white and lavender flowers. They were everywhere, adorning doorways, balustrades, windows and fireplaces. A corner of the library was reserved for Effie and Michael to receive guests. Her parents stood nearby, I was to Effie's left, and Michael's best man, another young doctor from St. Bart's named Jonathan Younger, stood to the right. Jonathan and Michael had known each other most of their lives; they had both attended the Harrow School. He had a very pleasant countenance and, according to Michael, a brilliant future in medicine.

After breakfast came the cakes, three of them. One was very elabourate, a dark, rich fruitcake scrolled in white frosting and orange blossoms. There were two small ones, a dark chocolate for Michael and a white cake for Effie. Hidden inside the cakes were charms for good luck, and Effie laughed when I threw tradition out the door and removed my gloves to fish for my favour. This rhyme went with the charms.

The ring for marriage within a year;
The penny for wealth, my dear;
The thimble for an old maid or bachelor born;
The button for sweethearts all forlorn.

I expected mine to contain the old maid's thimble, but much to my surprise, I received a button instead. Sweethearts all forlorn . . . was this my fate? I'd never wanted a big wedding. I remembered telling Victor about the marriage of some friends of Uncle and Aunt Susan. They had a simple ceremony to commemorate the union of two people without all the pomp and circumstance. No rich white silk, no spray of flowers, no tulle, no bridesmaids parading in silly dresses with lace flounces, not even a bride's cake. And no honeymoon, no wedding tour. They simply went to Richmond for dinner. Now, having taken part in the celebration of Effie's and Michael's love, the idea of having friends and family to share my commitment no longer seemed so foreign to me. Would I ever enjoy a day such as this? I doubted it.

The wedding cake was cut but not eaten. Traditionally, it was packed away for the 25th wedding anniversary, although I couldn't fathom biting into it twenty-five years later. But according to the baker, the heavy fruitcake was doused with liquor to preserve it for that special day far in the future, a day that for Michael and Effie would never come.

Right after the cake-cutting, Effie and Michael changed into travel clothes for they were leaving immediately for a honeymoon in Paris. She wore a simple blue dress, but travel or not, she could not resist an ostentatious hat. It was made of blue silk, with ostrich and peacock feathers, antique lace, and a vintage cameo. I helped her change and she gave me a flower from her bouquet.

I tried hard not to cry when they left. As they drove off in their carriage, everyone threw satin slippers. According to legend, if a slipper landed in the carriage, it was considered good luck forever. If it was a left slipper, all the better. I swallowed hard when I realized that not a single slipper had landed in their carriage. I pushed down the thought that it might be a terrible omen.

I slammed the journal shut. I wanted to read more, but I could not. The memories rushed back at me like thunder rumbling through black clouds. I simply could not bear them.

I hurried to the British Museum to find Sherlock.

15

I found Sherlock sitting on the floor and staring into a display case in the Asian room of the museum. I quietly walked up behind him and looked over his shoulder. In the reflection of the glass case, I saw him blink and smile.

He didn't say 'hello.' He greeted me by saying "I should have known."

"Known what?"

Then he turned his head, looked closely at me, and said, "Poppy, you've been crying."

"No, no. I'm fine."

"Are you sure?"

"Yes, really. It's nothing."

Nothing you would understand, I thought. *You weren't even there.*

"You were saying, Sherlock. You should have known what?"

"I should have known why Mycroft has stepped into this quagmire; why Mycroft *really* has his fingers in this pie. He wants to impress the Home Secretary. He doesn't want the slightest hint of incompetence at the new C I D. I read about the new Director— Vincent. Every time he was promoted, from Lieutenant to Captain to Colonel, it was in *The London Gazette*. Mycroft subscribes to it. Of course, the Home Secretary would hire someone like him to helm the new Criminal Investigation Department after the internal corruption that surfaced last year."

"Yes, I'm sure everyone is still thinking about the Great Turf Fraud mess. No wonder Lestrade and Mycroft are nervous."

The trial had indeed rocked the city because no one expected such perfidy from law enforcement officers. It came about when a rich Parisian woman, Madame de Goncourt, was the victim of two English confidence tricksters, men who were very adept at defrauding people after gaining their trust. The men, Harry Benson and William Kurr, convinced her to part with over thirty thousand pounds. Scotland Yard was called upon to investigate the scam, and the Superintendent of the former Detective Department, Adolphus Williamson, hired Chief Inspector Nathaniel Druscovich to bring Benson back from Amsterdam where he'd finally been arrested. Up until then, Benson and Kurr always seemed to be ahead of the game. It finally came to light that another detective, Inspector John Meiklejohn, was accepting bribes from Kurr to warn him when his arrest was imminent. Chief Inspector Nathaniel Druscovich and Chief Inspector Palmer were also implicated in the matter, and all three stood trial at the Old Bailey and were sentenced to two years in prison.

"But I shan't let Mycroft's political ambitions or Lestrade's anxiety stand in the way of my investigation into these murders," Sherlock said. Then he jumped up. "Now, Poppy, tell me about the autopsy."

I summarized the necropsy; he paced and nodded throughout. "You believe it was poison then."

"I do."

"I shall run tests to confirm it."

"Of course. Now what have you been able to find out here?"

He pointed to the Buddha in the display case. The statue was approximately thirty centimeters high and made of bronze. I'd seen it before but never given it its due admiration.

"It's very beautiful," I whispered, mindful of my surroundings. "I have always admired the artefacts in this room and I remember it from my last visit here with Uncle. It really does look just like the statue that was left with the body."

"This is a Buddha Vairocana. It's a Tantric Buddhist image from eastern Java, tenth century."

He turned around and sat cross-legged on the floor again next to the display case. I joined him there and faced him.

"How unladylike of you," he laughed.

I shrugged.

"Now, according to the curator, this is quite similar to many of the Buddhist bronzes of eastern India."

"Wait, Sherlock, Detective Inspector Lestrade was unable to see the curator. How did you—"

Smiling, he said, "I told him I was a reporter and that I was doing a featured article on the museum and promised a very favourable review of his tenure here. He was a bit reluctant at first, considering the last reporter tossed out his feature on the new exhibit in favour of writing an article about the murder. But he finally relented."

"I see."

"Now, as to the statue," he said, pointing. "See how Vairocana sits high on his throne over a double lotus base? Behind him is the back of the throne with a halo of flames and a royal parasol. Vairocana Buddha is sometimes called the primordial Buddha or supreme Buddha. He represents the wisdom of *shunyata*."

"Which is?" I asked, though I knew he would explain it anyway.

"It means emptiness. He is considered a personification of the *dharmakaya*, that which is free of characteristics and distinctions. When the Dhyani Buddhas are pictured together in a mandala, Vairocana is always at the centre. He is white, so he represents all colours. I've been speaking to Mr. Brown at St. Bart's. He is quite knowledgeable on such things," he explained. "In fact, he was here earlier. Apparently, he is quite the patron of the museum.

"The curator said that the Dharma wheel is one of the oldest symbols of Buddhism. It is used to represent Buddhism, just as a cross represents Christianity or a Star of David represents Judaism. It is also one of the Eight Auspicious Symbols of

Buddhism. A traditional Dharma wheel is a chariot wheel with a varying number of spokes.

"The circle," he continued, "the round shape of the wheel, represents the perfection of the Dharma, the Buddha's teaching. The rim of the wheel represents meditative concentration. The hub represents moral discipline. The three swirls on the hub are sometimes said to represent the Three Treasures."

"These three treasures . . . what are—?"

"The spokes," he interrupted. "They signify different things, depending on their number. But a wheel with four spokes is rare. They represent the Four Noble Truths."

"And what are the Four Noble Truths?"

"*Dukkha,* the truth of suffering; *samudaya*, the truth of the cause of suffering, *nirhodha*, the truth of the end of suffering, and *magga*, the truth of the path that frees us from suffering. The curator said that when this particular statue was acquired, there were documents relating to it that mentioned a four-spoke wheel, though a wheel with eight spokes is more common, and these concern things like the life journey, the cycle of birth, death, rebirth and so on. But they are irrelevant, according to the curator."

I was stunned to silence, amazed at the way his mind worked, like a sponge. I wanted to hear more about these truths, but again he continued, his words racing almost as fast as his brain.

Sherlock turned his head to focus again on the statute. "This Vairocana Buddha's hands represent a form of meditation that vanquishes ignorance. His hands are those of a teacher. So, truth and the end of ignorance . . . ."

Out of breath, he finally stopped speaking.

"Sherlock, this is all very interesting." *And confusing*, I added, mentally. "There are so many messages here. What does it all mean? How does it relate to the murders?"

He closed his eyes, let out a long sigh, and said, "I have no idea."

16

The next morning I woke to the warmth of a bright yellow globe which hovered over a pale, wavy, grey ribbon of clouds at the horizon. I pulled on a dressing gown and went downstairs to put on the kettle for tea. With Uncle and Aunt Susan in Scotland, I had their house in the city to myself, and it was soundless except for the tapping of my dog's toenails on the wooden floors and the whining of my complaining cat, Sappho. I hooked Little Elihu's leash to his collar and tied him outside behind the house, lest he decide to bite a passerby as he did on the day I met Sherlock. I left him to relieve himself, gave Sappho food and water, and finally her persistent meows changed to a soft purr.

A few minutes later, tea in hand, I let Little Elihu back inside, retrieved Effie's journal, and went into Uncle's study. It was a peaceful, albeit sparsely furnished room, for he abhorred clutter. His desk was a sturdy and substantial JAS Shoolbred, with heavy turned legs on brass castors, lined drawers and a well-worn leather top. The desk was, in my opinion, the loveliest and most useful piece of furniture in the house. Uncle told me that when he and Aunt Susan were gone, I would inherit it and everything they owned, for they had no children, and I was like their own daughter. I did not like to think about that day. I wanted them—and my parents and my brother Michael—to live forever. I had so recently lost Effie, who had died shortly after childbirth, and I could not bear the thought of losing anyone else I loved dearly. I cared little for furnishings or knick-knacks, but I knew that when the day did come, I would cherish this desk and every mark, crack, scratch and imperfection, for each would remind me of Uncle.

I sat down and opened Effie's journal. I skimmed her recollections of her wedding day again, which were not dissimilar to my own, and read on.

"You may wonder, Poppy, why I address these random thoughts to you instead of Michael. I know you will miss me, but I fear Michael would be unable to read my words at all after I am gone. There are things I must relate to you; things about which you must be warned. And there are memories I must share."

Once again, Effie warned me about Sherlock. She had said many times that he was dangerous and that I must walk away from him. Then her warnings became much more specific.

"You remember I told you about a boat . . . warned you not to board it. I have to say it again."

I did recall her vision. She had said that she'd had another dream. "Do not get on the boat, Poppy," she had said.
"What boat?" I had asked.
"The princess's boat."
And I had laughed at her. Why would I ever be on the boat of a princess?

"Many will die," the journal entry continued. *"You and Michael will try to help as you did at the train collision. But your medical expertise will be of little value this time."*

I flipped to the next page.

"The baby will come in February. He will come early. I thought I would have a daughter. I was going to name her Hope. But I see now that I was wrong. He is a strong healthy boy, Poppy. You must help Michael. He will grieve and he will not realize that he is jeopardizing our son. Do help him be strong, sweet friend."

87

August. This entry was dated in early August of 1876. The baby was not due until mid-April. She could not have even known yet that she was with child when she wrote this.

There was another entry in early September.

"It will be this time of year when the boat sinks. And you will be hunting someone. You and Sherlock. I see a bird, a dark bird. And something from the Far East. I know you will not listen, but please do not get involved."

I gasped. The Bird. The Buddha. She knew.

I could read no more just now and needed to persuade my mind to think about something else.

I closed the journal, rose and looked behind the curtain. Near the hem, in a pocket, Uncle kept the key to the right hand desk top cupboard. It did not fit any other drawer locks. I knew this because as a curious adolescent, I had tried each one.

Uncle kept things in this cupboard that he did not want to lose or that, when I was younger, he did not want me to see, like graphic diagrams of surgical procedures or ghastly photographs of wounded soldiers or homicide victims. Once, when I was only about ten years of age, I had opened it and found photographs of soldiers who had served in America's Civil War. Some were missing legs or arms; some were skeletal, having starved while they were imprisoned; some had a vacant, ghostly stare. Uncle did not scold me for opening the cupboard; he simply explained that these men were not likely to return to normal, for their emotions had been shattered, and once shattered, emotions did not mend. It was something that always came back to me now because Sherlock shunned emotions, entanglements, passion, or any sentimentality. I suddenly remembered that Uncle, staring at the photographs, had also said, "What a shame, a waste. How terrible to see someone suffer so and to force them to continue living like this. Better to end their misery."

Always curious about what interesting new and gory thing Uncle was hiding from Aunt Susan and me, I put the key in the lock and opened the cupboard. At the very top of a pile of papers, I found three photographs. One was taken on the day I graduated from nursing school, the second on the day I graduated from the London School of Medicine for Women. I turned the second photograph over and Uncle had written *Priscilla Olympia Pamela Price Yavonna Stamford, M.B., June 1877.*

I smiled. My lengthy list of names had long ago been shortened to 'Poppy,' though only relatives and close friends addressed me by my nickname. Victor Trevor, however, the man everyone had expected me to marry, always called me Priscilla.

The third photograph surprised me. It was a photo of Sherlock, Effie, Victor, and me. It had been taken at a dinner party in the spring of 1874, shortly after I met Sherlock. I had a miniature of the photograph that I had intended to place into a locket someday. I had forgotten that, at my uncle's request, Sherlock had a copy printed for him.

The memories of that year swilled around my mind like the last sweet sip of brandy at the bottom of the glass.

I was with Victor Trevor, who was then a student at Oxford. We were attending the final day of Eights Week, the four-day regatta on the Thames, when Little Elihu bit Sherlock's calf. Victor and I attended to his needs that day and continued to assist him for several weeks thereafter. Victor and Sherlock became friends and Sherlock and I worked with his brother Mycroft to apprehend the baby farmer about whom I had learned while attending nursing school at St. Thomas. I had overheard a suspicious conversation, related it to my uncle, who knew Mycroft Holmes who, in turn, enlisted me, and later Sherlock, to help with the investigation. That summer, Victor invited Sherlock to spend some time with him and his father at their country estate in Norfolk, not far from my own home, and my affections for him grew.

But a dark cloud hovered over the Trevor estate. A man from the Squire's past suddenly arrived, a man named Hudson who was married to Mrs. Hudson, who at that time was one of Squire Trevor's servants. His appearance threw Squire Trevor into a tizzy. Soon after, he received a letter from yet another past acquaintance and he fell deathly ill. When Sherlock set out to solve the mystery that so plagued Victor's father, he discovered that Hudson was blackmailing Squire Trevor, who had for many years hidden his unsavory past from everyone.

Sherlock summoned me to join him at Holme-Next-the-Sea where he had finally found the truth. He wished to discuss how to proceed—in other words, he actually asked for my counsel regarding whether to tell Victor everything he'd learned about his father. I joined him there and it was then that we finally admitted how we felt about each other. But Sherlock quickly recoiled from this love and the memories of the night we spent together, especially when, shortly after the squire's funeral, Victor discovered my true feelings for Sherlock—and Sherlock's affection for me. This ended their friendship and destroyed my relationship with Victor Trevor. Heartbroken, Victor left England to manage a small tea plantation in India that his father owned. Heaped with guilt over betraying his one true friend and infused with distrust of me for so easily having 'tossed Victor aside,' Sherlock retreated from me emotionally. He wallowed for a time in self-introspection. Though he was intent on finding the answers to all the riddles of life, love was too nuanced for Sherlock Holmes. He was enthralling, captivating, but unforgiving, particularly of himself, and this experience was yet another grain of sand added to the already vast shore of his knowledge of the unpredictability, absence of logic and disappointing nature of human beings.

I set the photographs aside and rummaged through the remaining papers and newspaper clippings in the cupboard. There were a few newspaper articles summarizing cases on which my uncle had worked with Scotland Yard, some legal documents, and several grisly photos taken during some of his surgical procedures. I was about to close the cupboard when I spied a small book. I took it out and stared, stunned, at the cover. The book was a series of essays concerning Tantric Buddhism. I leafed through it, scanning its contents. "The Truth of Suffering" was the title of the first section. Then the others followed: "The Truth of the Cause of Suffering," "The Truth of the End of Suffering," "The Truth of the Path that Frees Us from Suffering."

All the tenets that I had just learned of the previous afternoon.

I sat back in the chair, pondering. Sappho jumped into my lap and I stroked her long, ivory fur. Purring, she nudged her head against my chest, insisting on a further display of my attachment, so I nuzzled her nose and gently scrunched the fur on her head.

"Sappho, what am I to make of this? Why would Uncle be reading about the very things that relate to these murders?"

The cat arched her back and looked up at me as if to ask, "Why indeed?"

17

I bathed, dressed, made another cup of tea and went to Uncle's library, where I found several more books about Tantric Buddhism, most of them concerning specifically the Vairocana Buddha and the philosophy surrounding him. I retired to the drawing room, all the while ruminating on my discovery.

One night at dinner, Uncle had mentioned that he was pleased with the new global interest in Eastern philosophy. He gave a synopsis of the works of a German philosopher, Arthur Schopenhauer, who devised a philosophical system based largely upon his studies of it. Uncle was similarly intrigued with Henry David Thoreau, the American philosopher, who had translated a Buddhist sutra from French to English, as well as the works of Henry Steel Olcott, a theosophist, and Lafcadio Hearn, known for his books about Japan. My ears perked up at the mention of Japan as I remembered the many Oriental artefacts and paintings that adorned the walls of Squire Trevor's library.

But these brief summations of Uncle's readings were the extent of that dinner conversation.

Now I sat in Uncle's favourite wing chair near the fireplace and returned my attention to the little book I had found in his desk. The book explained, in simple terms, the basic tenets of the Four Noble Truths. I learned that the Buddha had set forth these truths during his first sermon after his 'Enlightenment.' Though the subject was complicated and confusing, the explanations were eloquent in their simplicity. *Even I can understand these*, I thought, as I read through them.

The Truth of Suffering: The First Noble Truth often is translated as "Life is suffering."

The Truth of the Cause of Suffering, teaches that we continually search for something outside ourselves to make us happy, but no matter how successful we are, we never remain satisfied.

The Truth of the End of Suffering: The first truth tells us what the illness is, and the second truth tells us what causes the illness. The Third Noble Truth holds out hope for a cure.

The Truth of the Path That Frees Us from Suffering. In the fourth truth, the Buddha prescribed the treatment for our illness, which is walking the Eight-Fold Path to become aware of oneself, one's feelings and thoughts, and gain a clearer picture of reality.

I leaned back and closed my eyes. Uncle Ormond was an avowed atheist. Though he had expressed an interest in various religions and seemed intrigued by Eastern philosophy and the ancient Oriental cultures, an interest that had obviously deepened in recent times, we had never discussed any of this in depth. I also knew that these books were recently purchased because I had lived in this house with Uncle and Aunt Susan since my early adolescence while I attended a private school for girls in London, and later while I went to nursing and medical school, and I was totally familiar with his library. I had never noticed these books and Uncle had never alerted me to them . . . uncharacteristic of him, because he loved to share with me the books he acquired on his frequent trips to the bookselling district on Newgate Street.

I opened my eyes and was about to close the book and return it to the shelf in the library when a slip of paper slid from between the pages to the floor. I picked it up and read a note that was written in Uncle's handwriting.

Only Buddhism locates suffering at the heart of the world. Why do pain and suffering exist? Siddhartha Guatama, c. 566 BC - c.480 BC. Compassion toward all sentient beings.

Then, he had written and underlined: <u>Abolish suffering altogether.</u>

What had stirred my uncle's new interest in the very things that Sherlock was investigating as possible clues to the British Museum Murders—a name I had affixed to them in my mind and which undoubtedly the newspapers would coin?

I returned to the Four Noble Truths. Suffering was the common denominator. Suffering and how to alleviate it.

How to alleviate it, I thought. How to end suffering. Euthanasia.

Hadn't Uncle mentioned this recently as well? Hadn't he and Aunt Susan discussed that very topic just the other night when he reminded her that even as far back as ancient Greece and Rome, before the coming of Christianity, attitudes toward active euthanasia and suicide were tolerant?

"Many ancient Greeks and Romans had no defined belief in the inherent value of individual human life," he'd said, "and pagan physicians performed both voluntary and involuntary mercy killings."

I had reminded him, as I thrust myself into the conversation, of the Hippocratic Oath which prohibits doctors from giving a deadly drug to anybody, not even if asked for. I had also reminded him of the edict of Thomas Inman, an eminent surgeon who had just died two years ago. "*Primum non nocere*," I said. "First Do No Harm."

And Uncle had promptly reminded *me* that, "Sometimes life is not worthy of life," and then expounded on the essays of Samuel Williams, who advocated the use of drugs not only to alleviate terminal pain, but to intentionally end a patient's life. "Williams' drive to legalize euthanasia has received serious consideration, Poppy," Uncle said.

I had turned on my heels but not before shouting, "No! Medication should be administered only to alleviate pain, not to hasten death."

Now, I slammed the book shut and marched back to Uncle's study to return the little book to the desk cupboard. It was unthinkable, what I was thinking. Which was that perhaps the victims were terminally ill. Which was that perhaps one had sought Uncle out to end his life and now Uncle was sending a message to others that they, too, could seek his help to end their suffering, their lives.

My mind raced. My thoughts grew darker. I'd often found Uncle deep in conversation with Mr. Brown at St. Bart's. Uncle said they talked about new medicines and engaged in discussions about Buddhism. What if my uncle had relieved the victims of their suffering and left, as Sherlock put it, a calling card, hoping to send a message that people need not end their lives in misery and pain?

I paced the floor. Had Uncle Ormond been to the British Museum lately? Yes, less than two months ago, we'd spent the day there when my mother came into London to visit with Michael and my little nephew Aleister Alexander, born just prior to Effie's death. He was just a little over a year old, and I had carried him from room to room, holding him close, hoping that somehow he would feel his late mother's warmth through my embrace.

Had we visited the room that housed the Buddha? We had. Had Uncle shown any particular interest in it? Lingered there to gaze at it? He had!

He had pointed it out to me specifically and said, "There is much to learn from these Statues . . . these symbols of how to vanquish ignorance and suffering."

I nearly passed out as the blackness of my thoughts and rekindled memories ravaged me.

Impossible. My Uncle? A killer?

And what had he told me as we treated the wounded at the scene of the horrible train crash near Oxfordshire on that blustery, rainy night in September of 1874? What had he said to me as he stopped me from trying to treat the two hopeless women who, pinned together by some part of the wreckage, were minutes from death?

I remembered now. Uncle had touched the hand of a man who was near death, and then another who was gasping his last. I watched as he moved on right past them. Without a word, he bent over the next man, who was sobbing like an infant.

As he opened his medical bag, I touched his shoulder and asked, "Uncle, what of the other two?" He stared at me, obviously puzzled by such a question. "They are close to death. Tonight I am a physician. Not a coroner." And on the way home, he'd said, "We should be thankful for those who died quickly. They did not suffer."

My thoughts, the absurdity of them, the uncertainty and brutality of them, choked my mind.

Uncle had moved on. He helped the living and left the dying. Was he also capable of moving the dying along a little faster? He certainly had the means and the acumen, and possibly the mindset, to do so.

Impossible. Or was it?

18

That afternoon, Sherlock and I met for tea at the same restaurant where I'd had lunch with Oscar. It was busy, even for a Saturday afternoon, but with autumn upon us and winter not far behind, many people wished to enjoy the balmy weather. We settled in on the sweeping, colonnaded Nash terrace and ordered finger sandwiches. When they served a pot of Indian tea, I immediately thought of Victor. I had written to him a hundred times, but all letters had gone unanswered. I wondered how he was doing at the tea plantation in India.

As if Sherlock had read my thoughts, he asked, "I often think of Victor when I have a flavourful cup of Indian tea. Have you heard from him?"

Shaking my head, "I doubt I shall."

"You have not heard a word?" Sherlock asked.

"Nothing, Sherlock. Pour me some tea, will you?"

We left it at that.

I knew that Sherlock still felt guilty about what had happened. He felt he had betrayed his only friend. I could never forget his words after we had spent the night, that one night, together. *I have betrayed my only friend in the world, and I have betrayed you as well because we both know a relationship is out of the question. I would not be a good husband and to be effective in my work, I must never marry. I must not succumb to love again. I never shall.*

It was true that I had not heard from Victor directly, but my brother received the occasional letter from him. Michael told me it was Victor's way of keeping in touch with me.

Several times he shared Victor's correspondence with me. Victor wrote of the long, humid days, the starchy, fibrous, green jackfruits that tasted like a combination of apple, pineapple, mango and banana. He described his house and his verandah with its moss-speckled walls. "Rat snakes forage beneath it when they are not glistening in the sun as they rest." In a recent letter, Victor had written about bees that settled in the hollows of trees; many of the locals left indentations in their walls so that the bees could build honeycombs in their homes. I had wanted to tell Sherlock about the bees in which he seemed so keenly interested.

Michael also had related Victor's descriptions of glossy black jungle crows with their harsh, guttural, grating squawk, and of the bluebottles that swelled around his home like an eager throng at a public hanging, waiting for the remains. I'd asked Michael what those were.

"Come now," Michael had said. "You know your Shakespeare. They are blow flies that like the smell of rotting meat and fruit. Victor says they curl and cluster around flowers with strong, disagreeable odors."

Unsurprisingly, Sherlock pushed his food around. He was never one to eat or sleep very much when he was focused on a problem. "I have confirmed the poison in the bird and the victim," he said. "It is, as I predicted, hydrocyanic acid."

Chemistry not being my forté, I asked about its attributes.

"It is colourless and lethal. It has a faint, bitter, almond-like odor, as you now know."

Now I understood why the word 'almond' had triggered his impatience at the fountain when he'd mentioned the word almond in connection with his diatribe on bee cultures.

"It seems to be quite effective as a rodenticide and is used in killing whales as well," he said. "A lethal dose can kill a human being in one minute."

"One?"

He nodded. "So now I know who, where, when and how."

"But not the elusive 'why.' And not the 'who' either."

"No. I know the victim's name."

"I meant the killer. The 'who did it?'"

"Ah, yes. Who committed the crimes? No, not yet," he admitted with a sigh. "But James Dixon is the identity of the man you examined yesterday. His young wife had reported him missing to the Metropolitan Police and his employer said he did not come to work for two days."

"Could it be a suicide, Sherlock?"

"Interesting you should say that. James was recently diagnosed with a brain tumor. I suppose he may have wished to end his life sooner rather than later. Before he suffered further."

I winced, trying desperately to discard the horrible thoughts that clouded my mind.

"His wife said that he had crippling headaches. There were gross personality changes as well. His employer noted the same. James possessed a high degree of mathematical prowess, but, of late, he could barely make correct change or tally up at the end of a day. Just last week he was given a rather abhorrent evaluation. The wife agreed that he could no longer balance their personal account. She urged him to see a physician."

"And did he?"

"His regular physician, one Dr. Price, whose knowledge of the brain, of any neurology whatsoever, is limited. He, in turn, referred him to a physician in Scotland."

"Scotland?"

"Dr. William Macewen, who is fairly prominent in the field. Dr. Macewen has attempted to remove brain abscesses."

"My uncle knows him, Sherlock. He mentioned that he intended to see him on this visit to Scotland."

Sherlock arched a brow. Then he said, "Dr. Macewen referred James to Dr. John Hughlings Jackson here in London. He has treated epileptics, and a few years ago accurately diagnosed a frontal lobe tumor in a young boy. The parents refused to allow him to operate and the boy died, but they did permit an autopsy and Jackson was able to confirm his diagnosis."

"Jackson," I said. "Sherlock, I have heard that name as well. Yes, now I remember. Uncle attended a meeting at the Hunterian Society, right around that time that we . . . that I met you. Dr. Jackson delivered the Hunterian Oration. He also delivered the Goulstonian lecture to the Royal College of Physicians a few years ago. Neurology is in its infancy, but Dr. Jackson is a pioneer in the field."

Again, Sherlock arched an eyebrow and nodded.

I recalled that Uncle described Dr. Jackson as an innovative thinker and a prolific writer. He'd read all of his articles in *The Lancet*.

"I did some research," Sherlock said.

Of course, he had.

"Dr. Jackson will soon be one of the initial contributors to a new medical journal, *The Brain Journal*, dedicated to clinical neurology. Its inaugural issue is scheduled for publication later this year. And your uncle is acquainted with him?"

"Uncle is a bit like your brother Mycroft."

Cutting me off, he scoffed, "He is nothing like Mycroft."

"I *mean,* Uncle knows . . . well, just about anyone who is anyone in the medical field."

"I must speak with him then, when he returns. When is he coming back to London?"

"Tomorrow evening, I believe. Aunt Susan was disappointed with the schedule. She wanted us to make a day trip on the *Princess Alice* to Rosherville Gardens at Gravesend."

All of a sudden, it struck me—something Effie had written about a boat. I shuddered now, remembering her prediction, her warning. I shook off the creeping evil feeling.

"To where?" Sherlock asked.

I had to smile. Sherlock hated to fill his head with trivial things and certainly a lazy afternoon aboard a paddleboat, moving at a leisurely pace along the Thames, or a day of traipsing through pleasure gardens and watching tightrope walkers or listening to the 'drivel' of fortune-tellers would not be a priority for him. He had never believed any of Effie's predictions, though he'd been shaken by her foretelling of the two horrible train collisions of 1874.

"Never mind," I said. "Did the victim's wife further elabourate on James' condition?"

"No. She was quite weepy and rather incoherent."

"Poor woman," I said.

"I would rather think to say 'poor man.' He might be alive today had she not convinced him to forego the operation Dr. Jackson offered to perform."

"But we know that Mr. Dixon was poisoned, Sherlock. He did not die of the tumor."

Then I realized we had not even opened the skull. We had not examined the brain.

"Indeed, he was poisoned. And I believe that when the other bodies are exhumed and I speak to the relatives, we will find some common denominator. The reason that all of them were poisoned, I suspect, was that they had in common something that could not be cured."

"I don't understand," I said, though I knew exactly where he was going.

"If teach man knew that his life was coming to an end, perhaps each of them wanted it to end sooner rather than later . . . and without suffering. Perhaps they sought the killer out."

I gulped down a glass of water for suddenly my mouth was dry as sand. "Sherlock, what you're saying . . . I have been wondering . . . thinking—"

"Do not hesitate, Poppy. I realize that most women are secretive but you are not most women. Speak your mind."

"Well," I said, "If you are right and all of these men were facing a slow and miserable but imminent death . . . if they were indeed suffering and unwilling to suffer more—"

"The statue . . . the Four Truths. You think that is the link. So do I."

"I don't know, but—"

I stopped and drank more water. He peered at me, studying my face, piercing through me with those intense blue-grey eyes.

"I am just parched, Sherlock," I said, draining the glass. "Now I do not know . . . but if they all were suffering . . . what if they knew that it would continue right up until death, and they wanted to just put an end to it and they found someone—?"

"Euthanasia, yes. I concur."

I nodded, but the word being spoken out loud made me nauseous.

"They were all found in the same way. All of them were peacefully at rest, as if in a coffin," he muttered, his face shadowed by his racing thoughts. "And the bird and the Buddha were placed right next to their heads! Poppy, you are more brilliant and logical than I thought!"

His face lit up like a child's viewing fireworks for the first time.

102

"Could they all have had brain tumors? Could each one of them have been diagnosed with that or something similar?" He was not speaking to me now. He was thinking out loud, probing his brain for the answer. "I think this is a distinct possibility. Poppy you are becoming a most valuable assistant."

"Is that what I am now?"

"Is that something you do not wish to be? I did not mean it as a term of reproach. Does that moniker somehow demean you?"

"No, I didn't say that, Sherlock."

But secretly, I still hoped that I might be so much more.

"So, as I said before," I said quickly to steer us back to Mr. Dixon's demise, "you likely have the what, where, when. Perhaps the why is that the victims wished to end their lives. But not who killed these men or why he—or she—did it."

"Someone who would kill for mercy's sake."

"Killing is not mercy," I said.

"Isn't mercy the very essence of euthanasia, Poppy? A merciful and serene end to a life that is no longer worth living?"

Once again, everything I had found in my uncle's desk and library, and his own words, rushed back to me.

19

Uncle Ormond and Aunt Susan were due home late Sunday afternoon or early evening. I spent most of the day contemplating if I should voice my suspicions to Uncle. The logical side of my mind reverberated a resounding 'No!' and my emotions kept step. How would I even broach the subject?

Uncle, I noticed you have several recent additions to your library, many of which relate to Tantric Buddhism, the Four Truths and the human condition, to-wit: suffering? Would you care to elabourate on these recent acquisitions and your intense interest in Eastern religion?

Or . . .

Uncle, why the sudden attentiveness to Buddha and the concept of eliminating suffering? Is there some personal reason for this concentration on the subject?

Or . . .

Uncle, five men have recently been murdered. Poisoned. In fact, I just assisted the Coroner with an autopsy of one of the victims. Have you heard anything about these events and would you care to share your thoughts?

Or . . .

Uncle, what are your feelings about euthanasia? Did you kill five men to relieve them of their suffering?

None of those questions could ever cross my lips. I knew that.

I tried to eat something. I couldn't. I tried to nap, but sleep eluded me, as it had the night before. I spent most of the day reading the books Uncle had purchased on the subject of Buddha and its doctrines. In the late afternoon, I decided to go for a walk.

When I arrived at the steps of the British Museum, I took a deep breath, and went directly to the display case that housed the Buddha. It was a truly beautiful artefact, worthy of its place in the museum.

My mind kept roiling back to the Four Noble Truths and what I had read in Uncle's books. The Truths were the essence of the religion and the philosophy entwined within it, and from my meager understanding, I gleaned that those who follow the doctrine believe that suffering simply exists; it has a cause; it has an end; and there is a way to bring about its end. Those who followed the religion did not think of suffering as negative but sensibly regarded it as a part of the world, the world as it is, and something that can be rectified. Pleasure is fleeting and leads only to an ultimately unquenchable thirst. In the end, all that is certain and unavoidable are aging, sickness, and death.

Buddha set forth a way, through the Truths, to deal with the suffering we face, be it physical or mental or emotional, and said that desire and ignorance lie at the root of suffering. He taught that without the capacity for mental concentration and insight, one's mind does not evolve and cannot grasp the true nature of things. Vices like greed and lust, hate and anger are derived from this ignorance.

It was a very reasonable and utilitarian way to approach the human condition and, though Sherlock subscribed to no religion that I knew of, it was not unlike his own tenets. Ignorance, to Sherlock Holmes, was the weed in the garden that invaded and blighted everything within it. He himself was ignorant of many things, but it was out of choice, for he focused on his own narrow interests and that which was necessary to his work. Nevertheless, he hoarded little packages in his brain attic, like my mother, who liked to purchase odd little gifts throughout the year and put them away for some occasion in the future when she might need them. And like Endelyn Stamford, Sherlock might forget for a time what he stowed away, but he always, always had a vague perception of what was tidied away in storage.

For a short time, I walked along Great Russell Street, and then turned left on Montague, the street where Sherlock lived. I toyed with the idea of dropping in, but he would likely be in the lab at St. Bart's anyway, fixated on his analysis of the results of the autopsy of James Dixon. I found my way to Russell Square, to Queen Square and Ormond Street, wondering as I always did if this was from whence came Uncle's name. After a very long meander, I somehow found myself at the Langham Hotel, where I had dined with Sherlock when he briefly visited London after the dog-bite incident that had initially brought us together.

At that time, the deep wound left behind by my dog and the sprained ankle that had not yet healed required that Sherlock remain on crutches but he had still made his way by train to London for a short visit. Over dinner, we discussed the baby farming investigation. Then a page and I helped Sherlock to his room. It was there he admitted he had feelings for me.

He showed me some books he had ordered to read during his visit. He talked about the room he was in—supposedly haunted. Just before I left, he encircled my wrist with those long fingers of his and said, "I just wanted a moment alone with you. You are a woman of soul and you touch mine—if indeed I have one—in a most unusual way."

And then he pulled me close. My lips were an inch from his and I could feel the heat of his breath on my cheek.

I could have cried out, but I did not. Instead, I brushed my lips tenderly against his cheek. Then I ran from the room because I realized at that moment how much he meant to me . . . and how dangerous those feelings were.

Now, standing at the entrance to the hotel, all those recollections flooded back. I quickly turned to make my way home.

As soon as I arrived, I took Little Elihu for a short walk, but suddenly I was exhausted and hoped that savoring those tender moments at the Langham, memories that were burned into my brain, would help me drift to sleep. I took off my dress, slipped into bed in my petticoats, and fell into a deep slumber.

I woke to hard knocking at the door. Night had fallen and there was no indication that Uncle Ormond and Aunt Susan had returned. I wondered if they had forgotten their key. I threw on a dressing gown and slippers, dashed to the door and opened it.

My brother Michael stood there, hair askew and plastered to his forehead, his face ashen in the pale light of the gaslamp above the entryway.

"Michael, what is it? What's wrong? Is it the baby?"

"No, he's fine. But Poppy, there has been a terrible disaster on the Thames."

"What?"

He brushed past me and we stood in the foyer. "A paddleboat. A paddleboat and some kind of iron cargo boat collided."

"What?"

"Just a few hours ago," Michael said, breathlessly. "Around half seven near Tripcock Point and Galleons Reach."

"My God, Michael, no!"

"I am on my way to Roff's Pier, to the steamboat offices, to see if I can be of assistance. Will you come?"

I cast off my slumber with my slippers, hastily changed and grabbed Uncle's medical bag, which, unlike my own, contained the most advanced surgical instruments and medications.

When we got to the pier, it was chaos and mayhem. Hundreds of people had already gathered to try to learn more about the extent of the wreck on the river and to try to find relatives and friends who had been aboard the *Princess Alice*.

The boat named for the princess, I thought, again recalling Effie's words.

20

I had thought that no horror could match what I had witnessed in Norfolk at the train collision. Too soon, I was proved wrong.

Chaos, panic, and mayhem really do not adequately describe the scene on Roff's Pier. Londoners were accustomed to fog, fire, riots, murders, and war—certainly war—but to witness the aftermath of this catastrophe right here on the Thames, to know that hundreds of passengers who had gleefully boarded the paddleboat near London Bridge that morning would never be seen again, was unfathomable.

Uncle had, over the years, become somewhat calloused to affliction and pain, and at the train wreck, I had somehow forced myself to harden, to momentarily filter out the gore and tragedy and misery enough to treat the injured, to move from one patient to the next, as is required in triage situations. My uncle's words at the train wreck when I started to fall apart echoed in my mind now. "Get hold."

But I was still often governed by my emotions, still vulnerable to empathy, perhaps because I refused to lose it, choosing rather to harbour that attribute to some degree, or perhaps Sherlock had awakened in me emotions that I had chosen to bury before.

Although Sherlock's general admonishment of religion still rang in my ears, I found myself briefly given to prayer. Though my great joy came from immersing myself in living in the present and how I might impact people's lives and be of help through my profession, and though I was reluctant to rely upon any promise of a 'better place,' I suppose I was unable to entirely abandon my faith. The particular brand of despair I was about to face once again— irrevocable injury and loss, fear, grief, sorrow and death . . . and the inconsolable people who were left behind . . . forced me to summon to my mind a kinder motif in the hereafter for the lost souls. I longed to believe in heaven, in a spot in the beyond with trees ripe with buds that hang like tapioca pearls and rosy blossoms. A place with humming rivers and streams, where babies, pink and wrinkled, remain forever nestled in soft grace and peaceful slumber. A place where aching eyes lift to the white trails of drifting clouds as the heavens filled with the sound of a choir of angels, whose throats swell with a fiercely joyous hymn.

As I treated the people who had almost drowned, I could not help but ponder those still in that river, and the immensity of the loss was almost too much to bear. It seemed to me that even the most heartless and insenstive person would forever see this madness in his dreams.

But there were those who found it within themselves to gather the facts and tell the affrighted, waiting world the number of casualties, the details, the news as it evolved. This task, and discerning exactly what had caused the calamity, fell to the reporters, spewing the information to the telegraph clerks at the post office, and to the authorities. And, of course, to Sherlock Holmes.

I did not seek out Sherlock nor did I see him at the London Steamboat Company's office at the wharf. Michael and I were too occupied with the mission at hand. Other doctors arrived quickly to lend a hand, of course, as well as clergy, police and the entire Woolwich community, who had congregated on the shore, most waiting for a scrap of news of loved ones. The sorrow on each face was palpable.

I was reminded of something Effie used to say. How drastically life can change in the span of a single moment.

At Rosherville Gardens at Gravesend—the very gardens which my uncle, aunt and I had talked about visiting that fine, sunny day until a glitch in Uncle's schedule prevented it—the news had cast a black pall over the area. The music and dancing stopped . . . for some, forever.

We had few details at that point. We knew that a steamboat, the *Princess Alice*, a 252-ton Paddle Steamer and one of the most popular of the excursion pleasure crafts on the Thames, left Gravesend at about six o'clock in the evening and was within sight of the Royal Arsenal, Woolwich, by eight. She was filled with some seven hundred merry day-trippers, many of them children eating oranges on deck and parents. No one was worried. On the bridge was Captain Grinstead, who had twenty years' experience, and Mr. Long, his first mate. It had been a perfect sunny day, the river was smooth as glass, and they had spent a joyful day at Rosherville, officially known as the Kent Zoological and Botanical Gardens. It was advertised as "The Place to Spend a Happy Day." As the sun sank, many sang and danced while the ship's band played as the steamer cruised up river. None anticipated that the trip home would be cut short at Tripcocks Point near North Woolwich.

Between London Bridge and Gravesend, the river winds with its biggest bend at Gallion's Reach. The ship hugged the bank to fight against the ebb. The moon was rising and she was in sight of North Woolwich Pier, half-way down the Reach near the city's gasworks at Beckton when a Collier, the *Bywell Castle*, approached Tripcock Point. The *Bywell* was heading down river. The two ships were near the middle of the river.

We heard that the *Princess Alice* cut between the Collier and the South Shore. The steamer swung broadside and was hit at full speed. I heard one survivor say, "The Collier seemed to hover over the starboard bow of the *Princess Alice*. I heard a rippin' crash as the sharp edge of the bow cut right into us. Shook and quivered. I heard a crew member say the *Bywell* . . . she drove right through to the engine-room." He paused, then added, "We was sliced in two."

Water gushed in; the forward part of the Princess Alice sank like a bag of rocks.

Another survivor said she lifted almost to the perpendicular, the aft part standing for a few moments, and then she was gone. "The last thing I heard before I was pulled out," he said, "was the screechin' of sea gulls."

There were a few lifeboats, but most were not accessible. Most could not swim. Many women wore voluminous dresses, pulling them down deep into the water because the fabric quickly became soaked. The *Bywell* let down ropes; a number of small boats attempted to rescue the drowning passengers. Only a few passengers were able to clamber aboard the *Bywell*.

I heard a survivor say that the *Princess Alice* was cut in two and, within five minutes, she was "completely heeled over and sinking in deep water," meaning she was leaning far over to one side and going under. I only knew what 'heeled over' meant because Sherlock had explained in maritime terms the sinking of the *Gloria Scott* from which Victor's father had escaped many years ago.

I watched as the dead were pulled from the water and taken to the Town Hall and to the boardroom of the steamboat company on the Wharf, both of which were turned into temporary mortuaries. Shells and stretchers laden with the dead continued to appear for hours. Most of the dead were women and children. I realized that there were more lost than saved. Some seven hundred passengers had journeyed on the *Princess Alice* that afternoon. Most perished.

When Michael and I entered the temporary mortuary in the boardroom, the floor was littered with bodies covered in sheets and sacks. We helped the police lay the corpses in order, put labels on them, numbers mostly, and continued to feel inadequate, waiting anxiously to receive those who we might actually be able to assist.

I went to the balcony outside the boardroom window to wipe away the sewage and soot from the four children who lay there; they were not much older than my nephew. I was overcome with a melancholy I could barely withstand as I washed the dirt from their pretty, innocent faces and their Sunday-best clothes, now cold and limp, wet and black from sewage and pollution that pervaded that part of the river. The site of the crash was immediately down river of the Barking sewer outfall, which was in the process of releasing raw sewage into the river when the collision occurred. Passengers were bogged down by the black, foul, poisonous sewage.

I imagined their last moments. People below in the two saloons, scrambling to exit, tumbling over one another, clutching and tearing at each other, women and children crushed in the stampede. I imagined mothers seeing their babies and toddlers wrenched from their arms, fathers trying in vain to shove through the mad crowd, trapped and unable to reach their children.

The captain of the Bywell, a man named Harrison, shouted orders to his crew to work the rescue. In a frenzy, they threw out life-lines and lowered boats and the ship's siren sounded, a cry for assistance. Captain Harrison dropped anchor to stop drifting downstream, not realizing that many drowning passengers were clinging to it. I heard in my mind the clank of the chain as the cable lowered through the hawse-hole. I saw the poor wretches who held to it pulled deeper into the watery grave.

Another steamer belonging to the same company and named the *Duke of Teck,* attempted a rescue, but by the time she arrived, the river was full of drowning people, screaming in anguish and begging for help. A passenger aboard the *Duke*, was hailed for saving several passengers. He had pulled six or seven women from the river. Although we heard other tales of amazing escapes, we heard far more stories of the pitiful screams of the dying.

The first body to be identified was that of a steward who had been in the service of the London Steamboat Company all his adult life. Another steward, however, survived. I was within earshot when he told a company official that he, William Law, was below decks in the saloon of the *Princess Alice* and heard a crash at around eight p.m. He ran up on deck, heard water rushing in below, and saw that the paddleboat was sinking. He rushed to the gangway and shouted to those below to get to the deck. "I ran into a young lady," he said, "took her onto my shoulders, and jumped overboard with her." They were now just two amongst a mass of those struggling in the water. He swam to shore, "but the young woman . . . she slipped away from me," he said, haltingly. "I lost her."

One of the *Princess Alice*'s engineers was also saved, but the captain, William Grinstead, and the remainder of his crew, were lost. The company's superintendent of the fleet, Mr. Towse, was on board with his wife and family, but he went on shore at Gravesend. His lifeless wife was brought to Woolwich; at that time, their children were still missing and feared lost in the dark river.

At midnight, officials at the Plumstead Workhouse were conscripted to do what they could to render help. Michael and I, and the other doctors at the scene, rendered treatment to the least injured survivors as they appeared, each rising from the slug like a phoenix from the ashes. They were taken to nearby infirmaries by an assortment of cabs and Black Marias, the patrol wagons used by the police.

As dawn approached, exhausted, covered with grime ourselves and bordering on shock, Michael and I stood on the dock, peering into the dark river, now eerily silent. "They will be pulling them out for weeks," he said, "Months."

I knew Michael was right. Staring out across the blackness, wondering what other horrors awaited us, I whispered, "I know."

It was when I turned to the sound of footsteps that I saw Sherlock walking toward us. He said nothing, I said nothing. I fell into his arms.

21

He held me close. "Are you all right? Poppy, are you—?"

I did not try to break the embrace. I looked up at him. "I am. I am fine. But Sherlock—"

He stroked my limp and sooty hair. "Thank God." Then he said, slowly, solemnly, "She had but two lifeboats. Two."

He pulled slightly away and looked down at me. He kissed my forehead. His expression, his manner, revealed his soul and, for a moment, he showed that he knew how this catastrophe would affect me, that he was concerned about me and that he did care for me, deeply. But I knew he would retreat from sentiment quickly. To save him from embarrassment, I squirmed from his arms. "I need not guess how you have employed your evening. You have been talking to people at the London Steamboat office."

"Quite so. Off and on. I have been talking to the steward who survived and a few others. Tomorrow, I shall widen my field of inquiries. I have just heard that there is a growing number of people who have heard about this and they've come out on trains from London to rummage in the wreckage and carry off curiosities. Lestrade has dispatched officers to prevent further vandalism, and I understand there will be two policemen posted day and night until the remains of the SS *Princess Alice* can be moved to the dockyard for examination and analysis."

"Dear God," Michael sighed. "Curiosities."

"Michael," Sherlock said, "you look a fright. As do you, Poppy," he added, clutching my hand. "They have tea and some food in the Town Hall. You should eat something."

"What about you?" I asked. "I imagine you arrived as soon as you heard and it's almost one o'clock."

"I had some chipped beef and a cold beer at dinner time. But now there is no time to eat or sleep. There is work to be done."

I knew there was no point in arguing with him.

On the way to my uncle's house, we stopped at Sherlock's place on Montague because he insisted that he could think better if he had his violin. By the time we arrived, Uncle had come and gone. Aunt Susan told us that their train in Scotland had been delayed, but as soon they arrived in London and heard the news, he set out for the wharf. Martha brought out a tray of tea, but Aunt Susan and Sherlock disappeared. Soon, Michael excused himself to go home to relieve Alexander's caretaker, who had been with the baby for at least ten hours beyond her shift. I went upstairs to my bedroom.

For several minutes, I think I simply stared into space. Then I washed my face, braided my hair and changed into a decent day dress. Inexplicably, it seemed important to me at that moment to appear composed before I went back downstairs. I heard violin music coming from my aunt's morning room.

I made my way down the hall and stood in the doorway of the morning room for a moment, listening. Sherlock rarely played an actual composition; usually he just plucked and scraped at the strings of the instrument across his knee while he was lost in thought. A few moments later, Sherlock stopped abruptly and looked at me.

"That was beautiful, Sherlock. What was it?"

"Vivaldi's Concerto for Violin in B Flat, Opus 4, Number 1. I know only a few bars. But your Aunt Susan found it soothing."

I glanced toward a corner of a room where I saw Aunt Susan leaning against the wall, listening.

"He is quite extraordinary, Poppy."

Sometimes, I thought. I simply nodded.

"I am quite exhausted," Aunt Susan said. She gave me a kiss on the cheek as she brushed past and went upstairs.

Sherlock returned his violin to its case and asked "Shall we go into the drawing room?"

I nodded again and followed him. He helped himself to a glass of port. "Your uncle won't mind?" he asked, raising his glass.

"No, he won't. And I'll join you."

I poured some port into a glass and took two long swallows, then settled down across from him in front of the fireplace. "Vivaldi died over a hundred years ago," he announced. "In Vienna. I should like to visit that city one day."

Then he stared off; he was momentarily unreachable.

"You seem pensive."

"Truth is the fruit of pensive nights and labourious days, Poppy."

Again, he retreated to that inaccessible part of himself. Finally, I asked, "What happens next, Sherlock? With the investigation?"

"They will continue to try to find the bodies. Many are still missing. The London Steamboat Company has already put in a bid to purchase the remains of *SS Princess Alice.* It will likely salvage the engines and sell off the rest. There will be some unpleasantness in all of that. And, naturally, there must be an inquest. As always, some legal bother, though I am sure long before it has even commenced, I shall have the answers to their questions."

"Does anyone have the least idea how this could have happened? Why the boats were in a position to collide?"

"While it is unusual for a captain with Grinstead's experience to make such a fatal error, I suspect that is what the facts will bear out. I am still balancing the matter in my mind. I find the conflicting stories a very serious impediment to the investigation. I fear it will be quite the menace to the inquest." He sipped his port, then sighed. "Mycroft was at the wharf, of course."

I squinted over my glass. "But why?"

117

"Because he would seek to spare Her Majesty all fear of future annoyance or—"

"But surely, Sherlock, a paddleboat colliding with a cargo ship is no reflection upon Her Majesty."

"The ship was named for her daughter. This catastrophe occurred on her river in her city. In Mycroft's mind, any calamity that befalls or occurs in Her Majesty's realm requires his inquiry and resolution."

"Perhaps he can help. His resources abound."

"There certainly is that," he said, and finished his port.

22

For the first time since I opened my practice, I was actually glad not to have many patients; I felt no compunction about hanging a 'closed' sign on my door. It enabled me to go to the wharf each day to assist the people from the community and the women from the workhouse who were tending to the dead. I also did what I could to console the grieving. Hope was lost for any more survivors.

I did not see Sherlock again until Wednesday when he was at the steamboat office, pursuing his investigation and assisting the police. We had tea that afternoon.

He asked how I was doing, and it was hard to reply. I could not stop seeing the faces of the children on the balcony or the many others in the make-shift mortuaries. Part of me shrank from the tasks; with my whole being I lamented those people who had boarded a ferry for an afternoon of amusement but had instead perished horribly, all their dreams and expectations swiftly and brutally dashed. The world could be a wretched place, and I wondered if the tragedy was caused by some failure on the part of the steamboat company . . . perhaps a faulty component that should have been replaced. So often, it seemed, people in high places had too much money and too little heart and cared nothing for the safety of others, even those customers who made them rich in the first place.

When I met Sherlock, I asked, "So, Sherlock, you are investigating the cause of the ship's demise. It would seem that you have decided to make a living by working for the police after all. Or the Yard?"

"No, I ask for no compensation for my contribution to the investigation of the *Princess Alice* incident. Though it is an interesting case."

An interesting case? I thought. Once again, Sherlock's ability to compartmentalize and suppress empathy baffled me. I hated to think of him as cold-hearted, but few of the seven hundred on the *SS Princess Alice* survived and he seemed interested only in the inquiry, the analysis.

"My reputation is growing, though," he said, "and occasionally I am remunerated. Most recently, by Reginald Musgrave."

"Reginald! I have not seen him in ages."

Not since the night he joined Sherlock, Victor, Effie and me for dinner, I thought, remembering the photo in Uncle's desk. It had been over four years.

"You do remember him?" he asked.

"Certainly. He was Victor's roommate at Oxford for a short time."

"Indeed. Shortly after Victor left for India, Reginald transferred to my college, and I ran into him now and then. Then his father died, and he returned to Hurlstone to manage the estate. I had not seen him since, but he called upon me early Monday morning to assist him with a small matter."

"Tell me," I said.

"As you may recall, Hurlstone is quite large and he employs many servants. One night, he couldn't sleep and wandered through the house in search of a book he had been reading. He happened upon his butler, a man named Brunton, who was in the library, staring down at a map. Reginald was about to speak to him when Brunton walked over to the desk and, with a key, opened it. He took out another document and proceeded to study it closely. Reginald then confronted him.

"Brunton had been in his family's employ for many years, so his behaviour shocked Reginald. He told Brunton to leave at once, but Brunton bargained for a week's time. A few days later, Brunton disappeared. Reginald and the servants searched everywhere for him; they even dragged the pond. Three nights later,

Rachel, a maid who Reginald later discovered was in love with Brunton, had some sort of breakdown. Then she also disappeared.

"After hearing Reginald's story, I went with him to Sussex and examined the papers in which Brunton had shown so much interest. It turns out one of them was a map and the other was a riddle of sorts, a document that had been handed down for generations in the Musgrave family. They call it The Musgrave Ritual. It was a series of questions and answers, none of which seemed to make sense."

"But you made sense of them, I take it?"

Sherlock smiled and said, "After a time, yes. I determined that the riddle was a series of clues and measurements . . . for example, a distance from an oak tree to something else. I found a peg hole in the lawn made by Brunton as he measured off distances. Once I went through all the clues, we started to follow the clues, and we ended up in a cellar where we found Brunton."

"Was he dead?"

"Yes, quite dead. It appears he found his way into a hiding place in the cellar, but he could not have lifted the stone slab by himself. I believe that he enlisted Rachel to assist him in his unscrupulous undertaking, much as that sailor from Squire Trevor's past enlisted Mrs. Hudson to help him blackmail Squire Trevor. They—Rachel and Brunston—could have lifted the slab together, but they would need support while Brunton went into the cellar to fetch the treasure. I saw her recently, by the way," he added.

"Who? Rachel?"

"No, Mrs. Hudson. She was visiting her son Morse who apprenticed under the owner of the art shop on Kennington Road. He's now the owner of the shop and employs assistants of his own. He's still short and stout. Anyway, he sells statues and paintings . . . in fact, I believe I may consult with him about the Buddha replicas. He is not yet very experienced, but he has several colleagues with expertise in art."

"Sherlock, you were saying that you ran into Mrs. Hudson."

"Oh, yes, she was in London to visit Morse and inspect some properties, and I ran into her at his shop when I went to ask him if he knew anyone who could verify the authenticity of what we found on Musgrave's estate. She's doing well. She has been saving to purchase a lease of a home here in London and plans to rent out rooms and offer light housekeeping to her tenants."

"That sounds like a good plan for her. Now what of Reginald's maid and the butler?"

"We spoke to the other servants and it seems that Brunton did not return Rachel's affections. She came to hate him. Based upon Rachel's sudden breakdown and subsequent disappearance, I have deduced that while he was down in the murky cellar handing up his finds to her, she became enraged and clouted him and let the slab fall back. Or perhaps she deliberately kicked the supports away and left Brunton to die. I suppose it is possible that the slab fell back into place by itself and she panicked. Whatever actually happened, Brunton is dead."

"Dear Lord," I said. "And was there some buried treasure?"

"In fact, there was. Some things that we found were of no consequence, but in the mire, we did find something that, though quite bent and battered and dull, was quite the treasure. It was a crown! The crown of Charles II."

"A royal crown buried in a cellar at Hurlstone?"

"One of Reginald's ancestors served as Cavalier to Charles II, whose father had handed the crown down to him, and he, in turn, gave it to Reginald's family. The riddle, this ritual as they called it, gave the clues to its whereabouts."

"That's quite fascinating."

"It's more than fascinating, Poppy, for I have been well compensated. Upon returning the crown to Her Majesty, Reginald was given several thousand pounds because his family had been

122

guardian of the treasure trove. He generously shared some of that with me. But best of all, I have bested the King of Controlling Catastrophies."

"I don't understand. Who—?"

"Mycroft! He had to report to the queen that his younger brother had recovered the missing crown. I must say, he did seem rather proud, in his own way. And I've enough money to keep me in beef and beer for some time to come."

"You really are living by your wits then."

He just smiled.

When we finished tea, I walked to St. Bart's with Sherlock, hoping to see my brother. We paused at a newspaper stand. The entire front page of *The London Times* was covered with a depiction of the paddleboat and the steamer and the crowds on the wharf. Authorities continued to drag the river and many bodies had been recovered, but hundreds were still missing.

"Have you seven pence?" Sherlock asked. "I have not had time to cash Reginald's cheque. I believe I spent the last of my coin on our tea."

Laughing, I handed him the pennies.

"Thank you. We shall stop at the bank on the way," he said, patting his vest pocket, "and I shall pay you back."

As he reviewed the front page story about the collision, I thought to myself how fortunate he was to have made such an impression on Musgrave back at Oxford. I had often wondered how Sherlock managed to keep a roof over his head or any food in his stomach. Living by his wits alone did not seem any more prosperous than my medical practice had been, and I survived only because I lived with Uncle and my parents were most generous with 'loans.' As far as I knew, Sherlock had had no extraordinary cases prior to deciphering Musgrave's coded documents, yet he wore very decent attire and maintained suitable lodgings in an upscale area, far nicer, for example, than the two-story row house in Finsbury Park where the victim James Dixon and his family resided. Sherlock told me that Dixon's wife was much younger than her husband and their son was an infant. Sherlock surmised that he had married late for most banks did not permit the men in their employ to marry until they had reached a certain level of salary. Employers were concerned that, family in tow and strapped for money, a clerk might be tempted to help himself to the contents of a drawer.

From everything that Sherlock had told me about his own past, the Holmes family was part of the landed gentry. Simply by virtue of the fact that Mycroft held a position of considerable importance in the government, it was likely that their father had been held in high esteem and had significant connections. But I doubted that Mycroft assisted Sherlock financially, and I deduced that he continued to receive some sort of subsidy from his eldest brother Sherrinford, who managed the family holdings.

Having finished reading the article, Sherlock tri-folded the newspaper and placed it under one arm. As we continued to St. Bart's, he said, "Your uncle . . . you said he's back from Scotland?"

I tried to hide my grimace. Uncle and I had barely spoken since his return. I was doing what I could at the wharf and Uncle had resumed his duties at the hospital. We rarely saw each other, but, in truth, I was avoiding him. I had trouble facing him for fear I would blurt out the ridiculous questions that swirled in my brain about his books and notations concerning Buddhism and suffering. They frequently blighted my thoughts, and I didn't know what to do about it. I repeated Sherlock's logical approach to deduction in my brain a hundred times a day. *Once you eliminate the impossible, whatever remains, no matter how improbable, must be the truth.*

And it was quite impossible, inconceivable to believe that Uncle was a murderer. The truth must lie elsewhere.

23

On Sunday, when I came back from a long walk with Little Elihu, I found Aunt Susan down below, mixing the ingredients for the sweet biscuits she was about to bake. When I looked around the kitchen, I realized that she and the servants were in the process of putting together an elabourate meal. Aunt Susan need not ever step into the kitchen, but it was not unusual for her to contribute her considerable talents for cooking and baking when she planned a special dinner party. In fact, she insisted upon it.

"Aunt Susan, are we having guests this evening?"

Smiling at me, she said, "Indeed we are." She turned to Martha and said, "Now pick the most excellent potatoes. They must be served smoking hot with melted butter of the first quality."

"Aunt Susan, who—?"

She turned back to me. "We're having consommé and pigeons comport. And also Fricado Veal."

"Uncle's favourite? The stew with mushrooms and garlic and saffron?"

She nodded. "We're also having pork loin and Florentine of Rabbit."

"My goodness, I haven't had that in ages. When Papa took me hunting, he always said there was nothing like it. But he didn't have to prepare it," I added, laughing.

I had often watched our maid Marie skin and bone a whole rabbit that Papa brought home. She stuffed it with a forcemeat made of bread, rabbit liver, bacon, anchovy, wine and herbs, then covered it with a veal stock white sauce, flavored with anchovy, lemon, eggs, cream and nutmeg, and let it simmer.

"Aunt Susan, who are the honoured guests?"

"Mycroft Holmes," she said.

"Mycroft!"

"And his brother Sherlock."

126

"Sherlock!" I screeched. "Now for the second course," Aunt Susan prattled on but I was still stuck on why the Holmes brothers were coming to dinner.

"But . . . why?"

She removed her apron and touched my shoulder. "Come into the drawing room, Poppy." She turned to Martha and Genabee. "I'll be back in a few minutes. Follow the recipe in the Elizabeth Acton cookbook for the pudding."

I shivered. The book had been a gift from Effie to my aunt. She had given it to me to take to Aunt Susan on the day I met Sherlock.

"Or it could be in Mrs. Beeton's book," Aunt Susan said. "And please finish cutting the ends off the *haricots verts*," she added with a flair of her hand, in her best French accent.

The girls looked at her blankly. "The green beans," I explained as Aunt Susan whisked me from the kitchen and up the stairs to the drawing room.

"Would you join me in a glass of wine?" she asked, pouring red wine from a decanter into a glass.

"No, thank you. Aunt Susan, why are Mycroft and Sherlock Holmes coming to dinner?"

"Sherlock invited himself, apparently," she said after taking a sip. "But Mycroft came to the hospital and expressed a need to discuss that horrible tragedy on the Thames. It's a week today, can you believe it? It is the sole topic of conversation, as you know, and the Queen has been unremitting in her inquiries about it. She has given special orders that all military resources in Woolwich are at the disposal of the civic authorities. Ormond said Mycroft told him that Friday evening, the latest estimate of the number of persons on board the *Princess Alice* was sent to Her Majesty, and they believe it nears eight hundred."

"But I heard the company's estimate. It was far less than eight hundred."

Nodding, she said, "I know. But Mycroft told Ormond that this is due to the fact that the company's calculation is based upon the fact that children in arms are not charged for on these excursion boats, and little ones under the age of seven are booked at half price. And there were a great many babies. The Coroner, at Friday afternoon's first sitting of the inquest, received an official communication about the number of turn-stile tickets, and the company now deeply regrets to say that eight hundred may be the lowest estimate. Seven hundred are feared drowned."

I listened solemnly. I could not speak.

"So, I presume Mycroft wishes to discuss this with your uncle."

"What has Uncle to do with inquiries and estimates?"

"Nothing. I suppose, nothing at all. But Mycroft has absolutely no true friends other than Ormond, and Ormond did, after all, spend his third year of medical school as a ship's surgeon on a whaling ship sailing for the Arctic Circle. So he is someone Mycroft trusts, and he has some maritime experience. This is simply conjecture, of course, darling, but I believe Mycroft is quite shaken by all of this, and the Queen is barking orders at him about resolving the matter as quickly as possible."

"But Sherlock?"

"He is fully engaged in the investigation as well, to the extent that he has apparently abandoned something else of a pressing nature. According to Ormond, Sherlock is quite concerned about you and would like the matter laid to rest."

"Concerned about me? Regarding the Thames accident? I don't understand."

She took my hand. "Poppy, that young man cares about you. Ormond said Sherlock told him that you are neglecting your medical practice, going to the wharf each day although there is, most regrettably, no need for your considerable skills as a physician."

"No, there are none left who need a physician."

I thought of the way we cleaned each face and put a number on its chest and placed whatever possessions had clung to the deceased in a tin box at its feet. I had meandered up and down the rows with relatives who were fearful they would identify a missing loved one. Many fainted dead away when they did. I could tell some barely hung on to their sanity. It was a grisly, awful thing, especially now that bodies were decomposing. I had heard that because of the number of unidentified bodies, the Coroner had ordered a mass burial, and I planned to go back to the wharf tomorrow to help with removing clothing, washing more bodies, and shrouding them for the make-shift ceremony.

Lost in my thoughts, my aunt's voice startled me when she spoke again.

"He wants you to move on."

"What?"

"Sherlock wants you to move on, Poppy."

Move on, I thought. *He wants my help on the British Museum Murders, that's what he wants!*

"Poppy, you must admit there is nothing more you can do at the wharf. Questions about the collision are now up to the civic authorities and people like Mycroft. Next week, the inquest will commence."

"I know, I know. Sherlock told me some of these things, and I have heard many discussions at the steamboat office. The Board of Trade is involved as well. Most believe that the captain of the *Princess Alice* broke some kind of rule and cut right in front of the cargo ship."

"My *point* is we must leave this investigation in the good hands of the authorities and people like Mycroft and Sherlock. It was a terrible disaster, but you need not continue to expose yourself to these horrors."

Speechless, I rose, poured myself some wine and drank almost the entire glass in one gulp. Then I turned to her and said, "I do not wish to dine with you, Aunt Susan, not with Sherlock and Mycroft and Uncle. I would rather—"

She cut me off. "Now, that's the other thing I want to speak to you about. You have barely spoken to your uncle since we returned from Scotland. He's very perplexed. What has gotten into you?"

"Nothing."

"Priscilla Stamford, do not tell me that there is nothing wrong. Your behaviour speaks volumes. Why are you angry with your uncle?"

"I'm not angry, Aunt Susan. I'm . . . I'm . . . ."

I'm afraid he is helping people die, I screamed in my head. *I am confused and upset and terrified.*

"Poppy, please tell me what is bothering you."

I couldn't. I lost my voice again.

"Dearest girl, I know you. You are never at a loss for words, and you have never ignored your uncle or me. Please, talk to me."

I said nothing.

She stood up, finished her wine, and walked to the door. "I shall not have you barricade yourself in your room whilst we have dinner guests, particularly someone as prestigious as Mycroft Holmes. I insist you join us. It is up to you whether you choose to engage in conversation."

I stood as well. "Aunt Susan, if you insist, then I shall see you at dinner."

Then I turned and ran to my room.

24

I sat at the foot of my bed, staring into space for a long time. Then I called to Martha and asked her to draw me a bath. Once finished, I tossed on a dressing gown, and she twirled and looped my hair up in an intricate style. When she left, I wore out the rug, pacing back and forth, to and fro, wringing my hands. *Move on*, I thought again. As if I could simply dismiss the appalling loss of life, a death toll even greater than that of the two Norfolk train wrecks combined.

I knew Sherlock's passionate nature first-hand, and I knew that Sherlock's emotions were not as shrunken as he let on. But he suppressed them these days, almost to the point of atrophy, and it could be chilling. I admired and respected his ability to be analytical and rational; I'd always prided it in myself. But his quest to completely repress his feelings until they were nothing more than a vestigial flicker was shocking. So why did I still find him so beguiling?

He was the confident centre of his own universe, unwilling to conform to social norms, independent, protective of his self-sufficiency, always in control, and driven in an almost primal fashion. He happily solved cases to relieve boredom, but often seemed to lack compassion for the victim. After Effie died, I remembered telling Sherlock that it was so hard to lose someone you loved. His answer? *Don't get attached.* My reply? *That hasn't worked for me.*

I treasured logic and deduction as well. I had always prided myself on being extremely observant and perceptive to details, on possessing a keen ability to focus and concentrate despite distractions, to predict human behaviour. With Victor Trevor, I had generally been calm, composed, restrained, and usually able to keep my emotions in check. Oh, occasionally I was wound a bit too tight. There were times I sprang from my coil like a cobra emerging from his basket, poised to strike. But generally, I was unruffled, self-possessed, collected. With Sherlock, when I was around him, I was intimidated, almost submissive at times, and far too emotional. I hated it . . . but relished it at the same time.

"Ohhh!"I yelled and took off my dressing gown.

I looked through my wardrobe and finally settled on wearing something that was out-of-date, out-of-style—Mum would have been mortified. But it was the same outfit I had been wearing on the day I met Sherlock, a pale blue skirt with ruffles, pleats and draped layers at the back, and a white blouse with wide lace. As I dressed, I found myself seeing Sherlock through the prism of that day, seeing him as the elusive man he was and had been all along, quintessentially icy on the surface, constantly shifting to meet the demands of his mind, and unattainable.

I glanced over at the hat on my dresser bureau. Effie had made it for me, and I had worn it to her funeral. It was made of bright blue fabric with a black lace ruffle around the narrow brim. It had a black feather plume and a short train of black tulle. Effie's early prediction seemed so eerily prescient.

"Poppy," she had told me, with a shade of deep concern on her face, "please stay away from Sherlock Holmes. He is dangerous to your heart."

"Dangerous? No, Sherlock Holmes, you are infuriating!" I yelled to no one, and hoped my voice did not carry too far because I'd seen the hansom cab pull up and Mycroft Holmes was by now knocking at the door.

I finished dressing, pinched my cheeks for colour, swept a brush through my fringe, and slowly walked down the steps to the dining room.

25

I did not say a word during dinner. I pushed my food around my plate and, anxious to retire to my room, I was about to ask to be excused when Sherlock changed the entire course of the conversation about the Thames accident—during which he had been his usually compulsive, aphoristic self—to the recent murders. As usual, he disarmed me with this unexpected swerve, though for the life of me, I didn't know why. The Thames accident was behind him; the murder case was not.

"A bird symbolizes the Lord Buddha—and freedom," Sherlock piped up halfway through dinner. "Did you know that many cultures believe the raven to be a symbol of impending death because the raven bird is believed to be able to smell death before it occurs? And in China, specifically, it is believed that the soul of the sun takes the form of a crow or a raven.

He turned to Mycroft. "So, it's even more telling that the birds left beside the dead men were ravens. Nothing particularly exotic but extremely representational, wouldn't you agree?"

Mycroft peered over his glass of wine and smirked. "Next my brother will be quoting Poe. 'Quoth the raven, Nevermore'."

"I hate that poem," Aunt Susan interjected. "And the raven, never flitting, still is sitting, still is sitting," she said. She recited another verse.

On the pallid bust of Pallas just above my chamber door;
And his eyes have all the seeming of a demon's that is dreaming,
And the lamp-light o'er him streaming throws his shadow on the floor;
And my soul from out that shadow that lies floating on the floor
Shall be lifted -- nevermore!

"That's the last stanza, Susan," Uncle said. "Those last lines depict the final step of the journey, the lifting of the man's suffering as he dies."

I swallowed hard and the lump in my throat would not budge. I did not want Uncle discussing this subject.

"I disagree, Dr. Sacker," Sherlock said. "That is not the meaning of the last stanza."

I stared at him. What? Sherlock Holmes analyzing poetry? Now *that* was truly impossible. I would have to speak to our friend Oscar Wilde to find out what he'd been filling Sherlock's head with.

"The raven's shadow most likely symbolizes sadness," Sherlock continued. "I do understand how some might interpret that last stanza as relating to the narrator's death, but they're wrong. Poe is discussing the narrator's soul; the words mean that the narrator will never be happy again. The shadow remains on the floor, and it is the narrator's soul that will never climb out from under that shadow of sadness. If someone has convinced you that he died, he's wrong, Dr. Sacker."

"Sherlock?" Uncle asked, his lips turning into a smile for the first time all evening.

"It's simple logic, Dr. Sacker. Whoever tells you that the narrator has died, ask him how a dead man can narrate a poem."

Now, for the first time all evening, I smiled as well, and Mycroft and Aunt Susan laughed.

"About the bird. I assume, Dr. Sacker, my brother has told you about the murders which have occurred near the British Museum."

I patted my lips with my napkin and started to rise. Aunt Susan tapped my wrist, and her eyes told me she wanted me to stay. I settled back into my chair.

"Sherlock," Mycroft said. "That is Her Majesty's business. You are not to pursue that further."

"Oh, dearest brother, how you do try to be that raven casting a shadow over me. When was the last time I allowed you to manipulate my life? Oh, yes, now I remember. I think I was three and you were ten."

"Sherlock—"

"As I was saying," Sherlock continued, "Now that it seems very clear how the Thames incident occurred—"

"The inquest has just begun, Sherlock. It is not clear at all," Mycroft interrupted.

"In fact it *is*, Mycroft. Quite clear. The vessel which ran into the *Princess Alice*, the *Bywell Castle*, was a screw collier going to the north, light in ballast and heading downstream from Millwall dry dock on her way back to Newcastle. She was built of iron and powered by a single four-bladed screw. At over 1300 tons, she was over five times as heavy as the *Princess Alice*, and she sat much higher in the water.

"Now, at about 7:30 p.m., the *Princess Alice* came round Tripcock Point and into Galleons Reach, heading into the sinking sun, on her way to Woolwich. The force of the ebb tide had pushed her to the north side of the river, so, to regain her bearing, she was in the process of turning and moving southwards to the centre of the river. Her new course took her across the bow of the *Bywell Castle*, which bore down upon her. It cut her almost completely in half.

"Captain Grinstead was not seen after the accident, of course, but he was observed at his post shortly before the collision. Beyond the fact that the tide was about two hours ebb, which would enable the *Princess Alice* to ease and stop sooner than the screw, which would be borne on the tide, it is impossible to discover any of the circumstances immediately preceding the collision. But survivors have confirmed that before the boats struck, there were cries from one to the other to keep out of the way.

"They have already started to inspect the wreck and the condition of the *Princess Alice* reveals it was utterly unseaworthy. It was literally broken into three parts. These so-called saloon steamers are little better than floating platforms, eggshells, that go down on the smallest contact with anything like iron or timber. The *Princess* was pricked out by plankin," he continued. "It is a mere platform, planked in. A description given to me by the Captain of the *Bywell Castle* of its condition is quite true. I don't know why anyone steps foot on them. The London Steamboat Company ought to be prosecuted.

"Passenger steamers have no business on the Thames hereabouts after dark. The river is full of heavy shipping, masses of wood and iron, not easy to control at certain states of the tide. The captain of the *Princess Alice* was out of his course and completely ignored the recent changes in the laws of navigation on the river. Captain Grinstead was avoiding the rush of the tide by making a circuit. They continually do this; there is not a day that passes when they don't risk the lives of their passengers."

He turned to me. "These steamers are like the hansom cabmen who think the London streets belong to them. Their captains believe that the river is theirs and that everyone else must get out of their way. These excursion steamers experience the narrowest 'shaves' in the busiest reaches and bends of the river, crowded as it often is with shipping, and they are, therefore, charged with sudden emergencies of navigation. But the *Bywell Castle* was too heavy and too slow, and she could not get out of Grinstead's way.

"As is usual in such cases, the accident is likely due to a misunderstanding, the one misinterpreting the intentions of the other. All the rules of sailing were cast to the winds in the moment of peril, each taking the wrong course to avoid each other's blunder." He turned to Mycroft, "So you see, dearest brother, the case *can* be concluded."

With that consummation of his discourse on the Thames accident, Sherlock turned his attention back to the British Museum Murders. I did not know it at the time, but before the evening's end, we would all be like the *Princess Alice* . . . cut in half, weeping from our gaping wounds, sinking to the lowest depths of a dark polluted river, drowning.

26

As soon as we finished eating dinner, the men retired to the library. Aunt Susan and I gathered dessert plates, fresh napkins and utensils to take to the dining room. The scent of Sherlock's pipe, sweet and strong, wafted through the air.

"Sherlock, pipes and libraries," I mumbled.

"What, Poppy?"

"Oh, nothing. I was just remembering a day that Sherlock and I met at the Bod at Oxford where he was doing research on laws against baby farming. He lit up a pipe despite the rules against it."

"That doesn't surprise me. His older brother is good at bending the rules as well."

I knew what she meant. Though Mycroft was the quintessential patriot, loyal to the Crown to a fault, he was certainly not above circumventing laws and protocol. I suspected he had long ago subscribed to the adage: 'the end justifies the means.'

Likewise, Sherlock was not above bending rules and breaking laws to solve a case. He did not rail against authority exactly, but he did not revere it either. When it came to crime investigation, he could be tart-tongued or lace his words with honey, whichever best served his purpose. He was always audacious, non-traditional, and mercilessly driven to uncover every shred of evidence without regard to convention.

We were placing biscuits on several platters on the sideboard when I heard Sherlock's voice. He was yelling at the top of his lungs.

"Are you mad, Mycroft? Are you insane?"

Aunt Susan and I quickly made our way to the library. Uncle was standing in the middle of the room with Sherlock in front of him, as if he were a royal guard protecting Her Majesty. Mycroft stood several feet away, near the bookshelves to the right of the fireplace, his arms crossed over his ample chest.

"Sherlock," Mycroft said with far more softness in his voice than I might have imagined, given the exasperated state Sherlock always elicited from him. "Even Lestrade wishes to speak to Dr. Sacker."

"Lestrade," Sherlock hissed. "That shallow, rat-faced—"

"Sherlock!" Mycroft yelled.

"If Lestrade is party to this, it is solely because *you* put him up to it. He has not an imaginative bone in his body. He's a black-eyed bulldog that you have on your leash."

"The best of a rather bad lot, I'll grant you," Mycroft replied, his voice drifting off. "Nevertheless—" He cleared his throat. "I simply need to ask Dr. Sacker some questions in a rather more formal setting, Sherlock. It is my duty to—"

No!" Sherlock roared. "You are not just asking questions! You have all but accused Dr. Sacker of committing multiple murders! I believe it's finally time to send a page to the sanitarium to have them fetch you."

My aunt finally injected herself into the conversation. "Ormond, what on earth is all this about?"

Uncle looked down at his feet, then stiffened and looked straight at Mycroft.

"My brother has lost his mind," Sherlock said, disdain dripping from his tongue.

"Mycroft," Uncle said quietly. "We have been acquainted for a long time. Since you were a boy. Good God, man, you just dined at my table with my family, and now you are accusing me of these atrocities?"

Aunt Susan ran across the room and slipped her arm through my uncle's. "Ormond, tell me what is going on."

Mycroft never took his eyes off Uncle's face. His icy stare, the darkness behind his eyes, sent shivers through my body. His intensity, the rigid stance and the astonishment on Sherlock's face muted everything else. The books, the wing chairs, the wooden

Eskimo statute that a sailor had whittled for Uncle on that arctic voyage years ago, all faded away. It was as if menace and malignancy had been hiding in plain sight.

Mycroft said, "Mrs. Sacker, Miss Stamford, I think it would be best . . . I think you might want to retire to the drawing room while Ormond and I continue this conversation."

"Conversation?" Aunt Susan asked, her strong emotions emerging with a howl. "You mean interrogation, don't you?" she wailed.

"Susan," Uncle whispered.

"No, Ormond. This is . . . this is . . . I don't know what this is." She slipped away from Uncle and marched up to Mycroft. "Get out of my house, Mycroft Holmes."

"Mrs. Sacker," Mycroft started to say, but she returned his frozen stare. "I said get out."

Uncle rushed over to her and took her hand. "Susan, it's going to be all right."

Mycroft blithely took a seat in a wing chair. "Mrs. Sacker, there have been several recent murders, all men. Each was found in the vicinity of the British Museum. I . . . we have deduced that the perpetrator of these crimes has medical knowledge and he is sympathetic to their plight. The medical and mental conditions of each man—well, they were all quite ill and unstable and unable to generate income to support themselves or their families. Each one had consulted with physicians, the very same ones that your husband recently sought out. In fact, a sixth body was found just this morning. Poisoned just as the first five men were."

"A sixth?" Sherlock said, a stunned look on his face. "Lestrade did not tell me."

"Because you are to have nothing more to do with this matter, Sherlock."

Mycroft fixed his gaze on Uncle again. "I spoke to Dr. Macewen and he said he had talked to no one about these matters,

140

except you, Dr. Sacker. Your whereabouts since you returned from Scotland have been rather sketchy and—"

Aunt Susan's vice was shrill now. "He has been at the wharf and attending to patients at the hospital!"

I was finally able to move my feet, which, until that moment, had felt as if they were cast in marble like the foundation of a statue. I dashed to Uncle's side and grasped his arm. "He has been at the wharf. I have been there each day since the Thames accident. I've seen him myself."

It was a lie, of course. I had never seen Uncle at the steamboat office or in the other temporary mortuary or on the docks. But we kept different schedules. That was all it was.

"These books," Mycroft continued, as if I were not even present. "In all the years I have known you, Ormond, you have never—" He stopped and sighed. "Ormond, I noticed them when I called upon you to discuss the findings of the coroner after the autopsy of James Dixon. The one in which your niece was the assistant. I went to each book shop in the bookselling district. It seems you have visited all of them and purchased almost every book in London on the subject of Tantric Buddhism."

He rose and went to one of the bookshelves and removed a book. He showed the cover to Uncle. "And this book of poetry by Edgar Allen Poe. You just purchased it six weeks ago. You have underlined several passages of *The Raven*, which your wife so eloquently quoted during dinner. Why? Why the new interest in Tantric Buddhism and poetry. *Poetry?* You, Ormond?"

I looked at Uncle's face. It was ashen.

Though Mycroft's deductions were confounding, what if they were true? What if all these men had chosen to end their lives and Uncle had helped them accomplish their goals? The shadow, the chasm between the uncle I knew and the person Mycroft suspected—that I suspected—was overwhelming.

141

"Please come with me willingly to the Yard, Ormond," Mycroft said.

Fearing Aunt Susan would take up the poker from the brass fireplace fender and club Mycroft with it, I went to her and tightly gripped her arm.

Mycroft replaced the poetry book on the shelf. "Will you come now, Ormond?"

"Ormond, no," Susan gasped.

"Uncle, don't go," I begged, now more terrified than ever.

"Stop this," Sherlock said, the vein pulsing at his temple. "Stop this nonsense right now."

Mycroft's steel-grey, deep-set eyes, although always subtle in expression, seemed vacant now, totally free of emotion. Nothing revealed what was going on in that dominant mind. "Oh, come now, Sherlock, are you going to thrash me like you did that boy at Harrow?"

Sherlock moved across the room in seconds, took his brother by the lapels and shoved him into the bookcase. They stood nose to nose and Sherlock said in a hushed but frightening voice, "Do not tempt me." He gave him another shove, stepped back and hissed, "I will get to the bottom of this, Mycroft. I will show you once and for all who has the better mind. Because you have lost yours."

Uncle donned his coat and hat and took an umbrella from the stand near the door. He followed Mycroft Holmes into the damp, dark night.

I attempted to embrace Aunt Susan but she bolted from the library and ran upstairs. Her absence and my uncle's permeated the room. Left behind, barely able to focus or breathe, I felt alone, more alone than I had at the wharf when I was often alone, the only one alive among desperate souls.

Sherlock crossed the room and put his hands on my shoulders. "We'll sort it out, Poppy. You and I. Do not worry."

"But it's my uncle, Sherlock. I cannot be involved in the investigation. He is like a second father to me."

"You must think of it as an autopsy, Poppy. You are not cutting into the person. You are simply attempting to deduce from the remains the cause of death."

"No! It's different. It's Uncle Ormond!" Then I swallowed my grief, looked up at him, and added, "Sherlock, the thing is . . . "

"What? What is it, Poppy?"

The paradox between the uncle I loved so much and the one I suspected was suddenly too much to bear alone. "The thing is . . . I have had suspicions about Uncle Ormond myself."

He looked incredulous. "Mycroft's suspicions—and whatever suspicions you may have—are unfounded. Quite impossible. We will investigate and offer another explanation. A plausible explanation."

Sherlock put his arms around me, and at that moment, I longed to recapture the feelings we had shared that night at Holme-Next-The Sea four years ago. I clung to him for a long time, neither of us speaking. Finally, he guided me to a chair and poured me a glass of port. We sat down across from one another near the fireplace.

As my dark thoughts slipped from my lips, unravelling like fragile threads that hold together an old, fraying quilt, he listened.

27

Finished with my port and revealing to Sherlock my list of suspicions, I sat back and glanced at his face, waiting to hear what he had to say. He seemed to have faded away from me. He was closed off, not speaking, motionless. His head sunk forward and his eyes fixated on the cold fireplace as if he were seeing something there in the ashes and residue that no one else could absorb. Then he lit his pipe and leaned back, watching the pale grey smoke rings spiral up toward the ceiling.

I was about to leave the room, to leave him to his mental gymnastics, when he said, "Poppy, I fully understand your qualms. I even understand Mycroft's display of mistrust of Dr. Sacker. In fact, I am already entertaining the notion that Dr. Sacker is bait of some kind. Nonetheless, there is hardly enough evidence to hang your uncle from the rope. You must trust me. I will catch the real murderer out. I do not want you to worry."

"But what if—?"

"Quite simply, your uncle is wrongfully accused. I feel it."

"You *feel* it?"

"I meant that as one progresses in this profession, one gets a sense of what matters, an ability to intuit that which is not clear at first. Did I not deduce that Mrs. Hudson was forced by her husband into helping with the blackmail scheme he devised against Squire Trevor?"

"So you admit to knowing instinctively that she was not a wicked person, that—?"

"Not at all. I claim no clairvoyance like that with which you and others invested in your friend Effie. There is no such thing as a sixth sense. However, through the actions and behaviour of a person, one can certainly infer certain things and predict future behaviour." Fingertips pressed together, teepee fashion, his elbows on the arms of his chair, he leaned forward and said, "Your uncle could not be the killer."

"Wait. You do not know my uncle that well. So you are admitting to intuition."

He shook his head. "I admit to no such thing. Your uncle is logical. He is a clever man. Brilliant by all accounts. Dr. Sacker would not leave a trail of clues. He would never allow evidence to be traced back to himself. Now, I must encourage you not to dwell on this matter any further, and if you will not help me investigate, at the very least, wash it from your mind."

"How can I do that? And why should I do that?"

His eyes were thick with thought, as if a dark syrup of data had seeped into his brain and he was stirring it about. Normally, I eschewed his incessant need for the most minute of details, but this time I hoped he could contain it and that he would not allow a single drop to slide through and away. I feared Uncle's life depended on Sherlock's ability to swiftly sort things out.

"Sherlock, Aunt Susan told me you were concerned about me. So, tell me, are you concerned about me, Sherlock?"

His eyes darted about and his lips turned to a frown. "Concerned? I am not concerned. Why would I be concerned? *Should* I be concerned?"

I had to smile a bit at the way he had prattled off the sentences, showing emotion whether he wished to or not, just as he had when he all but attacked his brother earlier in the library. He was trying so hard not to show it, but there was still something about me that moved him deeply. I felt *that*. And there was definitely an intense and perhaps neurotic attachment to his brother that gripped him, because his outburst had been as much a showing of disappointment in his brother's behaviour as it had been a defence of my uncle.

Taking a deep breath, I said, "Let me ask you this, Sherlock. Do you think that someone could be trying to cast blame on Uncle to avoid suspicion himself?"

"That is quite probably the most intelligent thing that has been said in this room all evening. Poppy, you are a gifted woman. You must not allow circumstantial evidence to interfere with your sensible, clever mind. I fear you are suffering from sleep deprivation or something."

"And so it's true. As Aunt Susan said, you are concerned about me."

"Your daily trips to the wharf, the way you are engrossed in the ritual of shrouding the corpses and trying to comfort the living . . . it borders on obsession. You are my assistant. I need you on other matters, and I need you to be rational and logical, able to judiciously sort the fact from the fiction."

"Sherlock, the victims . . . their families. I cannot simply dismiss them as you do."

He looked away and did not respond.

I took a deep breath and asked him to pour me another glass of port. He promptly complied.

"Sherlock, we have never talked about that night. That night at Holme-Next-The-Sea. Nor have we discussed the night of Victor's father's funeral."

He poured port into his own glass as well. "Now? When your uncle has just been arrested, you wish to discuss the night of Squire Trevor's funeral?"

"Did you not just tell me to wash Uncle's predicament from my mind? But Holme-Next-the-Sea . . . nothing washes that away," I said in a whisper.

He placed his glass on the table and palmed my cheeks with his hands. "Pray tell me, Poppy, what the point of rehashing that would be?" he asked.

Although his purpose was to inveigh on the topic—that being our fleeting flirtation with romance—as always, a blast of summer heat, a gust of fiery air, a tinge of warm gold as if the sun had just risen, slinked through, soaking my face and neck.

Sherlock's touch was the chink in my armour. I had tried to hate him. I almost did when he was somewhere else . . . when his hands and his eyes and his smile were somewhere else. I felt I was straddling the remains of what seemed like an ancient time in my life, a romance that had withered like dried mustard, and the stark truth of my present relationship with him. But when Sherlock was near, I travelled back to my dreams. I travelled back to the cottage, remembering the ripple of muscles just above his waist and the tautness of his arms.

Now I let my eyes roam down the slope of his shoulders and recalled my palms on them and the rise and fall of his chest as he slept and the sweet melody of the surf just beyond the window. I felt myself shudder and tremble.

I sighed and looked out the window, recalling the night that I had run into Sherlock at Oscar Wilde's recital four years after the death of Victor's father and Victor's departure for India. I had severely chastised him for failing to attend the wedding ceremony joining my best friend Effie to my brother Michael, Sherlock's sole friend now that Victor was gone. I had rebuked him for his failure to appear at Effie's funeral and scolded him for his refusal to come to my nephew's christening. But we had never discussed the night of passion we shared in the cottage by the sea, nor his immediate withdrawal from me afterwards, nor our momentary reconciliation in the ballroom in Victor's home, which was torn asunder by Victor's appearance, his jealous rage, and the violent fight that ensued.

"This is not the time for such reminiscences, Poppy," he said.

"I am certain you believe there will never be a good time to talk about love," I said.

"Love!" he shrieked, rising. "You want to talk about love? This is what I think of love. It is madness. It rips your innards out, it makes you reel with rage. It gives you a thirst you cannot quench

147

and a hunger you cannot quell. Your logic slips from you as if you are in an oil bath. You see with one crazed eye. You try to hammer it to stillness and nothing you do will smooth the pits and bulges. It is the strongest of metals and the most recalcitrant. It refuses to melt. It refuses to bend. You pound away but it does not yield. Instead, it reduces you to a feeble tremor!" He threw up his hands. "What has love done for your brother?"

"What has Michael to do with this?"

"He loved Effie and he lost her. He has barely survived that loss and has only done so because of people who helped him with the loss. Who would help me through it if I lost—?" He stopped mid-sentence. Then he added, "Who? Mycroft? Sherrinford?"

"Sherlock—"

Sherlock shook a clenched fist in the air. "Why must women do this?"

"Do what?"

"Women dwell in the past," he said waving a hand behind him. "They penalize when you do not explore the uncertain future. They reprove you when you are honest."

"I do none of those things."

I looked away and thought for a moment. I knew that lately I had not been very sensible or levelheaded where Sherlock was concerned—that fact was not lost on me. But I also knew that logic and rationality were my only imprimatur. I had to appeal to his logical mind if I were to sway him to my disposition on this matter. I surprised even myself by remaining so calm when I spoke again to him.

"I simply believe that we are compatible," I said. "You said it yourself. These feelings that you—that we have for each other . . . rather than let them get in the way, we should teach them to live side by side with logic and deduction. I think we should be open with each other. After all, we have never discussed the fact that I lost my innocence to you, that you immediately tried to push me out of your life, and then tried to seduce me again when—"

He pumped his fist into the air again. "You see? You embark on the very journey of which I speak. Talking about the past will not change it. Reproaching me for a momentary lapse that led directly to the end of your satisfying relationship with Victor and my burgeoning friendship with him will serve no purpose. Why do you seek to exhume our past history? To disinter it from its very solid place in—"

"In what? In your brain attic? In the depths of my heart? Do you even know where these painful memories are buried? Or if they are, in fact, buried, for I have not embalmed them."

"And you see some point in fossicking all of that?"

"I do."

"And what point is that, Miss Stamford?" he yelled. "It is inconceivable to me that under the present circumstances you wish to discuss—"

"Whether we wish to or not, we must be honest about our feelings, so that we can deal with them," I urged. I held fast to my composure and continued. "You must ferret out your emotions and acknowledge them, so that you can apportion an appropriate part of your life to them."

He sat down again and said, "I have no problem whatsoever knowing or dealing with my feelings. To begin with, I have few of them, and those I do, I choose to ignore. Absolutely nothing good can come of dredging up those youthful moments of indiscretion or allowing to spring to the surface a companionship that was best nipped in its nascent bud."

I wanted to lash out. With everything I was feeling about my uncle's predicament and all the emotions I had held back from Sherlock for so long, I desperately wanted to savage him, to strike him. But longing to get through to him, I rose, went to where he sat, knelt before him and placed my palms on his knees.

149

"It was not nipped in its nascent bud, Sherlock Holmes. Not for you and certainly not for me. You were my first . . . you are the only man that I . . . with whom I have ever . . . ." I heard myself start to stutter.

"Oh, can you not complete a sentence now?"

"You were the first man I ever . . . ." I felt my cheeks redden.

Finally he understood. "You mean you never . . . then you never . . . with Victor?"

"I was not in love with Victor. As I have told you a thousand times. But I am still in love with you."

"Love!" he shouted, taking up his glass of port again. "I tell you that I have no need of it!"

"That isn't true, Sherlock. I see that now. You cannot live with nothing in your life except cases and deduction. There is more to life than that for you. More to life than the work of your brain for you and more to life than medicine for me."

"Oh, no, Dr. Stamford, it is true. I have decided I cannot live without working my brain for there is nothing else to live for. Least of all love."

"You may try to suppress your thoughts and sensitivities *and* the physical sensations you feel when I am near you, but, Mr. Holmes, you make it clear in so many ways that you are fighting a battle you cannot win."

"No, you are wrong, and I was wrong to entertain foolish, youthful thoughts. I shan't give in to such a notion again."

"What youthful thoughts?"

"That I could—that there could exist any parabiosis of love and logic."

"You do not even realize that you still care for me, do you? When even the gift you gave me the other day is indicative."

"What? A stethoscope?"

150

"Of all the instruments in my medical office that require replacement, the stethoscope was the one you chose. And what does a stethoscope do, Mr. Holmes? It allows you to listen to internal sounds, to listen to the air breathing in and out, and to the sounds of the *heart*."

I returned to my chair and sipped my port, staring at him over my glass. We sat in silence for some minutes, yet I could tell he was as shaken as I had ever seen him. And at a loss for words, which was utterly impossible.

"Do you not understand, Sherlock, that whatever gifts are within my power to give, they are yours?"

He stared at me.

"Sherlock, must you dwell on the negative aspects only? Love is a true treasure."

"Treasures are fleeting, Poppy. They sparkle but only for a moment. Then they grow dim, dull, tarnished. They slip through your fingers. Love stops us, then makes us dance, then halts us yet again and cuts us off at our knees. It cannot stand the test of time."

"You're wrong, Sherlock. A *century* of wind and rain and all the elements cannot eradicate that night. It still stands, like a castle, like a fortress on the cliffs. Weathered, perhaps, but its stone is still strong."

He swallowed the remainder of his port. "No, Poppy. From afar, it may seem perfect, solid. But close up, it must give up its imperfections. As time carves into it, the flaws are revealed."

I stared back. "Its purpose has not been abandoned. It is an organic living thing and it is unfinished."

Finally, I rose and walked to the door. "I must attend to Aunt Susan. I will help you exonerate my uncle, and when we have done so, we shall revisit this conversation. Good night, Mr. Holmes."

28

After Sherlock left, I roamed the house to seek out Aunt Susan. I felt uncomfortable with myself, with the conversation I'd had with my miserable, loutish friend at such a time. A pang of shame washed over me for having dallied with Sherlock to engage in a discussion of our past when my Uncle had just been hauled off to the Yard, and my aunt was in a state of shock and concern. I thought I might retch.

Damn you, Sherlock Holmes, I thought. When I was with him, it seemed that my life stretched and pulled, slowed down and sped up. I could not understand my behaviour nor could I comprehend why he was so willing to entirely sacrifice the possibility of a full and balanced life for the immediate pleasure of solving a puzzle, a case, or a crime. Yes, criminal investigations were exciting. Being on the precipice of danger was exhilarating; I had to concede that. But the delicious and impassioned satisfaction he took in seeking the truth, no matter how horrific, and in being able to show everyone what he knew—always so much more than they knew—to the exclusion of all else . . . this I could not absorb. Had ever a man been such a conundrum?

I wandered from room to room and finally found Aunt Susan in my bedroom, sitting on the edge of the bed, the fingers of her right hand pinching the bedspread, the hat Effie had fashioned for me resting in the left.

I tip-toed across the bare wooden floor, trying to avoid the creaks so I would not startle her. "Aunt Susan," I whispered.

She looked up. Her eyes were rimmed in red, which came as no surprise, but the eyes themselves were hard as agates. I could see that she was angry, more angry than upset, and that was an emotion I knew to be inconsolable. I sat down next to her on the bed.

"Your mother ordered this coverlet from France."

"I remember."

"I had described one very much like it that I saw when your uncle and I went to France for the first time, and based just on my description, she decided she had to have one like it for you. And then I purchased one for you to have here to remind you of home. Does it remind you of your room in the Broads?"

I shrugged. "I suppose. Aunt Susan—"

"Now and then I imagine you wish you were back home, back in Norfolk at Burleigh Manor. It's so lovely there. So quiet. Do you fancy you'll ever go back?"

"Aunt Susan, this is my home now. London. Living here with you and Uncle. It has been for a long time and—"

She flipped the hat over and then back again. "Effie made a hat like this for me."

"I know."

"Only mine is the colour of dark red wine. I suppose you miss her terribly."

"Yes, I do, Aunt Susan."

"She told me once that you would go away one day. Far away. She told me this on a visit to your parents' home when you were both quite young. And then you came to live with us to attend school here, and I thought what she meant by far away was London. Here with us. But I wonder if she meant something else. Do you ever think about going far away, Poppy?"

Right now I would like to be in a distant land, I thought. *Anywhere but here.*

"Do you know how long Mycroft and your uncle have been friends?"

I shook my head.

"Fifteen years. The same number of years between them. Ormond was on a visit to see a friend of his from university who was teaching at Mycroft's boarding school. His friend—his name was Phillip—told Ormond that there was a boy in his class who needed help. He was not a pretty boy, not thin and athletic like your

Sherlock."

There it was again—'my' Sherlock. Why did everyone reference him thus? Why did everyone think of him as my Sherlock, except for Sherlock?

"Mycroft was—is brilliant, of course," Aunt Susan continued. "A bit lazy, from what Ormond tells me, but he was always focused, intent even then to be of service to Her Majesty. But he was odd, not like the other boys. Ormond talked to him, shared stories of his own unhappy childhood because he, too, had always been odd and friendless. He would visit Mycroft from time to time and they corresponded. By the time Mycroft graduated from Cambridge, Ormond had ingratiated himself to many in the House of Lords. With his influence and Mycroft's impeccable scholastic record . . . ." She paused, then asked, "Poppy, how could he do this to Ormond?"

I dared not breathe a whisper of my own suspicions. Aunt Susan would never forgive me.

"Sherlock will sort it out, Aunt Susan. I will assist him."

She cocked an eyebrow. "Assist him?"

"He thinks of me as his assistant in some of his investigations. Much in the same way that we worked together on the baby-farming matter, I shall—"

"No, Poppy. You are a physician. Your endeavours all these years have been toward that one goal. And I will not have you caught up in another criminal investigation. Ormond blames himself for your narrow escape from that woman, that baby farmer. I will not let you put yourself in harm's way again. Not even to help your uncle."

"I will be in no danger, Aunt Susan. I promise you."

"You think Sherlock will protect you, don't you?"

"I think you should try to get some rest, Aunt Susan."

Aunt Susan rose, placed the hat back on its stand, and smoothed the front of her dress.

154

"No, I am going to pay a visit to our solicitor. Ormond has often spoken to Mr. Havershal about the need for further reform, and he says that things have progressed. Mr. Havershal will be able to cross-examine the prosecutor and witnesses, and he can question the motives for bringing the prosecution, which in this case are completely spurious. And he can keep Ormond from saying more than he should. You know how your uncle gets, especially when specious accusations about something are set forth."

"Aunt Susan, it's late."

She shook me by the shoulders. "I don't care how late it is! Your uncle is in dire need of guidance in such a matter!"

She dropped her hands and tucked wisps of her dark hair back into her bun. "I shall return as soon as I can. Will you ask Martha to attend to things? The dishes and—"

I touched her arm. "I'll see to it."

"Oh, and Sherlock, I did not say goodbye. I must—"

"He let himself out, Aunt Susan."

"But I should have bid him a good evening. I should have—"

"Aunt Susan, don't think about that. Don't think about anything except Uncle."

"I rather doubt I will be able to remember so much as my name until your uncle's name is cleared."

29

I slept fitfully . . . I think I finally drifted off shortly before dawn, and a few hours later, I woke to light tapping on my door. Martha had come to offer breakfast, but I had no stomach for food. She also brought me a note from Aunt Susan.

Poppy, your uncle is still at the Yard. Mr. Havershal is there with him. I came home to change and for food to take to Ormond. Do not fret, we will sort this out. Go to work.

"Work," I said to myself. I had not been there for a week. "I should go," I said, again in a whisper.

I washed up, put on a brown morning dress that reminded me of the drab nursing uniform I had been forced to wear at the nursing school before I went on to medical school, and left the house. But instead of my office, I ended up at the British Museum. There might be clues there. The fact that all the men had been found near the museum had to mean something. There had to be clues to the identity of the real killer somewhere.

I went to the room with the Buddha statue. Staring at it, I thought, *What are you trying to tell us?*

I felt a presence. Someone was in the room with me. I swirled around and my eyes landed on a young man, standing in a dim corner. He was seventeen or so, and his brown skin, black hair, and sharp features betrayed his origin—India.

He approached me, smiling. Not sure if he spoke English, I simply nodded.

"It is beautiful, yes?" he asked.

Surprised, I agreed. "Yes, very beautiful. You're visiting here?"

His reply was delivered in impeccable English, but with a short, staccato accent. "I am in England to study."

"Here, in London?"

"No. Well, yes," he corrected. "I attend school here in London but I live in Hove. "It's in East Sussex on the south coast near Brighton. Do you know of it?"

I nodded.

"I live with my nephew and niece, my brother's children, and their mother, in a house my family owns."

"And your parents?"

"My mother died when I was very young and my father travels a great deal. He wants me to become a barrister, so I now study at the University of London."

"That's very admirable."

"But I do not like the law. I wish to study Shakespeare and *Coriolanus* and *Antony and Cleopatra.*"

I noticed his notebook and pen. "You wish to write?"

He nodded. "I have written poetry. And some stories and dramas." He bowed. "My name is Rabindranath Tagore. People call me Rabi."

"My name is Poppy. I am pleased to make your acquaintance."

He bowed again. "I have not heard this name."

I laughed. "It's a nickname. A pet name. A shortening like 'Rabi.'"

"I see."

"And what are you writing now, Rabi? About the Buddha?"

"No. But Buddhism teaches things I write about. I write about the essence of the love. And about time. Moments in time."

The essence of the love, I thought. With so much death and suffering and grief all around me, often I wondered if there were such a thing.

"May I hear it?" I asked.

"It is not finished."

"May I hear what you have so far?"

"The title, I think, shall be *Unending Love.*"

157

He had my attention. I seemed to be confronted by unending suffering these days, and I wondered if unending love was obtainable. Except that my love for Sherlock Holmes seemed never to end, and I so often wished it would.

Or did I?

"I call my poem this because 'unending' means that love is everlasting and immortal. It is a force felt by the entire universe," Rabi said, "not just one person. It is unquantifiable, and I think that the love we feel in this life will be passed on in the next and the next."

"I would like to think that, Rabi. Please, read me what you have."

"I have finished only the first and the last stanza. The first goes like this."

He read from his notebook. "I seem to have loved you in numberless forms, numberless times /In life after life, in age after age, forever/My spellbound heart has made and remade the necklace of songs /That you take as a gift, wear round your neck in your many forms/ In life after life, in age after age, forever."

"That is so beautiful. For one so young, you have a profound belief in the beauty and importance of love."

He shrugged. "I think the love we have will be felt in the next life, in all lives after, for once it is given to someone worthy, love merges with the memories of the universe. It becomes like an ancient tale, repeated over and over, and people who have met and loved in previous lives will meet again and again."

"I like that. The concept of timelessness."

"The moments we have now, Miss, in the present, are part of something bigger, something that is important in the past and the future. Our experiences are a part of something else, something larger, not just who we are, but who we were or might have been or might become. It is all connected."

I took in a deep breath. This boy was an old soul. "Is there more?

"A little bit. As I said it is not finished." He read from his notes again. "The love of all man's days both past and forever/Universal joy, universal sorrow, universal life/The memories of all loves merging with this one love of ours—/And the songs of every poet past and forever."

"My uncle says always follow your dreams," I told him.

"You have a talent, Rabi. Don't become a barrister. Write." Then I looked at the watch pinned to my cape. "I should go."

"You look sad."

I felt a flush to my cheeks. "Do I?"

"Yes. I am sad as well. I am missing home."

"Well, I hope you enjoy some of your time here in London."

"Thank you, Miss. But soon I will return to Hove, I think. And then, perhaps, back to Bengal. "

"Good luck to you, Rabi. I may not see you again."

The shadow of a knowing smile crept across his face. "Oh, but, Miss, of course, you will."

30

My office was musty and dim. I opened the drapes and windows to let in fresh air and light. I'd found notes on the door from two prospective patients I had missed, so after some housekeeping, I locked the door again and, with a pang of guilt, set out to their homes. By late afternoon, I had treated a woman who had burned her arm when she spilled hot water from a tea kettle and a boy with a sprained ankle.

I was reminded once again of Sherlock—of the day my dog bit his ankle and the severe sprain he'd suffered when he fell on the cobblestone. I'd had one of my brother's medical textbooks with me that day, and I read the symptoms of a fracture to Sherlock, partly to show him I had some medical knowledge, but mostly to distract him from his suffering and the irritating voice that accompanied it. Now, so much more certain of my abilities, I quickly examined the boy's ankle, wrapped it, told him to elevate it, and directed his mother to bring him crutches and keep him off his feet.

When I'd finished treating the boy, I hailed a hansom cab to go to Michael's home. He generally worked the night shift these days, so I hoped I would find him at home with the baby. They lived not far from a home Charles Dickens had once shared with his wife at Tavistock Square, near Tottenham Court Road, where Mycroft had purchased the Stradivarius for Sherlock. I needed to tell him about Uncle, and I longed to hold my little nephew Alexander in my arms. He was just eighteen months old and already resembled his mother Effie so much that it nearly broke my heart each time I saw him, yet I somehow felt close to her whenever I was with him.

When I arrived, Michael's housekeeper told me that Michael had taken Alexander with him to have lunch at Ye Olde Cheshire Cheese, a pub on Fleet Street.

"He took the baby to a tavern?"

"The boy likes the parrot, Miss."

"The African grey? Yes, Michael told me about her."

"I think her name is Polly. The bird lightens up the place. She chatters away, but rude she is, so I'm told," she added with a wink.

I hailed another cab and set out for the pub, a dim place with dark wood panels and vaulted cellars that some said were part of a Carmelite monastery many centuries ago. I paid the cabbie, navigated the narrow alleyway and went inside.

I spotted Michael with the baby on his lap right away. I felt my lips turn downwards. Since Effie's death, I feared that Michael drowned his sorrows far too often. He was in the company of two men. One was Michael's friend, Dr. Jonathan Younger, who had been his best man. The other man had his back to me.

I waved to Michael as I removed my cape, and he said a few words to his friends, picked up his pint and Alexander and came over to me.

"Poppy, what on earth are you doing here? And coming into a pub unaccompanied? Mum and Papa would be mortified."

"And when did that ever stop me?"

"I don't think you should—"

"Michael. Stop."

"Can I not be protective of you? Big brother's prerogative."

We sat down at another table, and I held my arms out to take Alexander. As he settled on my lap, he curled his pudgy little fingers around one of my curls. I was about to tell Michael about Uncle when he explained, "I'm just here to say goodbye to a colleague. You remember the chap who shares your birthday, John Watson?"

"Yes, you've mentioned him."

"Well, he's done at Bart's and off to Spike Island."

The name did not register.

"Netley?" he prodded.

"Oh, yes," I answered. "Royal Victoria Hospital. And he's the one who has been wanting to join the Army, yes?"

Michael nodded. "He was just telling us about it. It's a vast place, almost a town in and of itself. It has its own gasworks and there are stables, a bakery, and a swimming pool. Two hundred acres, I think John said."

I'd never been there, but I certainly knew that Florence Nightingale, a woman I greatly admired, had lobbied fiercely for a place to address the issues of the soldiers and their care. The Lady with the Lamp had served nobly during the Crimean War at the military hospital in Turkey and advocated for better sanitation, healthy food, and good health care, provided by well-trained doctors and nurses, for the wounded and sick. Thousands of British soldiers had died during the war and many fell to the ravages of cholera rather than the spray of bullets.

Uncle had attended the opening of the Sixth Session of the Army Medical at Netley when it replaced the school at Fort Pitt, which had always been regarded as a temporary measure. Later he joined the health reform movement to provide a better facility for the disabled soldiers. He had said that it was essential for England to have a medical school that flourished from the abundant wealth and professional knowledge that streamed so constantly to civil hospitals, so that the doctors who tended to sick and wounded soldiers understood their specific needs, much as railway physicians specialized in locomotive injuries.

"John says Netley even provides married quarters and a ballroom."

"A ballroom?" I asked, remembering my brief dance with Sherlock in the ballroom of Victor's home . . . the ballroom where they had come to blows over me.

He nodded.

"Is he married?" I asked.

162

"John?" Michael laughed. "No. But he's quite the ladies' man. He thinks . . . he seems to have a feeling that the treaty with the Afghans may not hold and there is some concern for the envoy in Kabul. So, like our friend Victor, he may be off to India—to join the British-Indian Army just across the border. They—"

"Michael, stop. Stop talking as if the Army is some sort of glamourous life. War is not glamourous."

"Exciting, though," he replied. "And I am single now, so.."

"Stop it. You have a son," I reminded him, stroking Alexander's pale hair. "Now listen to me, I've come with some urgent news."

Finally, he seemed to see the worried look I knew I wore and asked, "Poppy, what is it?"

"Have you been told of what's happening to Uncle Ormond?"

He looked puzzled and shook his head.

I recounted the events of the previous evening and his face flushed with anger.

"How dare he? Uncle Ormond a murderer. It's outrageous," he spat. "How dare Mycroft Holmes do such a thing? I'll contact Mr. Havershal at once."

"Aunt Susan already has, Michael," I said, bouncing the baby whose eyes were fixed on the parrot who kept exclaiming, "Rats!" as a new customer came through the door.

Michael gulped down his drink and said, "I shall go to the Yard at once."

I waited at the door while he bid goodbye to Younger and Watson. Then we left and hailed a hansom. Alexander settled on my lap and I hugged him close. "He's getting so big. Before we know it, we'll be playing noughts and crosses."

Michael said, "Beatrice will watch him for me tonight."

"Beatrice is a housekeeper, not your nanny. I can watch him until Levina arrives, Michael."

163

"Touch wood, we shall get this all sorted out and I won't be long, but Alexander would wear you out. You already look as tired as he is," he said, rubbing his palm over the sleepy child's blonde wisps of hair. "You spread yourself too thin, Poppy."

"As did you. And, Michael, I am concerned about you, too. About your health."

I paused a moment. I knew what grief was like. Hideous to experience and impossible to escape. I did not want to nag him about his drinking, but given the saturnine state of Michael's world, the melancholia was spiraling into ever-decreasing concentric circles, and I could not allow him to get trapped like a rat in a maze. "You must be strong and healthy to look after your son," I added.

"I know," he mumbled. "It's just sometimes . . . I miss her so, Poppy."

"So do I."

I looked out the window as we headed north toward Camden Town. I forced a smile. "Remember how happy we were not so long ago, Michael?"

"You mean when you had time to read Dickens and Eliot and Hardy and sail the Broads and still manage to study medicine? When Effie was about to open her millinery shop and planning our wedding?"

"Yes, all of that. I miss it."

I looked out again as we passed the British Museum and headed toward Marylebone Road. "We're almost home, Alexander," I said, cuddling him. "Will you give Aunt Poppy a kiss?"

He smiled and said, "Rats!"

Michael and I laughed. "You see? Happier times shall come again, Poppy."

I stared at him a moment and thought, *Will they, Michael?*

31

Michael immediately left for the Yard. I bathed and fed Alexander, then sat by his bed for a long time, watching him sleep. I could not stop thinking about the young poet I'd met at the museum. He seemed so certain of his faith, so confident that we would meet those we love again and again, that love would endure. I did not like to believe that losing a loved one meant losing a part of yourself forever. I knew that there was no way to inoculate oneself from the devastation of such a loss—unless you were Sherlock Holmes—but I did not like to think that Effie's parents, Michael and I to be so consumed by memories and the pain they induced that we could find no joy in living. I pondered the illusion, the hallucination I'd seen in the restaurant when I'd lunched with Oscar . . . the translucent figure with golden hair. I recalled Rabi's beautiful poem about unending love. If that were true, did that mean I would see Effie again? That she would see her son? And if I had that to hold on to, perhaps I could force the rawness of grief to subside. Perhaps I could let go if I found a very real reason to go on.

Pulled from my thoughts by the sound of Levina opening the front door, I ran to greet her, told her that Michael had been called into the hospital and that Alexander had been fed and bathed. Then, I hurried home.

It was almost dinner time when I got back to Uncle's house. I wondered if Aunt Susan had returned with any good news. I called to Martha and Genabee and when neither answered, I assumed they were below in the kitchen, preparing the evening meal.

It appeared that Sappho and my dog were the only ones present to greet me, which they did—Sappho with her loud 'meow' and Little Elihu with his happy whine. After I petted them, I released Little Elihu from the little cubbyhole beneath the servant's staircase, where he was kept when no one was about. We took a brief, brisk walk; then I gave him food and water and returned to the foyer. As I placed my cape on the coat stand, I lingered a moment and touched the stand tenderly. It was made of oak, in which Uncle's initials O. R. S.—the R. stood for Remington, his mother's maiden name—carved into it. The hooks were cattle horns from his grandfather's farm in Herefordshire, and the rail had been fashioned from parts of an old haywain. Uncle rarely spoke of his father; he had no use for him. But he'd exhibited fond memories of time spent on his grandparents' farm.

I went to Uncle's library, poured myself a glass of red wine, and took from a shelf one of his books on Buddhism. I flipped through the pages. Many were earmarked and most had Uncle's scribblings in the margins. In a section about love, the author talked about the Four Immeasurables known as the *Brahma Viharas*. It was like a prayer:

May all sentient beings have happiness and its causes,
May all sentient beings be free of suffering and its causes,
May all sentient beings never be separated from bliss without suffering,
May all sentient beings be in equanimity, free of bias, attachment and anger.

Below this were words allegedly imparted from the Buddha to his son. "Practice loving kindness to overcome anger," he had said. "Loving kindness has the capacity to bring happiness to others without demanding anything in return. Practice compassion to overcome cruelty. Compassion has the capacity to remove the suffering of others without expecting anything in return. Practice sympathetic joy to overcome hatred. Sympathetic joy arises when

166

one rejoices over the happiness of others and wishes others well-being and success. Practice non-attachment to overcome prejudice. Non-attachment is the way of looking at all things openly and equally. This is because that is. Myself and others are not separate. Do not reject one thing only to chase after another."

I realized that I had much to learn about love. I also realized that the hardest thing in the world was to practice bringing happiness to someone else without demanding anything in return. I certainly had difficulty behaving that way with Sherlock. I would willingly give him every happiness I could, but I *did* want something in return. Despite my proclamations of unalterable love, however, he seemed reluctant—no, incapable of doing that. Instead, in our most recent conversation on the subject, I almost felt accused of the gravest misdemeanour for expecting him to do so.

I skimmed through the book again and found another section on compassion. It was underlined and it struck me like a bullet had pierced my chest.

The definition is: wanting others to be free from suffering. This compassion happens when one feels sorry with someone, and one feels an urge to help.

The near enemy is pity, which keeps other at a distance, and does not urge one to help.

The opposite is wanting others to suffer, or cruelty.

A result which one needs to avoid is sentimentality. Compassion thus refers to an unselfish, detached emotion which gives one a sense of urgency in wanting to help others.

Wanting others to be free from suffering. I actually felt dizzy as I read the words. I sat down near the fireplace.

Hadn't Uncle professed to exactly this belief? That true compassion requires "an unselfish, detached emotion which gives one a sense of urgency in wanting to help others?" In slightly

167

different words, he had often explained this detachment to people who saw him as cold and aloof despite his dedication to his patients and the medical profession. Didn't he subscribe to precisely the Buddhist philosophy of relieving all suffering, extinguishing all suffering?

I slammed the book closed.

I called to Martha again and still getting no response, I finally went downstairs to the kitchen. I found her sitting at the long table where she rolled out dough and skinned rabbits, smiling, clearly rapt in awe of the man sitting across from her.

I took a step backwards and steadied myself for a moment. Seated across from Martha, sipping a glass of wine, was Sherlock Holmes.

32

"Sherlock!"

He rose and returned my greeting. "Poppy, I've been waiting for you."

I glanced at Martha, whose cheeks had reddened to a deep rose. Martha was a pretty little thing, about my age, with a face blooming with innocent beauty—a pert nose, pink lips, curls that cascaded down her back, thick and red such that any woman would cherish. I felt plain by comparison. I'd always felt too thin and too tall, too sharp-featured, and certainly too sharp-tongued. The angst I felt in that moment, the notion that Sherlock had spent hours entertaining her with stories, ogling her across the table, and she engaging him in her quiet way . . . the rising jealousy, the sinking feeling that Sherlock might prefer this beautiful but dull little wren who would simply listen instead of arguing or informing or infinitely attempting to display her intelligence, startled me and made my face flush with heat.

Martha rose as well and said, "I just made a roast chicken, Miss. I was just finishing when Mr. Holmes arrived."

"Thank you, Martha. I am not hungry but I am sure Aunt Susan will be famished when she returns," I said, as sweetly as I could conjure, though I believe it was through gritted teeth.

"She was here and left again," Martha said. "I'm to take some of the chicken and the other fixings to the Yard for your Uncle."

"Good. That's what you should do then."

I turned to Sherlock. "Have you any news?"

"I do," he said.

"Shall we sit in the parlour?"

"The library."

I glanced again at Martha, as she pushed a gleaming, stray tendril beneath her cap. For an anxious moment, I imagined her sitting at a dressing table in a voluminous teagown, in pale green, or

169

perhaps peach, with lace at the edges of its dolman sleeves. A '*cinq à sept*', worn during the hours when lovers were received, called this because, it was said, 'five to seven' was the only time of day when a maid wouldn't need to be there to help a lady undress and, therefore, discover her secret. I actually shook my head to judder the image from my mind. Then I turned and walked briskly up the stairs to the library with Sherlock at my heels.

I filled my wine glass again and offered more to Sherlock. He nodded and as I poured more wine into his glass, I asked, "So tell me, what news have you?"

"News aplenty. I've had my street urchins flushing out bits and pieces."

"Your street urchins? Oh, the orphans you employ to assist you in your investigations. I believe you fancy yourself an imitation of Fagin."

He laughed. "Indeed not. I'm certainly not a kidsman. Besides, I believe I should take offence, given Dickens described Fagin as grotesque," he laughed.

He was in unusally good spirits despite the dire straits Uncle was in and the fact that he was in the middle of investigating a serial killer. One who did not know—or understand—him might find his elevated mood odd or distasteful, but that was Sherlock, at his most ebullient when he was in the thick of working out a mystery, the more complex, the better. Banish the more parochial puzzles. Restless, always questioning, his merry, mischievous irreverance was always transient, as he clamored for something new, something less boring, even if it meant dueling with a criminal mastermind, a terrorist or a tyrant.

"And Fagin," he continued, "kept his troop of children captive and used them to pick pockets. I encourage no criminal activities. Nor do I beat them or leave them to be hanged."

"Sherlock, I was teasing."

His face shadowed. "I may have to resort to taking that persona, however."

"What do you mean?"

"In light of a rather surprising turn of events, I may have to morph into Fagin Holmes, keeper of children I teach to steal goods to exchange for food and shelter." He took from his breast pocket an envelope and handed it to me.

"A telegram?"

"From my brother Sherrinford. Read it."

I opened it and was shocked at the content. Sherrinford had written that he would suspend all further stipends or subsidies unless Sherlock refrained from 'involving himself further in our brother Mycroft's ventures and concerns.'

I looked up at him. "Sherlock, why?"

"It's Mycroft's doing. For whatever reason, he does not want me involved in the British Museum Murders or in attempting to exonerate your uncle."

"I don't understand!"

"Nor do I. And this is a bit of an inconvenience. I am quite certain that, in time, I will eke out a living in my newfound profession, but I am only just beginning."

"You do have the money from Musgrave."

"Indeed, and that shall have to last for a bit. They won't intimidate me. Neither Sherrinford nor Mycroft. I am going to solve this case."

"I know you will."

He drank some wine and said, "Sit. We have much to discuss."

He settled in a wing chair and I sat in the other one. "Tell me."

"Well, I've had the children watching the comings and goings at the British Museum."

"And?"

He leaned back and closed his eyes, momentarily lost in his thoughts, his hands scraping the invisible strings of the invisible violin that he imagined was resting on his knee. I wished that, instead of a grand piano, I had a bevy of violins from which he could choose when he visited, infrequently as that might be.

His eyes popped open. "Young Archibald observed one gentleman of Asian descent who works there. Apparently, he keeps very odd hours and Archibald saw him meeting with a man very late at night behind the museum. There was some sort of exchange. Archibald is almost certain that the Asian man handed the other man a small statue. But it was too dark for Archibald to be certain, and, additionally, Archibald's observations are less than reliable because he had with him an infant."

"An infant?"

"Archibald is imperturbable, but of late, he is straddled with his youngest brother Billy, who is still in nappies."

"And how old is Archibald?"

"Ten or eleven."

"And he is living on the streets with this baby?"

Holmes shrugged as if it should come as no surprise.

"We should do something, Sherlock. Aren't you concerned at all about the danger in which you may be putting these children?"

"They can be a problem, I admit. I do calculate the limits to which I am justified in putting them in harm's way."

"Well, then, this baby—"

"I shall see to its care." Then there came a second shrug which made it clear that he was not interested in pursuing further discussion of the infant's welfare.

"So, this man with whom the Oriental man from the museum met could be the killer," I breathed out.

"Possibly. Or it could be some sort of preliminary conference to arrange for the true exchange of the poison. Where to obtain it and so on. I should think the mercy killer would prefer something a bit more private. He might not be present at the suicide."

"Suicide. But this man—if we are correct—he is ending a person's life! That is not suicide. And as for mercy—"

"Poppy," he said quietly "I do not believe that this particular enterprise involves anything but merciful intentions."

I thought a moment. Could a person be so tormented that he asked to be put out of his misery? Could anyone be in so much discomfort that he wished to relinqish the last moments, so steeped in emotional crisis or physical pain that he was no longer comfortable in his own presence? My life was far from perfect. My romantic entanglement was a disaster. My best friend was gone. Now my beloved uncle was in gaol. But underneath it all, my nerve endings still fired with the staggering sense of being alive.

"But that does not make it right, Sherlock."

"No, it does not. More importantly, the perpetrator must be found to exculpate Dr. Sacker." He sighed, rose, slammed his glass down so hard on the mantel that I thought it would shatter. "Damn Mycroft!"

I rose and put my hands on his shoulders. "I am grateful, Sherlock. Grateful for your persistence and your faith in Uncle. As I told you, my own has been a bit shaky of late."

He brought his hands up and clasped mine. Our eyes met in that familiar way, and I knew both of us were remembering the touches, the caresses, and the warmth of that night in the cottage.

173

But the depth and the authenticity of his feelings were almost imperceptible. He quickly discharged them, dropped his hands to his side and released mine, turned and looked into the mirror for a moment. I could not discern what reflection he perceived. He turned around and said, "I have a plan."

"To catch him out?"

He smiled, nodded, and said, "Of course!"

We sat back down. I sipped my wine, drinking in every word as Sherlock, ever unable to resist an opportunity to display his dramatic talents, very slowly unfurled what he knew, what he needed to know and how he planned to apprehend the British Museum murderer.

33

"First of all," Sherlock said, "I believe we have already established that all the victims had one thing in common. Each was dying or debilitated in some way by a mental disorder."

"How do you know this?"

"You remember that Mr. Carttar ordered the exhumation of the first four bodies?"

"Yes."

"I made a point of being present at the autopsies and I have read through their medical histories."

My status as a novice detective had its advantages. I had not yet learned how to ignore the law, but Sherlock was a putative expert in such endeavours. Even if Sherlock never achieved fame and fortune, he would definitely make an indelible impression on anyone he met, fooled or engaged in his great game. Once again, I was struck by what an interesting brain his was to inhabit. "And just how did you obtain those?"

He grinned. "First, I talked to relatives of each of the deceased. At first blush, it appeared there might be a common denominator with Dr. Price, James Dixon's regular physician. But he diagnosed only two of the victims, James Dixon, and the third man. I then sent two of my little friends to see Dr. Price, and, when I learned the names of the other doctors who treated the other men, I sent the boys to them. While the doctor examined one boy for feigned injuries, the other boy slipped into the anteroom and found the appropriate medical file."

I smiled. "Clever." Then I forced a frown. "Clever, but dangerous. If the boys' ruse were—"

He waved me off. "*They* are the clever ones. I chose them carefully. The boy who pretended to be hurt should be an actor and the other one . . . well, I discovered not long ago that he reads quite well and retains every word, as if his mind could photograph them."

"Truly?"

"He did not spell correctly each symptom or disease, but I availed myself of medical textbooks your brother loaned me months ago and looked up the necessary details. Now, the second victim was Jonathan Hartwig. He came to England after America's Civil War ended. Well, he was sent here to live with relatives by his mother because no one could handle him. Mr. Hartwig was a soldier in the Union Army. He spent considerable time in a Confederate prison camp called Andersonville."

Instantly, I recalled the photographs of prisoners of war that Uncle had in his possession. Emaciated, broken, all with vacant stares as if their minds, their very souls had been extracted.

"This place, this prison in the state of Georgia, was under the command of a vicious, savage man named Henry Wirz. Some fifty thousand soldiers languished under the brutal torture of this man; nearly fifteen thousand perished."

"Dear God."

"Yes, if there is one, one might wonder why he did nothing about it. At Wirz's violent hands, Mr. Hartwig endured countless beatings, starvation, and every form of cruelty and deprivation. He was finally released when the camp was closed in April of 1865, but the effects have lingered. He had what they call in America a 'soldier's heart.'"

"Uncle has explained this to me," I said. "It is when a person's mind simply cannot manage horrors he saw and the suffering he endured, which is beyond the range of any normal experience."

"Yes, yes," he said. "Severe traumatic events, the repeated threat of death. Now, according to a cousin with whom I conversed, Hartwig was tall of spirit before the war. Studious, a treasurer of books. They were an appendage to his well-being. He had planned to become a professor of rhetoric. Yet, he felt compelled to do his duty. He was captured and sent to Andersonville in the fall of 1863.

The cousin could not recall exactly which battle or campaign he was involved at the time.

"When he returned home, he had changed completely. He could not read or even speak coherently. He complained that he could not seem to purge the terrible memories and that he had frightening nightmares. His brother took him hunting as a diversion, and Hartwig went completely out of control at the sound of the guns firing. His family thought he might benefit from a complete change of scenery and sent him here, to England, to the family farm in Dentdale, deep in the northern Pennines."

"In Yorkshire."

"Yes, near the Tyne Valley. I know it well," he said.

I had never been, but my father and brother had gone on a hunting trip there, more for Papa to bird-watch than to hunt. Papa had described the lush valley of High Gup Gill and the beautiful rivers and wild alpine plants that grew nowhere else. And birds, of course. Pied flycatchers, redstarts and wood warblers, and glorious songbirds like song thrush, mistle thrush and blackbirds.

"It's supposed to be so beautiful there. So restful. But Mr. Hartwig still found no peace?"

"Unfortunately, no. This affliction of his mind—it is quite persistent. It displays itself in amnesia, negative feelings about oneself, lack of interest in much of anything," Sherlock explained. "They said that Hartwig seemed to feel alienated, that he was easily startled, had grave problems with concentration, and could become violent and aggressive. And he suffered from the recurring nightmares and sleep disturbances." He shook his head. "What a waste of a young mind. He was but twenty when he came home."

"So he is—was just thirty-three when he died?"

"Yes. He was unable to adjust, even in the peaceful surroundings. He ran away and the relatives could not find him. Somehow he made his way to London earlier this year. He may have been living on the streets. It is highly improbable that he could find employment, other than perhaps as a cook or washing dishes in a pub. Somehow he made his way to a Dr. Elkins who could not help him." He shook his head again.

"The third victim, Arthur Flincher, saw the same physician who treated Dixon, Dr. Price. Flincher suffered from a disease with which I am not very familiar, a shaking palsy first detailed by a Dr. James Parkinson over fifty years ago. It causes—"

"Tremors, slowness of movement, rigidity and postural instability. Yes, I know of it. Many also suffer from incontinence, blurred vision, uncontrollable eye movements. There is no cure."

Nodding, he said, "And the fourth victim, the man discovered a week before Dixon, one Andrew Baker, sustained a head injury in a carriage accident. He was, according to his family, never the same. According to the notes of his physician, a Dr. Aldridge, he lost many of his cognitive functions and was dismissed from his employment. Now, we are still tracking down the medical history of the first victim, a man named George Blake, and that of the sixth victim whose name Mr. Carttar has not revealed to me. I shall find it out, naturally, and I am certain his death will be of similar circumstances."

"So," I soliloquized as I paced, "their difficulties were all related somehow to the brain, and all experienced life-altering symptoms."

"Yes. Precisely!" He jumped up excitedly and took from his pocket a newspaper article. "But look at this. It's not unlike our baby-farming case. You remember Mrs. Hardy was foolish enough to wrap dead infants in papers with her address and that we were also able to trace her through newspaper advertisements?"

"Of course, I remember."

"Well, while I have little respect for the sensationalizing of the media, once again the newspapers will help us find our killer."

I looked at the classified advertisements on the page.

"Which one—?"

"The one that says, 'And my soul from out that shadow that lies floating on the floor

Shall be lifted -- nevermore! Suffer no more.'

"Do you see how it has been signed? '*The Raven. British Museum.*' The mercy killer is directing them to seek help from him, Poppy. Every man had a copy of that advertisement in his pocket."

34

As I gazed at Sherlock, I saw in his eyes exactly what I had spotted when he came up with his scheme to catch the baby-farmer. He would answer the advertisement. He would meet with the killer himself. Likely by himself this time, however, and the risk be damned. The confrontation was inevitable and fraught with danger. The memories of that harrowing night he had arranged to meet the baby-farmer, Margaret Hardy, infused me. I had accompanied him as part of the subterfuge, been dragged down an alley by her partner and daughter. I'd nearly been killed.

"I have a better way," I said. "A bit more cautious, but—"

He could not help himself; he had to interject his own remarks. "You have not even heard my plan yet. You don't know what—"

"I *do* know what you plan to do. I have studied your methods."

He rose and stood in front of me. "Poppy, you are in a considerable state of excitement, and it is understandable given your uncle's predicament. Not to mention your preoccupation with our—with other things. But you must hear me out."

"No, Sherlock, it is you who must listen. We do not know the identity of this Asian man young Archibald saw at the museum. He may be the killer, he may not. He may be the one who prearranges what follows or simply be giving the killer the Buddha statues, or he may, as you say, simply be a messenger. I shall go to the museum and see if I can find out who he is."

"I will go. I shall talk to the curator and—"

"And tell him what? That you are following up on the story you are writing, and oh, by the way, that to complete it, you need to know the identity of an Asian man who keeps strange hours at the museum?"

Comprehending my logic and my eagerness to once again involve myself in this adventure, his face went momentarily grey and his eyes became restless. "I am discerning a leitmotif here, Dr. Stamford. You inject yourself into an investigation, cavalier about the jeopardy, and making yourself quite vulnerable. Do I deduce a strange affinity for endangerment? Or is it simply that you wish to make yourself indispensable to me?"

He took a few steps, turned away from me, then snapped back to face me. "Or do you simply wish to be in my company?"

Though he was correct in his assumption, I inwardly raged as he said it, but I kept my voice steady and paced as I disavowed them. Paradoxically, of course, I knew they were correct. In my fantasies, I was always by his side, whether he liked it or not.

"It is the aggregation of the circumstances, Sherlock. Your ploy with the museum curator is finished. You cannot use your disguise as a reporter yet again. I believe, for the time being at least, Mycroft will be keeping his eyes on you, rather than on me. And you still need to find out more about this sixth victim. Perhaps you can also extort some information from Detective Inspector Lestrade about why Mycroft has singularly focused on my uncle in this matter. Or from that nice young inspector who was so eager on the baby-farming case, Inspector Hopkins. Meanwhile, I can go to the museum and try to find out something about this mysterious Asian man that your street urchin observed."

He stared at me, perplexed. Finally, he said, "I am all attention, Poppy. Tell me what you will do. And pray, do be precise in the details."

"I shall visit the museum. I shall ask if there is anyone knowledgeable about the artefacts in the room where the Buddha is kept. It seems logical to me that if there is an employee of Asian descent, it would be him to whom I shall be directed. I will have Archibald in my company. I realize it was dark when he observed the exchange, but hopefully he will recognize the man. Can he keep his wits about him if he does?"

"As I said, Archibald is quite imperturbable. But he will likely have little Billy with him."

"All the better. Who would suspect a young woman on a visit to the museum with her younger brother and her infant son?" His eyebrows arched. "Indeed. But one moment . . . assuming you are introduced to the man that Archibald saw and if, in fact, he does identify him as the man he saw the other evening, what shall you do then?"

"I—" I stopped and stumbled. I had not thought quite that far ahead. "After a brief conversation about the art in the room, I will ask if he knows anyone who might fashion a replica of the Buddha. Archibald will have expressed an eager interest in such things. We shall see where it leads from there."

"But if it appears that he is the man, that he is in any way involved in this nefarious pursuit . . . if he is the artist who recreates the Buddha, he must be apprehended."

"The replicator shall be apprehended when he delivers the replica to me. If he is involved, but not the killer, you can get him to talk. Or he may alert the killer . . . or the killer may be suspicious if he is keeping tabs on his artist and he may be nearby. And you will be nearby as well."

He paced the room, shaking his head. "This is all speculation. It will take too long. Who knows how long he would require to make the replica?"

"I shall tell him time is of the essence because Archibald's birthday is imminent and I wish to give it to him as a birthday gift. I shall offer him a substantial amount of money if he can produce it very quickly."

"Again, conjecture. Poppy—"

"Sherlock, I know you. If I could see through a mirror to all the years you were growing up with a father who seemed disappointed in you and a brother who seemed to overshadow you, I would say that you are once again trying to be bigger, better, smarter. You *are* all of those things but let me help you prove it, and without getting yourself killed. We shall exonerate Uncle, catch the killer and—as you said, show Mycroft once and for all who has the better mind."

"You will depart at the slightest indication of danger? You will swear it?"

I nodded.

There was a long silence, during which Sherlock stared at his reflection in the pane of glass above the fireplace. Then he turned to me. "I am going to talk to Mr. Brown again."

"The apothecary? Why?"

"He has knowledge of the ingredients in this poisonous potion. He is also a member of an ornithological society. There may be some clues there, given the killer places a bird at the crime scenes."

"What if Mr. Brown is the killer?

"Hopefully I can confirm that. Now, there are many details which I should desire to know about what you are going to say, and I must also coach young Archibald before we take this course of action."

"Yes, but we have not a moment to lose. And Sherlock, there is one very large detail to discuss before we embark on this adventure."

"What is that?"

"Have you something that poor Archibald can wear that is suitable for a patron of the British Museum?"

Nodding, he smiled.

35

A few minutes after Sherlock left, Aunt Susan came home. I was so elated to see her, I burst into tears as I ran to her.

"Is Uncle with you? Did they catch the killer?"

Her face was drawn, her eyes frightened like a trapped animal and the expression she wore was drained and haggard.

"Aunt Susan, tell me."

"He has not been charged with anything, according to Mr. Havershal. But he is locked away. Poppy, he refuses to speak to anyone. Anyone! He does not admit guilt, from what I understand, but he says nothing to exculpate himself from these ridiculous accusations."

"If they have not set forth a charge of prosecution, then how can they keep him?"

"For further interrogation. That's all Lestrade would tell me. Mycroft refuses to speak to me at all."

"Is there not some law to prevent this? Must they not—"

Before I could finish my sentence, she had walked to the library. She poured herself some port and drank it quickly. Then she poured herself another and went into her morning room. She sat down on the piano bench and I knelt at her feet.

"Aunt Susan, talk to me."

She tinkered on the piano, playing a few notes from *The Maiden's Prayer* by Tekla Badarczewska. It was incredibly popular and Uncle had purchased the score for her last Christmas. Suddenly, she stopped and gazed at me. "As I said, there has been no indictment yet. But there will be, I am certain of it."

"And then?"

"Mr. Havershal says that the prosecutor, judge, and jurors have great discretion, much flexibility in interpreting the law. I don't know what that means, really. Once charged, Ormond will have to plead Guilty or Not Guilty. If he confesses—"

"He will not confess. He did not do this."

"But he also won't speak! And refusing to plead is deemed the same as pleading guilty. Then evidence will be presented and Ormond must explain away the evidence against him to prove his innocence. From what I am told, Ormond has access to the poison used to kill these men. He has spoken to all the physicians who treated the victims and diagnosed them. Mycroft told Mr. Havershal that there will be witnesses who will describe him as cold, as someone who has frequently voiced his approval of euthanasia. He does not go to church. He makes no overt affirmation of the sanctity of life. He—"

I stopped her mid-sentence. "Of course, he believes in the sanctity of life, Aunt Susan. He's a surgeon. He saves people's lives. If you could have seen him at the train collision. If you—"

This time she interrupted. "Did you see him at the wharf, Poppy? Did you ever really see him there?"

I did not answer.

"Do you remember that discussion we had not long ago at dinner? Do you remember he said that sometimes life is not worthy of life? Those were his very words. And he went on and on about his advocacy of the use of drugs to intentionally end a patient's life. He agreed with the legalization of euthanasia. He has said so to people at the hospital."

"How do you know this?"

"Mycroft told Mr. Havershal. And Detective Inspector Lestrade and Mycroft's people are now talking to everyone at the hospital who ever heard Ormond say anything on the subject."

"There is nothing to tie Uncle Ormond directly to these murders, Aunt Susan."

"Mr. Havershal read to me from an old case, Poppy. The case of John Donellan. He said that . . . that . . . wait, I wrote it down." She pulled a slip of paper from her pocket. "This is what the judge read to the jury in that case."

She read the excerpt of the judge's jury charges to me. "A presumption, which necessarily arises from circumstances, is often more convincing and more satisfactory than any other kind of evidence because it is not within the reach and compass of human abilities to invent a train of circumstances which shall be so connected together as to amount to a proof of guilt. . . . But if the circumstances are such, as when laid together bring conviction to your minds, it is then fully equal, if not more convincing than positive evidence.

"He called it circumstantial evidence," she added. "So if there is enough, Ormond could be hanged for these murders. He said people have been convicted on less."

I opened my mouth to speak but nothing came out.

She drank down the rest of the port and ran from the room.

36

As part of the plan we had discussed, the next day I went to St. Bart's to meet Sherlock and Archibald. It had rained the night before, so I trudged through the black mud. The soot that vitiated the air filled my lungs as I made my way to the hospital. Blazing fires and cheery hearths gave way to dust and smoke and fog. Nothing squelched it, and I had taken to washing my face at least three times a day. A dustman called out "Dust-ho!" as he approached in his high-sided horse-drawn cart, his youthful carrier beside him with his large wicker basket. The old man still wore an old-fashioned 'uniform'—a fan-tailed hat, loose flannel jacket, velveteen red breeches, worsted stockings and short gaiters to protect his legs and feet. And the street sweepers were out and about, their clothes sullied with cascades of blacks, covered from head to foot with dirt and grime. They reminded me of the children on the balcony after the Thames disaster. Even though the sewer system removed much of the filth from central London, it shifted upstream to Beckton and Crossness, and when the sewer was discharged, as it had just been on the night of the crash, the river, as described in *The Times*, hissed "like soda-water with baneful gases, so black that the water is stained for miles, discharging a corrupt charnel-house odour."

And I knew that Sherlock's little friend Archibald came from some back-street, some pig-sty littered with decayed vegetables and fish guts, bones and bottles and oyster shells and rags. The idea of children living in such turmoil turned my stomach. I hoped Sherlock remembered to find appropriate attire for Archibald. I doubted the boy owned anything except the clothes on his back.

I said hello to several people in the hospital corridors, but they ignored me. It unnerved me—what game was afoot about which I was unaware?

I had almost reached the lab when I saw Michael running toward me. He pulled me into a supply room and shoved a newspaper at me. "Have you seen this?"

I looked down at the page. The headline read: ***Ostrich Farming in South Africa.***

Michael's eyes followed mine as they left the ostrich article and swept down to the headline that read: *Terrible Accident on The Thames.* Below it was an illustration. Its caption was, *"Recovering bodies from the Thames after the Princess Alice Disaster."* The article that followed read:

> At high water, twice in 24 hours, the flood gates of the outfalls are opened when there is projected into the river two continuous columns of decomposed fermenting sewage, hissing like soda water with baneful gases, so black that the water is stained for miles and discharging a corrupt charnel house odour.

Of course, I already knew that swallowing water from this part of the Thames at that time was fatal. Few victims died in the actual collision. Most suffocated and drowned in the toxic combination of raw sewage and industrial pollutants. I felt the bile rise up in my own throat and looked up at Michael.

"I'm sorry, Poppy. It's another article I wished to have you read. Turn to the next page."

Now I saw what had so excited and agitated him. The headline at the top of the second page read:

SUSPECT IN FIVE MURDERS IS PHYSICIAN AT ST. BART'S HOSPITAL

"Oh, sweet Jesus, Michael!"

"You didn't talk to anyone who might have leaked this to the press, did you?"

"No" I whispered. "I've spoken only to you and Aunt Susan and Sherlock."

"Well, surely neither of them would speak to a reporter."

I fixed my eyes on the article again.

A prominent physician, Dr. Ormond Sacker, is being questioned in connection with six murders. Dr. Sacker has worked at St. Bart's Hospital as a surgeon for over a decade and currently engages in pathology work as well. He resides with his wife and niece in the Regent Park area.

According to sources at the highest level, though Dr. Sacker is patently implicated in these crimes, thus far, he has refused to confess or even to speak on the matter.

In recent weeks, the bodies of six men have been found near the British Museum. The sixth man was found in the same condition as the others, likely poisoned, with a blackbird, also poisoned, positioned near his head and a small replica of a Buddha statue that is on display in the museum. An employee of the museum, Mr. Morris Engelwood, discovered the body. Employees who had exited the museum just minutes before Mr. Engelwood had not seen anything unusual near the premises. Even if it was too dark to see the body of this man, it is impossible to suppose that the employees who preceded Mr. Engelwood would not have tripped over it had it been there when they left.

The inference is therefore this: if the man was murdered where he was found, the deed was done in the short period of twenty minutes. This is the approximate amount of time the police say a medical expert or someone with knowledge of chemistry would take to do it.

The five previous victims have been identified as follows:
George Blake, Jonathan Hartwig, Arthur Flincher, Andrew Baker and James Dixon.

The identity of the most recent victim is being withheld until family members have consented to its release.

Neither afternoon patrons nor employees heard or saw anything that led them to suspect that foul play was going on around them. A watchman was on duty at the back door to the museum at the time the assassin was operating, yet nobody heard or saw anything likely to rouse suspicion. The silence and secrecy around these senseless killings wrap them in an impenetrable veil of mystery for the moment.

As in former cases the murderer seems to have been almost miraculously successful in securing his retreat. The public cannot fail to be impressed with one fact—the apparent bravado of the assassin. Until now the assassin has clearly baffled all ordinary means of detection, reveling in leaving behind these ominous clues to taunt the police. The patrols in the area have been trebled but a source at the highest level of government has indicated that, with the detention of Dr. Sacker, the investigation—and the killing spree—have likely come to an end.

I felt ill. My eyes blurred and I felt myself sway into Michael's chest. All I wanted to do was to repair to our home in Norfolk where there was light dancing on the rivers and my father's music as he tinkered on the piano, and my mother's chattering. Michael was silent, as was I, and we remained so for several long moments.

"Would Mycroft have spoken to this reporter? Are they about to charge Uncle?"

"I don't know. Darling, I don't know, but I wanted to warn you. We must keep the newspapers from Aunt Susan, if we can."

"Yes, yes of course."

"Now, the reason I was able to catch you just now is because Sherlock told me you were coming . . . and about what you are up to . . . and I am here to put a stop to it. You are not going to the museum on this insane mission of his."

"It was my idea, Michael, not Sherlock's."

"Then he has driven you to the brink of insanity as well. I'll have none of it."

"Michael," I said, shoving the paper into his chest, "now more than ever, we must do everything we can to catch out the real killer. Uncle must be exonerated."

"But the authorities—"

"The *authorities*—one of Her Majesty's own—have done this to Uncle. And I am going to undo it as swiftly as possible."

He crossed his arms and stood in front of me like a beefeater and would not let me pass.

"I shall scream, truly I shall, if you do not let me by."

"Poppy—"

"I mean it, Michael."

He heaved a sigh and stepped aside. I knew he was angry but I didn't care.

Nonetheless, I had scant faith in my ability to remain composed, and even less confidence in young Archibald's thespian ability. I doubted that he had been Sherlock's protégé long enough to have acquired his penchant for disguises or his flair for the dramatic. As I stepped into the lab, I was very close to tears and even closer to telling Sherlock that I could not accomplish the mission.

37

Sherlock was fussing with the bow he was attempting to tie at Archibald's thick neck. Archibald was dressed in a two-piece lounge suit made of wool twill in a tartan pattern and held a black top hat in his hands. He was tall and his arms were muscular but the rest of him was like a scarecrow.

"The single-breasted jacket is all the rage," Sherlock said.

"I know. It's an *Albert*. Michael owns several."

I felt a tear slip from the corner of my eye.

"Poppy, what's wrong? If I may so express it, you look positively saturated with fear."

"Do I? It's that I just saw the newspaper and—"

"Oh, yes, that drivel in the *Evening Standard* about your uncle."

"Drivel?"

"Well, it is, is it not? Nonsense. And quite to our advantage."

"In what possible way could public accusations of my uncle be—"

"The killer, Poppy. The killer can more easily be flushed out. The newspaper says that Dr. Sacker refuses to speak, does it not? So, if he knows anything whatsoever about the murders, he is not telling it, and now the murderer *knows* he is not talking. Dr. Sacker probably knows nothing about them, at all, of course. But in any event, the killer will feel free to pursue his course or he shall seize this opportunity to flee before he is found out. I have some theories about the identity—"

"Then tell me!"

"Not yet. I never guess. But we must act quickly before he is able to escape. I have my young charges all over the city. At the docks, at the railway stations—every one of them. They are keeping watch."

"But if they do not know who to look for, Sherlock—"

"Actually, they do. Now, are you ready to proceed?"

I sighed and turned to peruse Archibald's disguise. Though I had never met him, I knew it was a remarkable transformation from what he must look like on any given day, since he was living in the slums.

I looked down at his tubular trousers and saw that there was some revision required. They were supposed to be at equal length at knee and ankle, but one trouser puddled at the floor, covering one of the short ankle-length boots.

I took a deep breath. The youth was here at the ready, eager to do Sherlock's bidding. I knew that I could not back out now.

"No Billy today, Archibald?"

"No, Miss. Me bruva's wif Mum."

"Well, that's good."

I had thought a baby would enhance my disguise, but we would manage, and I was glad their mother was actually looking after the little one for a change.

I dropped my bag, took off my cape and offered it to Archibald.

"Wha' are yer doin'?" he asked.

"Put the cape around you and drop your trousers. I need to fix your pants leg."

"Wha— . . . .?"

"A bit of field triage, Dr. Stamford?" Sherlock quipped.

I grimaced.

"Just go along," Sherlock said, grinning.

Archibald took off his shoes and wrapped my cape around to cover himself from the waist down, took off his trousers, and handed them to me. I retrieved a needle and thread from my bag. Archibald glanced at Sherlock in puzzlement.

"A lady always comes prepared, Archibald," Sherlock quipped. "And in this case, arguing with her is of no use. This particular lady always has the last word."

I quickly turned up the hem and basted it, then broke the thread with my teeth and handed the trousers back to Archibald. He slipped them back on and handed my cape back to me. I tossed it over the back of a chair.

Sherlock started to fashion the tie again and I nudged him out of the way. I had watched my father many times. I positioned the tie around Archibald's neck with one end about two inches longer than the other end. I crossed the long end over the short one, pushed it under with my thumb, pulled the long over the short to form a bow with the other end, using my thumbs and forefingers. Then I pulled the second piece behind the first, made another loop and brought the first end up and under the loop.

I glanced over at Sherlock. "Where did this suit come from?"

"Sampson's. We made a quick trip to Oxford Street. And before you ask, Sampson owes me a favour, so he sold the suit at a discount."

"What kind of favour?"

"You don't want to know."

I was quite certain that I did not.

"Straighten up, now," I instructed Archibald and he pulled back his wide shoulders and puffed out his chest. I lifted his chin with two fingers and resumed my tie endeavour. Holding the longer piece of the bow firmly, I pushed it behind through the knot. I pulled the looped end to lengthen the bow and tightened the knot. I stepped back to appraise my masterpiece and said "Success!"

"She is a woman of many talents, Archibald. Put your shoes back on."

As the boy slipped into his shoes, I said, "Braces would have helped."

"To hold up his pants?" Sherlock asked. Returning his eyes to a book, he grumbled, "Hadn't thought of that."

I went over to him and touched his shoulder. "What's this? A medical textbook?"

"One loaned to me by your brother."

I reached over and flipped the book to the cover. "Theodore Wormley's *Micro-Chemistry of Poisons Including Their Physiological, Pathological, and Legal Relations*. For second-year medical students, yes?"

He nodded. "There is some brewed tea over there on the table. Help yourself. You, as well, Archibald."

Archibald quickly poured himself a cup of tea, but as he brought it to his lips, he paused and held it out to me. "Suga', Miss?"

"Yes, Archibald. Thank you."

He put a spoonful of sugar in the teacup and handed it to me. Then he poured himself one and wandered over to a shelf filled with jars of organ specimens, likely waiting to be analyzed after recent autopsies.

"I looked up the possible uses for the poison that killed all of these men," Sherlock said. "For example, bitter almonds contain three basic components: benzaldehyde, glycoside amygdalin and hydrogen cyanide, which is also known as prussic acid. The toxic compound glycoside amygdalin, present in bitter almond oil, affects nerves and make them insensitive to any sensation, even pain. This induces numbness and anesthetic effects."

"I vaguely remember this from medical school," I said. "But because of its toxic nature, it is for external use only, as an anesthetic. Bitter almond oil cannot be digested. It will cause vomiting."

"Yes, apparently it is an effective purgative, but the dose must be very low and mild or it may have severe adverse effects. As we well know." He opened the book again. "Listen to this, Poppy. It says here that it's not only found in almonds, but can be obtained from many fruits which have a pit, like cherries, apricots,

196

apples. Many of these pits contain small amounts of cyanohydrins and mandelonitrile and amygalin that slowly release hydrogen cyanide. Just one hundred grams of crushed apple seeds can yield seventy mg. of hydrogen cyanide. I have just learned that it is present in tobacco and wood smoke as well. Something for further study.

"Now, here is something quite fascinating, Poppy. There is a theory that hydrogen cyanide is a precursor to amino acids and nucleic acids. Some believe it played a part in the origin of life."

"The origin of life?"

"It is speculative, of course."

"Well, in this case, Sherlock, it is the origin of death. And Archibald and I must be about our business."

I pulled the bow tie taut again and Sherlock handed Archibald his hat. "Now, your accent will give away your humble beginnings in the East End, so speak as little as possible. Try to pronounce the 'g' at the end of words like singing or ringing."

"Say again?"

"When you speak, Archibald, you drop off the g' in words that end in 'ing' so you say, singin' instead of singing. And you don't pronounce your 'T's in words like 'bottom.' You say 'ba-ahm.' Now try this. Say, 'I don't like you.'"

Archibald stared at him for a moment and hissed, "Righ' now, Mr. 'olmes, I don' fu'in li'e yer!"

I covered the broad smile on my lips.

"Do try it again without the profanity. Slowly, Archibald."

"I don' fu . . . I don li'e—"

"No. I *don't*," Sherlock corrected, emphasizing the 'T' at the end of the word. "Pronounce the 'T,' please."

"I don't," Archibald repeated, spitting out the 't.' "I don't like yer."

"You. I don't like *you*. Say it again."

197

Cheeks reddening, parroting the words very deliberately and with painful emphasis, Archibald said, "I don't like you."

"Fine. That's fine. Just let Dr. Stamford do the negotiating, will you?"

"Oh, fu' that," Archibald said, pronouncing the 'T' at the end of 'that' very, very hard.

Sherlock leaned toward me and muttered. "He's a bit rough around the edges, but he's a good lad."

"All right, then, Archibald. Are you ready?" I asked.

"A' course I am, Miss."

Sherlock raised an eyebrow, then held out the door for us and said, "Good luck."

38

"Archibald, have you eaten today?"

He shook his head.

"Then before we go to the museum, you must have a decent meal."

"Bu', Miss, I—"

"Remember what Mr. Holmes told you, Archibald? Arguing with me is of no use."

"Yes, Miss."

"Now, some restaurants do not permit ladies, even with as fine an escort as you. We shall find one that is more progressive. Wilton's, I think, on Ryder Street, just off St. James. Or, no, The Criterion. My mother likes to dine there when she comes to London to go shopping in Piccadilly."

"Wha' eve' yer say, Miss."

He ate everything in sight. But between mouthfuls of roast and potatoes, he told me a little about his background. He could have been one of Dickens' characters in *Oliver Twist*. He and his friends had been leading a subhuman life in the darkest of London's slums. He lived in an area of Whitechapel, the East End's crime-infested hub. Years later, I would recall this conversation. I'd realize I knew someone who actually lived in Jack the Ripper's hunting grounds.

"Your father is dead?"

"Naw," he said. "Me fatha's in Spitafields."

Spitafields was one of London's poorest areas with broken down houses, most rotting from attic to cellar. Uncle volunteered on occasion at Providence Row, where the Sisters of Mercy had created a night refuge for destitute women and children. He had described it and Brick Lane and the other streets in the area as a dark, uneasy place brimming with haggard, skinny women, and children with sunken eyes and pale faces and empty stares.

"So he's alive, then. Your father."

"'e is. But I wan' nothin' t'do with 'im. 'e spends mos' of 'is time in molly 'ouses."

"In what?"

"Chummin' with ova men 'ho fancy 'im. 'e finks 'e's th' wrong sex."

"Oh," I mumbled. "Oh," I repeated with a gasp.

He continued to munch on the last of the bread, and I finally asked about his mother.

"She's a barmaid. Never meant to 'ave me. Billy t'either. But along we come."

"Billy's father?"

"Someone else. I come alon' afore me dad figured 'e wanted t' be a woman 'sted of a man. Don' know 'ho Billy belongs t'. Mum used t' be a laundress. Lived in a 'ouse in Thrawl Street and then with a bloke in George Street, but they gots kicked out for drinkin'. She moved down in Miller's Court on the north side a' Dorset Street, ya see. Finks Billy's dad was th' owner of a chandler shop on Dorset. Billy looks like him. Stout with blue eyes and pale. Looks a bi' like the Chandler bloke. But maybe a guy 'ho works at the gas works on Stepney. 'e gives 'er nice dresses. Like yours."

I knew the area. A place where women paraded along Commercial between Flower and Dean and Aldgate or on Whitechapel Road, soliciting clients. I could not even begin to speculate what kind of life these children had.

"Your mother doesn't take care of you or Billy?"

"She's awright. She tends t' Billy when she can."

"And what about you? You have to take care of him a lot."

"Aw, e's no bova." He shrugged and ripped off another chunk of bread.

He's no bother? I thought. *He is just a child himself.* Aunt Susan had always wanted children and could never have any, and here was a woman who had produced two and cared little for either.

As if he had read my mind, Archibald said, "We does awright, Miss. We get fed and 'ave a bed now and fen a' the Union. Kin't smoke fere. Bu' i's fem old ones I worries 'bou'."

"The old ones? The elderly people, you mean."

He nodded. "They kin't 'ave even a cuppa fru th' day. Only one in th' mornin' and one in th' evenin'. At nigh' fey ge' a hunch a bread and a tad of bu-ah. Maybe a bi'-a-gruel and a dip in th' copper now and fen."

I couldn't stand it. Poor people, hungry people, maimed or sickly, and all they received each day were two cups of tea, some oats boiled in milk or a slice of bread, and a cup of hot cocoa. These misfortunates had little choice . . . go to the Whitechapel Union or live on the streets, and likely to die too soon in one or the other.

Archibald dabbed the last of the bread in the skim of gravy from the beef roast. "Say, Miss, fem fings I saw in th' lab. Fey was parts a people?"

"Yes, Archibald. Organs taken from bodies after death."

He thought a moment. "Fey don' ge' fem from graves, does fey?"

I doubted that Archibald had ever read Mary Shelley's *Frankenstein* or Dickens' *Tale of Two Cities*, which had certainly popularized the image of the Resurrectionists, who were often eminent physicians who snatched bodies or employed grave robbers to supply them, so that they could study colours of death displayed in various stages of bacteria in corpses. Putrefaction was an important factor in the timeline of death . . . the subtle green that appeared twenty-four to forty-eight hours post-mortem; the feathery black along the vessels; and the black blotches that would smear the face and torso and limbs after four or five days. That was when the final never-to-be-forgotten stench of death permeated the air.

201

The poorly maintained city graveyards gave off their own peculiar smell as well. I shuddered, remembering the mortuaries near the dock after the Thames disaster. It was not inconceivable that Archibald knew grave robbers. Perhaps he had even been approached to participate in such activities himself. Hopefully not by Sherlock, though he'd mentioned back at Oxford that, for purposes of research, he had 'come across' severed heads and legs and arms, likely provided by those undesirables who made a living dismembering with crowbars, axes and saws.

"Why do you ask about such things, Archibald?"

"I 'ears fere's good money in i'. I 'eared they does i' 'andsome, they does. Nearer on four pounds, sometimes five. 'ave a mate 'ho give up crackin' cribs fer it cos 'e says 'e 'ad a nice spree over it."

"It is illegal, Archibald."

He lowered his head. Then he said, "We best be goin', Miss."

"Yes, we should. Now, remember Sherlock's instructions, won't you? You won't say much. I will tell them that you stutter a bit and that you are shy. And if you recognize the Asian man you saw—if we indeed meet one—then you are to remove your hat and walk away as if to study something on display. You'll remember, won't you?"

"Yes, Miss."

I paid for our lunch, and Archibald stood, poked out his elbow for me to slip my arm through his, and placed the hat on his head.

As we walked up the steps to the British Museum, Archibald turned to me and asked, "Fem grave robbes . . . yer said wha' fey does is illegal?"

202

"Yes, it is."

"Bu' Mr. 'olmes tol' me yer kin learn all sors a fings from dead people."

"Yes, a scientist can learn things, like when the person died and what caused it. But there are proper channels, legal ways to obtain corpses to study."

"Oh," he muttered as he opened the door for me.

I did not like his preoccupation with the subject, but when he did not say anything else, I chose not to pursue it.

We made our way to the curator's office but were told he wasn't available,' no doubt due to the unwelcome notoriety of the museum in relation to the murders. When I explained my interest in the Buddha statue to the clerk, he cocked an eyebrow. "Is this about the Buddha and the bird left at the murder scenes? Because if it is, we have no comment."

I feigned ignorance. "I don't know what you're talking about, sir. Murders? Here? In the museum?"

"No, just out . . . never mind. The curator is not available. I can direct you to someone in the Oriental Department, if you wish. Your name?"

I decided to lie again. Sherlock had undoubtedly given a false name when he masqueraded as a reporter to talk to the curator. I was certain of that. I was uncertain, however, if there were any other newspaper articles floating about that might list my name as the niece of the accused. I decided to use one of my middle names . . . and Sherlock's surname. "My name is Olympia Holmes," I lied.

"Follow me then, Miss Holmes."

He took me to a small office near the Oriental Department and introduced me to a man who had just joined the staff of the British Museum. He was about Sherlock's age and his name was Theophilus Goldridge Pinches. In the course of our conversation, I learned that he had been employed in his father's business as a die-sinker but broke from his father's clutches to follow his amateur interest in cuneiform inscriptions and Assyriology.

"Very admirable, Mr. Pinches. What do you do here?"

"Painstaking work, actually. I am trying to translate some Babylonian tablets which relate to the Battle of the Vale of Siddim that we have recently acquired, and I am planning on writing a book about Assyrian grammar and late Babylonian forms of characters."

"An ambitious enterprise. My brother Archie"—Archibald nodded and tipped his hat—"is hoping to join the staff of the British Museum one day as well. He is particularly interested in the artefacts relating to Buddhism. And no, this has nothing to do with the murders about which the clerk has only just informed me," I lied. "We come here often, Archie and I, and he would like to study the tenth-century bronze Vairocana? Of course, we know it is impossible for him to remove it from the premises, but I was wondering, do you know any artist, someone who could replicate one for him? His birthday is coming up and it is all he has talked about."

"I have not heard him utter a word," Mr. Pinches observed.

I placed my hand on Archibald's shoulder. "He is rather shy." I leaned toward Pinches and whispered, "And he stutters. He is a bit embarrassed by it. But he is very, very keen on Asian art."

"Well, young man, I wish I could introduce you to Augustus Franks. He is the Keeper of Antiquities. He has been here for over a decade and he is very knowledgeable. But, there is someone else who may assist you. Follow me, please."

As we walked up a flight of stairs, Pinches said, "Only a few objects were acquired from Asia until recently, but our collection is now one of the world's largest, mainly because of a series of donations. The first was from Hans Sloan who acquired quite a bit of Japanese material from a family in Germany. A physician in the family, Dr. Kaempher, was quite the world traveller, and he led an expedition to Japan. There is also the Bridge Collection of East and Central Indian Sculpture and—"

"Quite interesting," I sighed, running out of patience. "But Archie is really quite intense about his research into Chinese culture and Buddhism."

"I see," said Mr. Pinches. "Perhaps he should broaden his horizons."

When we arrived at the room that housed many of the museum's treasures of ancient Asia, Pinches stopped in front of a large gilded bronze statue. Golden and luminous, the goddess stood over 140 centimeters high. Her enviable hour-glass body was naked from the waist up. A lower garment, tied to her hips, hit her ankles at the hem. Her right hand reached out as if she were giving something away. Atop her head was a high crown with some kind of medallion.

Clearly mesmerized by the deity's large exposed breasts, her narrow waist and ample hips, Archie gazed up at the regal goddess. "Who is she?" Archie asked.

"This is our figure of Tara," Pinches said. "Her legend goes like this. At the beginning of time, the oceans were churning and a poison was created that Lord Shiva, a Hindu deity, drank, thus saving the world from destruction. Tara took Shiva on her lap and fed him with her own milk, a milk that could counteract the poison. This statue was found in the early 1800s on the eastern coast of Sri Lanka. She was subsequently acquired by the British Governor at the time, Sir Robert Brownrigg, who later donated her to the museum. Although," he added, "there is some speculation that Brownrigg took the statue from the last King of Kandy when that country was annexed. 1815, I believe.

"What do you think, young man?" Pinches asked.

Archie's eyes were still riveted on the statue. "Strewth, she's a bonnie pa—" He stopped and, in a hushed tone, said very slowly and cautiously, "God's truf . . . truth, she is a beautiful girl."

205

Pinches gave me a puzzled look but continued. "She was not on display for three decades," Pinches said. "Too erotic, some thought. But her purpose is solely religious. Then again, she was likely hidden from the general population in Sri Lanka as well. Only chosen priests and monks were able to admire her. Ironic, isn't it? Well, now, let's see if Mr. Feng Zhèng is about. He is Mr. Franks' assistant. He speaks very little English, but he reads quite well, and he has been invaluable in helping us catalogue various acquisitions. Just down this hall now."

Feng Zhèng, I thought. *He has to be Chinese. This really could be the man that Archibald saw.*

I took a deep breath, slipped my arm through Archibald's, and we followed Mr. Pinches down the dark hallway.

39

Feng Zhèng was definitely of Chinese descent. His skin had a yellow cast, his hair was jet black, and his eyes were angled somewhat downwards. His nose was rather flat and roundish. He had a round face but a strong jawline. When he stood, I called upon my powers of observation and heard Sherlock's voice in my head. How often did he say that people see but do not observe? I knew few Asian people, but Aunt Susan employed a Chinese washerwoman, and sometimes her husband accompanied her when she dropped off clothing. Neither was more than five feet tall. I believed most Chinese people were small in stature, so Zhèng was far taller, more broad-shouldered, and more athletically built than I would have expected. And, though his face was cordial, there was a flicker behind his eyes, like he was retrieving information from his memory bank. The expression was somehow familiar to me. I'd seen it with Sherlock when his mind was busy working out a problem.

Zhèng wiped his brow with his sleeve and cleared his throat. "Ah, Mister Pinches, what can I do for you?" he asked haltingly.

Mr. Pinches introduced me and asked, "What do you say, Zhèng?"

"Ah, shi, shi. Ni hao. Hello, hello. Please to meet you." The 'please' came out as 'pwease.'

"I am pleased to meet you, too, Mr. Zhèng. This is my brother Archibald."

Archibald muttered hello but immediately removed his hat. He turned to me. "I think I will g-g-go over to the d-d-d-d display case," feigning the stutter.

I knew that this signal meant Mr. Zhèng was the man Archibald had seen in the alleyway, but I proceeded, I hoped, as if the gesture meant nothing. "All right. I'll be right over."

207

It took a while for Mr. Pinches to explain to Mr. Zhèng what I wanted, for it appeared that Zhèng spoke only broken English and Pinches spoke little Chinese. He walked us over to the statue of the Buddha and pointed to it. In a very slow and deliberate manner, he explained to Zhèng that I wanted a small statue like the one in the case. He stopped to explain to me what he was trying to tell him. He said he was telling Zhèng to make (chu pin) a little (xiao) fake (jia) Buddha for me. He pointed to the statue and said, "Like this one in the display case, Zhèng. Only smaller," he added, touching his forefinger almost to his thumb. "Xiao xing. Small size."

Zhèng thought a moment, the nodded his head in understanding. "Ah, shi, shi."

"Can you ask him, sir, if he can actually make one, what will it cost?"

Pinches thought a moment, then asked, "Zhe duo-shaov qián?"

"I can do, quick-quick. No dollar. No dollar. I do all time for Mr. Brown at hospital."

Pinches' interest piqued. "Mr. Brown?"

"Mr. Brown at St. Bart's?" I asked.

"He . . . uh . . . he make medicines," Zeng said. He became very animated. "Shi, shi, Mister Brown at St. Bart's."

"I believe he is the apothecary," I told Pinches. "My brother . . . my other brother . . . works at St. Bart's."

Zeng motioned to us to follow him back to his little office. He pointed to a shelf. "See? One almost done, I give you."

"No, no. I couldn't take one that's meant for Mr. Brown."

"Ah," he said, a shadow crossing his face. "Shi, shi. I make you another. You come back ming tian."

"Ming tian?"

"Tomorrow," Pinches explained.

208

"Shi, shi," Zhèng agreed, nodding his head furiously. "Tomorrow."

Sherlock and I had agreed to have him deliver the replica to my uncle's home. I took a piece of paper from the desk, retrieved a pen from my bag and wrote down my address. "Mr. Pinches, can you explain to him I'd prefer to have him deliver it to this address, tomorrow afternoon? Before Archie's birthday is over."

"Oh, shi! Birthday boy?" he asked pointing.

"Yes, for his birthday. Tomorrow. Ming tian."

Then he yelled, "Happy Birthday!"

Pinches gave him a scowl, put a finger to his lips, and said, "Sssh."

Nodding again, Zhèng parroted the 'Sssh.' "Shi, shi, quiet."

Pinches turned to me and said, "I will negotiate a price for you, Miss Holmes. But I think I need to get an interpreter in here. These dreadful events . . . I understand that a replica of the Buddha was left at the scene of each crime. Mr. Zhèng may know something."

"Indeed. And it should be reported to the authorities. I have a . . . a cousin at the Yard. I shall advise him forthwith that he should speak with Mr. Zhèng." I took him aside and asked, "Sir, I take it you do not think Mr. Zhèng had anything to do with the murders?"

"Feng? Good heavens, no. He has a great reverence for life. He won't even kill a bug. Just the other day, he tried to help a bird with a broken wing. No, I must say this Mr. Brown certainly should be a suspect, given his access to chemicals and his expertise in mixing them."

"Of course." Then, in a louder voice, I said, "Very well, then. As to the price, any amount within reason. This will make Archie very happy. How do you say thank you and goodbye?"

"Thank you is 'Xie Xie' and goodbye is 'Zāi jiān.'"

I repeated the words and Zhèng bowed to me several times and gave me a broad smile as I left.

I grabbed Archibald's arm and hurriedly guided him out of the museum. "That was the man you saw?" I asked as he scrambled down the steps. "You are certain?"

Archibald said, "Dead sure."

"All right. You run along and find Sherlock and tell him. Tell him everything that just transpired at the museum. Try St. Bart's and if he isn't there, then go to his residence on Montague Street. Do you know where he lives?"

Archibald nodded.

"I'm going to talk to Detective Inspector Lestrade . . . and visit my uncle." I turned to hail a hansom and Archibald called out to me.

"Miss . . . Doctor Stamford?"

"Yes, Archibald?"

"Fanks. I'm 'umbly fankful, for ever'thin'."

I smiled and waved as he took off running in the other direction.

40

I told the cabbie I would pay him thrice his fare if he got me to the Yard in record time. He raced through the streets, and I had visions of joining the litany of victims I had treated after carriage accidents. Sherlock had told me his mother had died in one . . . my mind went back to the conversation on the day I'd gone to Oxford to attend to his injuries as he was still recovering from his nasty fall and the dog bite. He'd played his violin, something from the *Lieder.* He had told me about his parents, his brothers, his Uncle Charles, who could choose a stranger and by observing him for moments only, deduce his occupation and recent activities. That day seemed so long ago, a lifetime ago.

We arrived at the Yard minutes later. I paid the cabbie, jumped out of the cab and ran up the steps and inside. I sought out Detective Inspector Lestrade.

"Detective Inspector, I have some information for you. There's a man who works for the British Museum. I just saw him. He makes the tiny Buddha statues. He makes them for—"

He cut me off, took me by the elbow, and escorted me to a quiet corner down the hall.

"Detective Inspector, this man, this Chinese man, he makes the replicas for Mr. Brown, an apothecary at St. Bart's. An *apothecary*, sir. Mr. Brown has access to the poison that has taken the lives of these men. He is a member of an ornithological society. Birds, sir. Like the ones left at the scene. You need to—"

"Who told you to go and talk to this man at the museum?"

"What? Did you hear what I said? It's Mr. Brown, the apothecary at St. Bart's."

"Quiet!" he hissed. "Dr. Stamford, please keep your voice down. Why are you meddling in this case?"

"Meddling! Aren't you listening to me? You must let my uncle go and arrest Mr. Brown. It's obvious—"

Just then I heard heavy footsteps coming up behind us. I turned. Suddenly I was facing Mycroft Holmes.

"Detective Inspector, I'll have a word with Dr. Stamford, if you please."

"Of course, sir," Lestrade said and hurried down the hall.

"Dr. Stamford, did my brother put you up to this?"

"Did you hear what I said? You must do something. Go arrest Mr. Brown and let my uncle out of here."

"Did your aunt not tell you? Your uncle has been taken to Newgate. Just a few hours ago."

"What!" I gasped. "But he has not even been charged. He—"

"He has been, Dr. Stamford. That's the reason for the transfer."

"No, this is not possible!" I yelled. I collected myself for I refused to behave like a whining fool and paced for a few moments. "The man at the museum, the Asian man. You have to listen to what I'm saying. He told me he has made statues for Mr. Brown. Surely now you will listen to reason."

His lips pursed and he glowered at me. "We are speaking to all persons of interest in the matter. I suppose it was Sherlock who has involved you yet again."

"Last time I worked with Sherlock on an investigation, *you* involved us."

He grimaced again.

"Both of you must cease and desist. Let the authorities do their job."

"But—"

Fixed on holding back my tears, I pulled my shoulders back. "Mr. Holmes, can you at least assure me that you will . . . that you will process this information and proceed accordingly?"

"I assure you we are doing everything possible to solve these murders, Dr. Stamford."

212

"But you won't let my uncle go."

"No. We won't."

I thought about his words for a moment as I paced again. Obviously, he did not consider this case solved, and that meant he did not think Uncle was the perpetrator of the crimes. What game was Mycroft playing?

I turned and asked, "Then can I see him? Will you let me visit my uncle?"

"Your aunt asked to accompany him, but I was able to reason with her. I just sent her home. You do not want to go to the prison."

"I most certainly do. Please, Mr. Holmes. I just need to know . . . He probably will not speak to me about any of this either, but I need to see him with my own eyes. To know that he is all right."

He fidgeted for a moment. "Well, given your help to us in the past—"

"Yes, do I need to remind you again that you yourself involved me in the Angel Maker investigation and nearly got me killed?"

"And you were of great service to Her Majesty. But you—and my brother—have no business in this matter."

"I—"

"However—"

I opened my mouth to speak again and he gently placed his forefinger briefly against my lips. "However, under the circumstances, with you being a respectable doctor and all—"

"As is my uncle."

"Well, I might be able to arrange for a short visit. We shall tell the Warder that you are a doctor and that you wish to attend to his health and well-being."

I nodded, holding back the tears. I refused to let anyone see me cry.

41

A short time later, Detective Inspector Lestrade escorted me to a police coach. Every minute seemed like a day, a week, or longer. I kept seeing the prison in my mind. I'd read about it, heard stories.

It was thought that Newgate Prison dated back to the thirteenth century, when it was the fifth gate to the city. A new prison had been built in the late eighteenth century, and it had been remodeled once or twice. Then the building was badly damaged by fire, and it was rebuilt just the previous year. At that same time, as a result of the Prisons Act of 1877, conditions were supposed to change. The prison bore an ugly history of appalling conditions. It had often been crowded with half naked women and their children, most waiting for transfer to prison ships that would take them to the Colonies. Prisoners under sentence of death were kept shackled and apart from other prisoners. Murderers were fed only bread and water for the final days of their lives before ascending to the gallows. Their only permitted visitors were prison staff and the "Ordinary"—the prison chaplain.

Now, it was to be used only for those awaiting trial and prisoners sentenced to death awaiting execution, but those rules were not strictly enforced. I knew that it still housed all manner of prisoners who had committed heinous crimes. They could be taken right next door for trial at the 'Old Bailey,' the Central Criminal Court, the trial venue for all of London's most heinous criminals.

As if he were reading my mind, Lestrade said, "Newgate is better than it was, Dr. Stamford. These days, they don't keep most prisoners in irons and the food is better. And friends and family can visit occasionally."

Faint praise, I thought. Uncle should not be in prison at all!

"I inspected Newgate once myself," he went on. "There's a small anteroom near the entrance where there's a collection of castes of the heads of the recently executed, taken after execution, of course. One of the detectives—you know him, Stanley Hopkins, Sr.—he's very interested in them. He's an amateur student of phrenological science."

Phrenology . . . a pseudoscience that focused on measurements of the human skull in the belief that the brain contained very specific functions and that different parts of it controlled character, thoughts, and emotions. I did not dispute this necessarily, but I didn't believe that measuring the skull had anything to do with a mind's capacity, a man's ability to think. *I wonder what would someone make of the measurements of Sherlock Holmes' skull, a skull that contained a brilliant mind, but a mind that controlled all emotions?*

"Some time back, I did see the irons in which prisoners used to be confined," Lestrade continued. "And the cells. Prisoners who are sentenced capitally are taken to the condemned cells, and they do not leave them again except to go to the chapel. Those cells are in the old part of the building, toward the back. They have narrow port holes that give a view of Newgate Street. The prisoners pass through the kitchen on their way to the gallows. Then the guards take them to a chapel to see the Ordinary.

"I've been told that some murderers are buried under a flagstone passageway," he said. "Quick lime makes short work of the bodies. Now some, while they are waiting to take that last walk, scratch their initials in the wall. Most can't even stand, though. They just faint dead away, so they put them in a chair and, as a bolt is drawn, it crashes to the pit below and—"

You are a dolt! I wanted to scream. *Sherlock is right! You're thick-headed.*

Instead, I said, "Stop. Please, Detective Inspector. I thank you for the history lesson, but I would rather not know anything more about this place where my uncle is being wrongfully detained. And I would rather you concentrate on apprehending the real killer."

Ignoring Lestrade for the rest of the journey, I looked out the coach window at the blur of buildings as we passed, and I listened to the hooves of the horses striking the streets. Though Sherlock always greeted Lestrade as if he were a friend, he did so mainly so he could keep in touch with what was going on at police headquarters. Lestrade always seemed eager to please Sherlock, and Sherlock delighted in any news of unsolved crimes; but down deep, Sherlock thought Lestrade lacked imagination, that he was deficient in the skills and knowledge one needed for detective work.

They did, however, share one common trait . . . they lacked the good sense and were too insensitive to realize they were hurting someone's feelings.

"Anyway, Newgate is not that way anymore," Lestrade said. "I'm sure your uncle is just fine."

We soon arrived at the corner of Newgate Street and the Old Bailey. I looked in despair at the granite building. It had few windows, an empty niche here and there, and some shabby, eroded carvings. All of it, everything about it was gloomy, stony, and cold. The dome of St. Paul's loomed large against the sky behind it.

"Wait here one moment," Lestrade said. "I need to talk to the Warder to arrange the visit."

I nodded.

When he went inside, I followed the wall of the gaol to a roadway. There were people milling about, most smelling strongly of spirits. A guard pushed several people aside and told me to come into the yard. Blurry-eyed and disoriented by the events of the day, I followed him.

"You don't belong with the likes of them out there," he said. "This is where the gallows are kept," he added. "And where the whippings take place. Over there is the Debtor's Door. They come out of there to be hanged. It's what you came over here to see, eh?"

I felt sickened. I could not flee quickly enough. I ran back to where Lestrade had left me and saw him pacing.

"Where did you go off to? Never mind. Come with me, quickly now."

I followed Lestrade, cautiously keeping within a few inches of him.

We went up some narrow steps, into the turnkey's room, and then along a dark hallway. At the end, we came upon a small open court surrounded by very high walls. Not much light or air or warmth could ever find its way into this well. "We are facing the women's wing of the prison," Lestrade said.

I saw a chary of windows, strongly grated, and shivered.

A guard turned the locks, removed the heavy bars and we ascended another staircase, this one of stone. There were suites of chambers on either side.

"This is where prisoners are kept while waiting to stand trial," Lestrade told me.

We passed through many rooms and corridors, dark and close and foul smelling. It was a forbidding place, cramped and narrow.

"Are you taking me to Uncle Ormond's cell?"

"No, I've arranged to have him brought to the chapel to visit with you."

"But—"

"I don't think your uncle would want you to see him in a cell. Like I said, the Warder is letting me bring him to the chapel."

"But, Detective Inspector, how can I see to his health if I don't see where they are keeping him?"

"Dr. Stamford, please."

"Tell me. At least tell me what the cell is like."

"Dr. Stamford, I must insist you stop asking—"

"I need to know, Detective Inspector. I need to know what Uncle is faced with."

He heaved a sigh. "He's alone. There's a water tank and a basin and a bed roll. He can have a Bible and books, a plate and a mug. And there's a stool and a table. And a window."

"He does have a window?"

Lestrade nodded. "High up and double-grated. It does get intensely cold in inclement weather."

"How cold?"

"Cold enough that prisoners suffer almost beyond endurance, so I'm told."

I thought of Mr. Hartwig, the victim who had been imprisoned during the American Civil War. I thought of the horrible agony he had experienced and the lasting effects of his confinement.

"It is only September. Uncle Ormond will not be here when it gets cold," I said, more to reassure myself than anything else.

Finally, we arrived at the chapel, and he motioned to me to sit down. I took a seat in one of the pews to the left of the pulpit. Then Lestrade disappeared.

I looked around the chapel. It was neat and plain, with galleries for male and female prisoners. I'd read Dickens' descriptions of the chapel in one of his books. In later years, remembering this day, I would return to a passage and read it over and over again. He said:

There is something in a silent and deserted place of worship, solemn and impressive at any time; and the very

218

dissimilarity of this one from any we have been accustomed to, only enhances the impression. The meanness of its appointments - the bare and scanty pulpit, with the paltry painted pillars on either side - the women's gallery with its great heavy curtain - the men's with its unpainted benches and dingy front - the tottering little table at the altar, with the commandments on the wall above it, scarcely legible through lack of paint, and dust and damp - so unlike the velvet and gilding, the marble and wood, of a modern church - are strange and striking.

I squirmed and looked at the pulpit. It faced the communion table. To the right of the pulpit there was a box for the Governor of the gaol, and the Chief Warder's seat was beneath that. Between the stove and the reading desk below the pulpit was the harmonium for music during services. Then my eyes fixed upon 'the condemned pew.' Dickens had described the pen as well:

There is one object, too, which rivets the attention and fascinates the gaze, and from which we may turn horror-stricken in vain, for the recollection of it will haunt us, waking and sleeping, for a long time afterwards. Immediately below the reading desk, on the floor of the chapel, and forming the most conspicuous object in its little area, is THE CONDEMNED PEW; a huge black pen, in which the wretched people, who are singled out for death, are placed on the Sunday preceding their execution, in sight of all their fellow-prisoners . . . .

Often, during the service, the coffin that awaited the prisoner was placed by his side in this pen. I'd seen Auguste Pugin's painting of it once—this chapel, that pew with a coffin waiting for its occupant. The other prisoners would be asked to pray for the soul of the condemned man. I had no doubt they prayed only for their own.

Imagine, Dickens wrote, *what have been the feelings of the men whom that fearful pew has enclosed, and of whom, between the gallows and the knife, no mortal remnant may now remain! . .*

. Think of the hopeless clinging to life to the last, and the wild despair, far exceeding in anguish the felon's death itself . . . .

I shuddered as a miserable foreboding came over me.

Uncle would never sit in that box. Never. I would move heaven and earth to keep that from happening, and I knew that Sherlock would as well.

42

Lestrade opened the door to the chapel and I saw Uncle Ormond next to him in the hallway. I had not seen him since Mycroft incarcerated him. He wore a different set of clothes, ones that Aunt Susan must have brought to him . . . pants and coat made of a midnight blue fabric and an ivory shirt. He looked tired and untidy, but otherwise like himself.

I bolted from the pew, ran to him, and threw my arms around him. He stroked my hair and held me close. He turned to Lestrade and said, "Thank you."

"I have to stay right here in the doorway, Dr. Sacker. You understand."

"Of course," Uncle said, and he guided me to a pew just a few feet away.

"Uncle, I have news."

I quickly explained to him my trip to the museum and my brief exchange with Mycroft, and I told him that Sherlock had launched his own investigation. "You will be out of here in no time."

"Poppy, you shouldn't have come. I keep telling your Aunt Susan to stay away as well. And you must stay out of this. You and Sherlock. Please listen to me, dearest girl. I've tried to reason with Sherlock. I thought he would be rational. He told me what the two of you have been up to but—"

"You've spoken to Sherlock?"

"He's come every day to see me. Several times a day, in fact."

"Well, then you see how focused he is on your release. Uncle, why is this happening? Please talk to me. Talk to Mycroft and make him see—"

He smiled. "You do sound like Sherlock. He ranted on and on about 'What is the point of your incarceration? What object is served for you to place yourself in this miserable, violent

221

environment?' And then we were off on this long, protracted discussion about the misery of the world, the pointless suffering, and he wondering if the world is ruled by chance when he is certain that is quite impossible." He chuckled. "He said that life is stranger than fiction, that in fiction you can almost always foresee the outcome, but in real life, human reason rarely surfaces."

"Uncle, this Mr. Brown, the apothecary . . . you must know him. Is he capable of committing these murders?"

"All of us are capable of despicable acts."

"No, not all. Not you."

"You believe I am innocent."

"Of course, I do."

"That is not what Sherlock told me."

I felt the blood rush to my head, which started pounding. For a moment, I was afraid I would be sick right there because I felt nauseous and frightened. "Sherlock told you . . . he told you that I . . . ." I stammered and stumbled. I could not find the words.

"He said you confided your doubts to him."

I would thrash him. I would beat Sherlock's face bloody!

"He explained to me," Uncle said, "that you had found my scribbles in various books. That you pondered my long absences. It was a comfort."

"What?"

"I did not know why you refused to speak to me for days on end. At least now I know why. And I understand."

"Uncle, I—"

"Poppy, I have been considering the dilemma of euthanasia for a very long time. The meaningless suffering some have to endure. The lack of dignity so many experience when they are terminally ill. I have had many conversations with like-minded people and one urged me to explore the teachings of the Buddha. I am not a religious person, as you know."

He stopped and looked up at the pulpit. "An odd place for us to be meeting, isn't it?" he asked solemnly. "An atheist and an agnostic. Unless you have changed your mind on the matter of God's existence."

I looked down. I truly was unsure of my beliefs.

"There is much to be learned from the Buddha, Poppy. From the Four Truths. Especially the Truth of Suffering. That *life* is suffering. Sherlock asked, 'What is the meaning of that?' as well. It is difficult to calculate, to measure humanity or its components. The great problem with. . . ."

His voice drifted. "But Sherlock decided, in his infinite youthful wisdom, that even this must serve some purpose, must tend toward some end."

He sighed. Then he said, "I asked you to read the article that was published in *The Lancet* a few years ago. The one by William Dale. You remember it?"

I nodded. I'd read it long ago, long before I entered nursing school or medical school. I didn't want to reproach him. I loved Uncle more than ever. So I answered, "Yes, I remember it. He wrote about telling a patient of his fate and using medications like opium to relieve the pain, but that is not the same as euthanasia, Uncle."

"No, but opium, and other drugs, certainly are a great boon to allowing a person to depart this world less filled with terror." He picked up one of the books that he had placed on the pew. "I want you to read this, too. You remember our discussion about Samuel Williams?"

"Yes. It was a heated discussion."

"Yes, it was, as they so often are with you," he laughed. "Well, his essay was published in this book called *Essays of the Birmingham Speculative Club*. They are the collected works of members of a philosophical society. Williams' essay was very favourably reviewed in *The Saturday Review,* as I recall." He

223

tapped on the book. "He proposed that in all cases of hopeless and painful illness, it is the duty of the physician, if it is desired by the patient, to use chloroform to deliberately hasten death. The remedy must be applied only at the express wish of the dying person, of course."

"But this method leaves the sick open to terrible abuse," I said. Then I thought, *My God, he's lured me into a medical-philosophical discussion!* "Uncle, I did not come here to debate the moral implications of euthanasia. I want to get you out of this place!"

"But you must think about these things. You must! Poppy, I have long tied my self-esteem to my skills as a surgeon, but often they go unrewarded. It is a great burden at times, my inability to save every patient, my inability to cure every sick person who crosses my threshold, to alleviate the suffering of those who cannot be cured. It diminishes me.

"You must see the same pride and ego in your Sherlock. For him to be unable to solve a case? Unthinkable! But he must stop. Both of you must stop. In due course, this case *shall* be resolved."

Hearing those words, I knew, I was one hundred percent certain that Uncle had nothing to do with the murders. But he *knew* something.

"You didn't do these horrible things. But you do know who did, don't you?'

Though I pleaded with him, he refused to answer me. Finally, he picked up a second book. "I want you to read this, too."

"Uncle Ormond, I don't want to read. I don't have time to read or discuss human frailty or morals or mortality! I have to help Sherlock get you out of here."

He shoved the books at me. "In this book are David Hume's *Essays on Suicide and the Immortality of the Soul*. He wrote them over a hundred years ago."

"How did you—"

"I asked Sherlock to bring them to me."

He closed his eyes and recited words he had obviously memorized from Hume's book. "What is the meaning then of that principle, that a man who tired of life, and hunted by pain and misery, bravely overcomes all the natural terrors of death, and makes his escape from this cruel scene. That such a man I say, has incurred the indignation of his Creator by encroaching on the office of divine providence and disturbing the order of the Universe? Shall we assert that the Almighty has reserved to himself in any peculiar manner the disposal of the lives of men, and has not submitted that event, in common with others to the general laws by which the universe is governed?"

He opened his eyes and patted the book. "Promise you will read these."

How often he had said these words to me and how I wished to be a child again. I tried to invoke those times in the past, when I was a little girl and he and Aunt Susan visited my home in Norfolk, and then, far more recently, when I came to live with him so I could attend school in London. I tried to see through the shadows to those lovely moments when Uncle read to me or discussed with me some pressing social issue, even if I were too young and inexperienced to fully appreciate it. I had never turned a deaf ear to him.

I took the books and held them to my breast. "Yes. I promise."

He leaned back and looked at me. "You have done something quite remarkable, Poppy. You have allowed Sherlock to break through that wall of his, the one he created to protect himself from being hurt and to protect others from him. You allow him to see himself, to see his reflection and temporarily cast it off, to break through and make a connection, much as your aunt did with me. But I still want you to be careful. I do not believe he can ever free himself entirely from his own constraints or patterns. He has a need to manage himself, restrict himself to focus on his work and only his work. He may never be able to entirely shed that. You must protect yourself from being hurt, Poppy."

He rose then. He gave me a look that was so very familiar. The one that said, 'This conversation is over.'

He gave me a hug and a peck on the cheek and murmured, "Now go home."

Then he walked over to Lestrade and they disappeared.

When Lestrade returned to escort me back to the Yard, we repassed the quadrangles. The walls were curiously exactly the same height as the lovely houses on Newgate Street. They were daunting, clearly a huge barrier to any escape route.

"One sweep did escape, Dr. Stamford," Lestrade told me. "He placed his back in the angle of the wall, and by pressing his hands and feet against the masonry, he worked himself up the wall. When he reached the top, he let himself fall on his back, turned around and crept along. He jumped on a roof and entered a balcony. Nearly frightened the woman who lived there to death. Since the prisoners wear regular attire, he passed completely unnoticed and was at large for a time. But they captured him eventually. Now the walls are smooth and the top is spiked. There will be no more escapes in that way."

I hurried with Lestrade to the police carriage, and once we were on our way, my mind tumbled with the image of that prisoner who was able to escape from Newgate. I'd dreamt of Uncle in a prison cell since he'd been taken away. I had tossed and turned, thinking about him being in a place like this and trying to figure out what I could do about it. I had considered the most absurd options. Planning his escape with Sherlock, approaching Her Majesty. And now, having seen the prison for myself, those thoughts and images pierced me like a hot poker.

43

Determined to convince someone to listen to me, I waited until Lestrade went into the Yard, then went around to the side of the building and entered through a different door. Lestrade nowhere in sight, I asked to see Detective Hopkins. I was directed to a large office where the detectives sorted out cases. I tapped on the door but no one noticed me at first.

I spotted Hopkins right away. I think he was dressed in the same inexpensive, tweed suit he'd been wearing the day we met four years ago. Though he had aged a bit and looked wearier, he still sported the eager smile and the intensely alert eyes. Hopkins was tremendously interested in new scientific breakthroughs; hence, his interest in phrenology, which seemed to be taking England by storm. He studied Sherlock's methods with intensity and often tried to apply Sherlock's forensic science methods to his own cases. Sherlock thought well of him, and he had mentioned several times that despite the fact that Hopkins had supplied some crucial evidence that assisted Sherlock in tracking down the Angel Maker, Hopkins had had limited success in climbing up the ladder at the Yard. Hopkins was a few years older than Sherlock, and he lamented the fact that he had not progressed more quickly.

Hopkins also had high aspirations for his son, Stanley Hopkins, Jr., who was at that time about seven or eight years of age. He came from a long line of law enforcement officials, and he hoped that when his son grew up, he, too, would join the police force or engage in private detective work. According to Sherlock, Hopkins secretly hoped that his son would become Sherlock's disciple. I knew—and disapproved—of Sherlock's interactions with the boy. Sherlock had told me that Stanley, Jr. was a bright child who showed great promise; he thought nothing of showing the boy gruesome artist's renditions of crime scenes and delighted in the boy's enthusiasm when he asked about them. I recalled that one evening when we were at dinner after Sherlock had spent some time with the child, Sherlock said, "Young Stanley Junior might be my protégé one day—except I'll be over forty years old and retired by the time he's of any use to me."

I'd countered with, "Oh, come now, you'll never retire, Sherlock. What do you think you're going to do? Buy a house in the country and keep bees or something?"

He'd said, "I might just fancy that."

Now that he was playing apprentice to Dr. Haviland with his bee colonies at St. Bart's, I half-expected him to do precisely that.

I must admit I rather hoped that Stanley, Jr. would benefit from Sherlock's tutelage, if detective work were indeed his bent, but I also wanted him to emulate his father, for Stanley Senior had a pleasing personality and people skills, a characteristic Sherlock sorely lacked.

As I entered the office, to my surprise, I also saw Sherlock when he turned around. He'd been facing a great board with drawings—crime scenes, I believe—but now he was pacing back and forth as if he were a panther on the prowl.

I closed my eyes, and my mind flashed back to our first few encounters. Back then, when we first met, he had been strong and driven, yet awkward and fragile, eccentric and often disagreeable, a bundle of contradictions. He was still eccentric and anti-social, but he was more focused now, always intent upon unlocking an enigma. When he solved a puzzle, his face took on the patriotic glow of a proud soldier.

I opened my eyes and watched him speaking to Hopkins. I could tell that this case was like a maw, the gullet of a voracious, insatiable beast into which Sherlock had fallen prey. I could tell that it was incomprehensible to him that his own brother was blocking him at every turn. It was like Sherlock was an army forced to fight on two fronts, or a firefighter called to put out a blazing house. He sees the flames engulfing the structure. He feels the heat on his skin. He gets into position to fight the fire, equipped only with pails of water, but each time he puts out a section of the fire, a gust of wind ignites the dying embers again and they shoot to the roof.

I tapped on the door again. This time, all eyes turned. Hopkins and Sherlock hurried over to me.

"Poppy," Sherlock said, "tell him to listen to me."

Hopkins cast his eyes downward. Then he looked at me. "Unlike Mr. Holmes, I am an official member of the police force. I am subject to rules and regulations and the law in instances where he is not."

"Oh, Hopkins!" Sherlock squawked. "You are subject to incompetent leaders, failed institutions, and feckless city officials. Do you not apply my methods at every turn? Do you not study the science of deduction and see the evidence more clearly?"

"I'm in a different position, Mr. Holmes. And that impacts how I may go about solving cases."

"Use your ingenuity, man! Think for yourself. Have I not told you a hundred times that the others see but they do not *observe*?"

This was classic Sherlock. Willing to take risks that the case required of him. Willing to bend rules, toss them out, if necessary, to bring down the perpetrator of a crime.

"My dear Detective Hopkins, how many times have you come to me and asked for my assistance? Granted, sometimes I say, I am busy, I hope you have no designs on me tonight, but then, when you made it known that you were not clear about your case, that you could not make heads or tails of it, that it was too tangled a business for anyone—except me—to resolve, did I not always invite you in, offer you a cigar and a cup of tea with lemon, and help you sort it all out? Have I not always said, 'Do sit down and let me hear about it?'"

Hopkins' face turned red.

Sherlock turned on his heels to face me. "Why have you come, Poppy? Shouldn't you be bandaging a scraped knee or something?"

I bit my tongue. I stared at him a moment, still wanting to flog him for revealing my doubts to Uncle. And now, his insolence and rudeness made my blood boil even hotter. "Must you always be so insensitive?"

Then I turned to Hopkins and forced a calm voice. "Sir, I have some information I would like to share with you. Information that can exonerate my uncle."

Before Hopkins could get a word out, Sherlock said, "Wiggins told me what transpired at the museum, Poppy."

"Wiggins? Who is Wiggins?"

"Archibald!" he yelled, clearly losing his patience. "The boy who accompanied you to the museum—his name is William Archibald Wiggins. On the streets, his friends call him Bill. His mother was so knockered, she named her second son William as well, so I've taken to calling him by his second name. "

Detective Hopkins shook his head and looked at me. "Do you see what I mean?" he asked me. "He is outside the law. He employs children . . . street urchins and beggars like this Wiggins character." He turned to Sherlock. "And Mr. Holmes, this is one method I can neither condone nor endorse . . . using destitute children who live by stealing, scampering around our streets like vermin—"

"They needs must fend for themselves," Sherlock retorted, "but I do not encourage them to steal, sir. I simply employ them to go places I cannot and hear things I cannot. I compensate them for the information they acquire on my behalf and they are good little spies."

I shuddered, again thinking of the tiny babe that Archibald cared for most of the time. He was just a child himself. All of them, all of these deserted, abandoned children belonged in warm, cozy homes, and in school, not living dirty and ragged on the streets of London.

"Detective Hopkins, is there somewhere we can speak privately?" I asked finally. "Please, sir, you always listen to Sherlock and—"

"I have already spoken to him about the man at the museum, Poppy," Sherlock said. "And I have spoken with Mycroft. And Gregson and Lestrade as well."

Ignoring him, I said, "Detective Hopkins, I think that you should question Mr. Brown. He knows how to mix medicines; he's interested in birds and mercy killing and Buddhism. He's a patron of the British Museum and a man at the museum makes little replicas of—"

Sherlock abruptly grabbed my wrist, dragged me out of the office and down the hallway. "Poppy, what are you doing here?"

I yanked away from his grip. "Sherlock Holmes, if you ever grab me by the wrist again, I shall make good on my prior threat to flog you with a riding crop!"

He winced but he did not apologize. "Why are you here?" he asked again in an impatient tone. "Did you not get the note?"

"What note?"

He sighed. "I told Archibald to go to your house and tell your Aunt Susan and your mother to spend the night in a hotel. They were to leave a note for you to join them if you came home."

"To spend the night at . . . what did you say? My mother? What are you talking about?"

"I ran into Michael at St. Bart's earlier and he told me that your aunt had sent a telegram to your mother about the situation, so your mum decided to be with her sister during this difficult time. Michael was on his way to pick her up at the train station. I sent Archibald to wait for them at the house to tell them to spend the night at a hotel and to leave a note for you if you returned."

"Sherlock, I don't understand."

"Something is about to happen, and all of you may be in danger."

"What? What is about to happen?"

"Poppy, just this once, listen to me. Don't be stubborn and headstrong. Do as I say."

"Sherlock, if something dangerous is about to happen, then come with me."

"I cannot. I must see this through. Every instinct I possess cries out to do so."

"Well, I am going to Uncle's. If my mother has come, I must go to see her. And unless you tell me what is going on, I am not—"

He stopped me with a kiss.

It is utterly impossible to describe how it felt. It had been four years since our lips had touched. I pulled away to catch my breath but his lips met mine again. The torrents of tears I had shed over this man faded away. The hustle of the Yard, the officers, the investigation faded away, replaced in my mind by the aroma of wildflowers and the sounds of seagulls. My head rested on a soft white pillowcase embroidered with gold edges like a priest's chasuble, and candlelight danced against pink and azure curtains. I could almost taste traces of sweet wine and smell the scent of it on Sherlock's breath. We were tender and submissive to each other. We were without quarrel, without words for none mattered and none would suffice. In the years that followed, I would often lie in bed until morning thinking back to that time and that moment.

I pulled away and looked at him. "Sherlock, there's not a bit of use to you—"

He kissed my parted lips yet again and said, "Stay the night with me. If you won't stay at a hotel, stay with me."

I had trouble breathing. My skin went hot at the words, which he uttered in a husky voice laced with a distinct tone of mystery. I melted immediately. No flash of lightning could have rendered me so completely helpless. It seemed that no matter how I endeavoured to stop this affliction, no matter how dreadfully he treated me at times, no matter how hard I tried to hide my feelings, he possessed an instinctive perception of exactly what I was about. He saw in my eyes my affection. He knew that he occupied my thoughts. He knew that I was easily persuaded to form my mind to his and that at the slightest provocation, I would yield to him.

"All right, Sherlock."

He grabbed his cape from the coat tree and we left the building.

44

When we arrived at Sherlock's residence on Montague Street, he kissed my forehead tenderly. Night crept over the city, so he lit the gaslight fixtures that flanked the fireplace. He told me to make myself comfortable while he put on the kettle.

I took off my cape and looked around. In the corner on a coat stand hung a clerical costume, one of Sherlock's disguises, I presumed. I recalled that he said he'd recently masqueraded as a priest while investigating a burglary at the medieval St. Pancras Old Church. I smiled to myself, imagining how must have looked to passersby . . . over six feet tall, slimly built, with sallow face and fake dark moustache and beard, disguising his sallow complexion, a black felt hat drawn over his forehead.

I glanced at the breakfront bookcase to the right of the fireplace. It held many books I remembered from his room at Oxford where I'd tended to him while he recovered. Texts by Pasteur and Lister, works by Aristotle, Wilson's *The Arte of Rhetorique*, Gilbert Austin's *Chironomia* and Sheridan's *Lectures on Elocution*. Books on anatomy and new treatises on the blossoming field of forensic science. New editions of Fitzherbert's *Great Abridgement of the Law* and *The Statutes of the Realm. London*. Many others had been added to his reference collection since he left Oxford. I was leafing through Cicero's *De Oratore* when I felt his breath on my neck.

He put down the teacups and I turned to face him. How eagerly I welcomed the warmth that sneaked along my skin as he seized my hand and led me swiftly past the kitchen and into a dark room. I pondered what had made his heart of coldness suddenly swell with such eager ardour, but that thought quickly dissolved as he pressed his chest to mine. I was vaguely conscious of the bed and a small dresser. I bumped into the open door of a wardrobe, but, like a cat on the prowl, he seemed to have a remarkable ability to see in the dark. Still holding my hand, he felt his way among the

235

furniture, closed the wardrobe door, and sat down on the bed. Then he pulled me down with him and kissed me again.

I broke away, barely able to catch my breath. "Wait, Sherlock. Before we . . . before I . . . we must talk first."

I didn't really want to talk. I wanted to relive the night we'd spent in the cottage in Holme-Next-The-Sea, that one night when he had given into his youthful desires. I wanted to enjoy this moment outside the confines of distraction and intrusion. To give into wildness, to push away confusion, to stop dissecting my feelings, and his, and simply devour him. To trace my mind to that happy night, that cheerful ghost of a night when the paroxysms of our bodies expressed every hidden thought and fantasy. When I actually still believed with all my heart that the impossible was possible.

But I could not proceed without receiving some explanation as to why, after four years, he wished to take me to his bed.

"Sherlock, do you love me?"

He pulled back. He pulled away. "Love again. What does that mean?"

"What does it—" I paused to suppress my anger again. Sometimes I truly wondered if Sherlock had suckled poison at his mother's breast. But I also wondered if I were his Tara, the goddess Archibald and I had seen at the museum, the one whose milk could counteract the poison.

"Sherlock, I am trying to understand you. I know how much your work means to you. I understand that that your intensity has propelled you down this unusual path. I mean, you work as though your life depends upon it. So why now? This, why now? I mean, when you finish a case—"

"When I finish a case, it feels as if I were hanging over a cliff. It feels like I am in a constant dance with gravity. If I do not work, I get socially bizarre and agitated."

When you do *work,* I thought, *you are socially bizarre and agitated!*

"Then why are we here if you have concluded that you cannot make room for love in your life? If you refuse to admit you fell in love with me?"

I felt him staring at me through the darkness. He rose, lit a candle, ran his fingers through his hair and leaned against the wardrobe. There was no mistaking his tortured brow and his regret at the stirrings of sexuality that hammered to the surface when he was with me.

"Falling in love," he said, "means losing control."

"Yes. It does."

"And despite your intellect and your education and your usually very logical mind, you have a strong, natural turn for this sort of thing, Poppy. I do not."

"You did feel it, Sherlock. At Holme-Next-The-Sea. Why is it that you cannot admit it?"

His eyes betrayed him. I observed that he was suddenly in a thoughtful mood. He was either striving to recall something in his memory—or to bury it away, seal it from his consciousness forever.

Finally, he said, "Love. It feels like you catch your reflection in a mirror and what you see there is not you. Your knees go, your skin is on fire, and you can feel your internal organs, your heart, your kidneys, your lungs, all of them are burning and beating. And the irony is that you want to keep feeling that way! You are awash in the fear that you will be unable to sustain the intimate relationship! It is my belief that you cannot. You cannot sustain love."

"I don't believe that."

"I refuse," he continued, "to find myself in that vast graveyard of human beings with broken hearts. The earth is scorched with the dying embers of their useless feelings—the remainder of them, for they burn out—and it is littered with such fools. Look at your brother, for example. No, I will not join that dead wake."

I understood, I really did. I had watched my brother go from his exuberant new life to despair. The frenzy of his love for Effie had died; the fiery furnace expired when she did.

But if only I could convince Sherlock that logic and love could co-exist—a theory he had put forth himself the night of Squire Trevor's funeral. If I could stir him once again to joy, light a flame, make him quiver as he once did, and split his stone heart, I would trade castle for dungeon and mansion for hut.

"My work gives me a similar feeling, and it is one that *is* sustainable. I am charged with this obligation to solve cases and I must tend to that end at all times.

"With love," he continued, the pace of his words growing faster and faster, "too much is left to chance. With work, I am the master. I am . . . I am like a chorus master. I can be the best. I can even benefit from certain factors that are out of my control. I can cultivate voices in the dark, I can manipulate them, rearrange the positioning of breaths in each vocal part so that certain phrases have a richer tone. I can capitalize on nuances. The work . . . the work is grueling . . . seeking out the evidence, scattered as it may be, memorizing it and churning it into a set of facts that will hold up in the court case. The relentless, rigorous work is of no concern, though, because it is a means to an end and in that end is joy, an almost savage joy."

I clenched my teeth. Usually, even if his voice grated me, I heard only liquid diamonds. But my frustration with this monologue rose; it was like listening to my bitter grandfather's dementia-fogged ramblings about the Afghan War, his remembrances of lingering sadness and loss so long after that we could barely stand to listen.

"And so," I said, sighing, "it shall always be about the next case. And the next. And nothing else."

"Yes, when one ends, then I must audition the players for the next performance and achieve that sublime satisfaction all over again. It is the only way to leave the monster behind."

I wanted Sherlock to want me more than his work. I wanted him to love me, to realize that he already did. But perhaps that was the fatal flaw. I was not sure that there was any way to make him see it, and I did not want to settle for less. Still I pressed on.

"Sherlock, there is more to life than solving the riddles. More than investigations and cases and victims and criminals. More than medicine! Is it really so utterly inconceivable to you that we can share all of the mundane details and interludes of mediocrity that life can offer up? Can't we try to edit out the inconsequential differences between us, and have a life together? Enjoy the little things? Can't you keep an open mind?"

"I do have an open mind, Poppy. And the little things . . . do not think that I see them as unimportant. The details are important. They can be infinitely the most important in solving a case."

I threw my hands up into the air. "I'm not talking about cases, Sherlock! I'm talking about . . . about flowers like those you left for me at the cottage. I'm talking about—"

"I know what you are talking about, Poppy, and I am not immune to emotions. I am not inhuman. I seek admiration and appreciation, like any man. But I know myself. I know wherein my serenity of spirit lies and I best abate my anxieties through my work."

"Have you never thought that perhaps fate brought us together? That my dog biting you was meant to be?"

"Fate. Fate is surely difficult to comprehend. And it seems to me that fate can bring as much misery as joy. Were Archibald and his little friends fated to be born into such a miserable life? I yearn for peace, Poppy. I do. But the flesh is transient and I aspire to something higher."

"You sound like someone who wants to be a priest. Sherlock, for heaven's sake—"

He gave out a sigh like a man too weary to take another step. "Let us say that I simply feel called upon to trace evil to its source. And now that I know it, I must go out for a short while, Poppy." He went to the dresser, took something from a drawer, and tucked it under his waistcoat. I realized it was likely his pistol.

He walked over to me, kissed my forehead and said, "Stay here. Promise me you will stay here and if you insist, we will talk more when I return."

"Don't go, please."

He turned toward the door.

"Sherlock, this was a ruse, wasn't it? A ploy to keep me away from Uncle's house. You are going after the killer, aren't you?"

"I must take the risks that the drama asks of me."

"But, Sherlock—"

He sighed. "I don't know what you think is hidden at the bottom of this roundabout conversation."

"But—"

"Poppy, impose no further tax on my patience or time!" he bellowed. "I have drawn the large cover. The animal has broken the cover and now the hunt begins. Do not leave, Poppy. Do not exert yourself in your reckless fashion and follow me," he warned.

With that, he hurried from the bedroom and I heard the door to the hallway close.

45

In the wake of this soliloquy, I went back to the lounge and sat down in a chair near the fireplace. I had to face the fact that Sherlock might never embrace the possibility that each of us could gain as much as we lost. I still believed that there was something hidden 'at the bottom of this roundabout conversation,' that we could renew that hopeful flight of fancy we'd shared; that we could invest in it, widen that sliver of a connection upon which we could mutually agree and liberate it.

I was unsure what I feared most and endeavoured to avoid—a life without Sherlock in it or one that bound me to him. My upbringing, especially my uncle's influence, had exhorted me endlessly to move forward, steam onward, to carve my psyche into a rather efficient machine, but Sherlock held me hostage. My feelings for him clouded my mind so much that logic sometimes receded. The disconcerting reality was that I alone could exhume that logical self. That I alone could make the decision to distance myself from Sherlock Holmes or accept him for who he was and stop trying to assuage his infinitely impossible personality, his moroseness, his darker side, his coldness.

I wanted to shape the clay from which he was made, cast him in bronze and stare at my towering hero forever. I wanted to erase the vulnerability, mend the broken pieces and banish the blustery veneer. But those qualities made him who he was . . . an odd man, a fearless man who smiled at death, who beat death. I wondered if Uncle was right. Was there any way at all to make that leap, for me to take him as he was, detached and unapologetic? Could I succeed in looking past his flaws and the disappointments and hone in on the pleasures we enjoyed in each other and the things that set us in motion to begin with? Could Sherlock ever let down his guard long enough to say goodbye to the fear that isolated him so he could let me in? Could I stop giving into the fury and sadness and let go of those emotions and simply appreciate his brilliance? Could I ever stop suffering the anxiety of my own insignificance? Was there a way for us to recognize that among the multiple choices of futures that stretched out before us, the array of possibilities available, we could mutually elect the most positive one?

And if not, was there really any way to leave this man who wielded so much power over me?

I sat there for a long time. Then, like a sudden gust of wind sending a chill through the room, I thought of him, alone, unprotected, standing toe to toe with the murderer of six men. Sherlock drove me insane at times. He drove *everyone* insane at times. But I was shackled by my affection for him. Love is, indeed, an obstinate shackle, and my heart ached too deeply when I tried to break from it.

Overcome by the prospect that Sherlock would harrow this danger alone, I blew out the candles, turned off the gas lamps, and tossed my cape over my shoulders. Then I rushed down the stairs and out to the street. I hailed a cab and blurted, "Regent Park. And please hurry!"

46

On the way to Uncle's house, instead of thinking about the danger Sherlock was in, I tried to distract myself by concentrating on all the things I would say to him when this case was resolved. It was fantasy, but I still foolishly wanted to believe that my relationship with Sherlock could rise, like a phoenix, from the ashes.

Ashes, I thought. Sherlock was forever scrutinizing ashes, like he had that afternoon in the lab. Cigar ashes, pipe ashes, ashes from a fireplace, ashes from ashes! Sherlock had convinced me that each kind of tobacco has a different smell, a different look, and thus, a different quality. Given the prevalence of the habit—every man seemed to indulge in smoking a pipe or rolling a cigarette—I supposed it was possible to use it as a means of identification.

Then there were thumb and hand prints. Prints on a letter, prints on glass. He'd corresponded with Sir Henry Faulds, a Scottish surgeon who had established a mission in Japan, about Faulds' work in using fingerprints to identify a criminal.

"This man," Sherlock had told me, "is convinced, as am I, that the pattern of ridges is unique to each individual. In fact, when his hospital was broken into, the local police arrested a member of his staff, whom Faulds believed to be innocent. Faulds collects fingerprints."

"He what?" I had asked.

"He studied ancient fingerprint markings on caves and started a collection of prints. He recently discovered that someone had taken a bottle of alcohol from his office. The police accused one of his medical students. But Faulds matched the student's fingerprints which he had on file to those on a cocktail glass and compared them to those left behind at the crime scene. The prints were different. On the strength of that new evidence, the police released the man they had suspected of the crime and caught the true thief. The Yard should take note of that, but they have not.

Faulds has even written to a man you admire very much, Poppy. Charles Darwin. He keeps trying to persuade the Yard to establish some sort of fingerprint identification system. They are, as usual, sorely lacking in vision."

I glanced out and saw some street orderlies, young boys dressed in frock, leggings, boots and shiny hats, risking life and limb as they scurried about the streets with scrapers and brooms to rake up mud and horse dung. I sighed. Many were no older than Archie and they laboured from late at night to late morning for the astronomical sum of five shillings a week and the right to dip into a pint of hot cocoa. By the end of the shift, they were covered in dust and slop and horse muck and mud.

Mud stains, I thought. Sherlock endlessly tested them. And rust stains, stains caused by fruit juice, and blood stains, of course, for he was also convinced that testing it could determine whether the blood was old or new and that it could lead to identification of a criminal. My brother Michael had told me that often in the wee hours, he'd catch Sherlock out in the lab, dissolving blood in water, adding white crystals to it, and then adding a transparent liquid.

I thought back to the day I had watched him test it.

"These are the steps one must take to identify the type of hemoglobin in blood," he'd said.

"I don't understand," I'd said.

"Oh, Poppy, use your brain—it's slightly less ordinary than the average person's! Now, I want to be able to differentiate the types of blood that run through our veins."

"Types?"

"Yes, yes! Determining the type of hemoglobin in the blood will lead to less erroneous identifications. Don't you see?

244

Soon we shall be able to separate one wild, unruly savage from another by his blood!"

He had added water to a drop of human blood, mixed the contents, added a pellet of sodium hydroxide in a crushed, crystalline form, and mixed it until the crystals dissolved. What was left was a brown dust at the bottom of the test tube. He had not perfected this procedure yet, but I was certain he would. Because he was focused. Because he was mono-maniacal. Because he would not let anything else in. Because he kept his emotions in check and avoided entanglements and commitments to the fair sex.

But there was more to Sherlock's single-mindedness, his devotion to examining ashes or deciphering codes, than that one explanation. Sherlock really did ponder whether there was anything beyond this life and, in his own way, I think he—like many others—sought his own form of the Fountain of Youth, some achievement of immortality. Though he had thus far refused to take credit for any crimes he helped the police to solve, he feared obscurity. He intended to write a monograph of his findings about ashes and hemoglobin. He often said he wanted someone to memorialize his adventures. And somehow I knew, even then, that it was only a matter of time until heads of state and royalty, murder and revenge, treasures and guns, chases and dramatic captures in the city's swirling fog—the stuff that aspiring writers dream of—would pepper Sherlock's life. Once again, I felt inadequate. Thinking it through, I was perforce reminded that I could never compete with such mysteries and escapades! Life with a country doctor, a family, hanging ornaments on a Christmas tree—how trivial and mundane, how boring and ordinary all of that would be to someone like Sherlock Holmes.

Yet, hadn't he demonstrated how deeply he felt for me? On my nineteenth birthday—was that really four years ago?—he had given me a drawing of the archangel Michael and compared

245

me to the 'warrior-angel,' writing, *"What a likeness of you, the avenger of the little ones murdered by the Angel Maker."*

And hadn't he once said, *"You know that I relish silence and stillness, but when I am not with you, I miss the sound of your voice . . . Is it time for me to show you how I feel?"*

Remembering that confession now, I started to shake, just as Sherlock had shivered that night at the cottage when he admitted that he cared for me. He was truly afraid of what was about to transpire between us, and he had told me that he was shaking because "of what happens to me when I am with you. Because I cannot control my emotions where you are concerned. I cannot keep my distance from you. Because I have these feelings and my body keeps betraying me and I would . . . I fear I would neglect my work . . . ."

It always came back to that. His work. His destiny. Such a complicated man was he. Devoted to solving crimes, yet unwilling to formally join the Metropolitan Police. A scholar and an avid reader, but lacking in interest in so many subjects that others found fascinating. Skeptical about religion, yet could quote it as a clergyman quotes the Bible chapter and verse. Less and less interested in theatre, despite his flair for the dramatic, yet fond of Shakespeare.

Once, when we had been conversing on the banks of the river near my home in Norfolk, I'd asked what play he liked best. He told me *Twelfth Night*, though he'd immediately passed that off as a deference because he was born on January sixth.

"I like that play as well," I'd told him. "It's about love."

"I suppose," he said, "But we must not forget that the play symbolizes how love can cause pain. Some characters see love as a curse, one that disrupts their lives. Some suffer pain from being in love. Orsino, I believe, depicts love woefully as an appetite, 'which cannot be satisfied.' Olivia sees it as a plague. All these love-struck victims . . . they suffer. And doesn't Shakespeare also show that love is exclusionary? He demonstrates that some people find romantic happiness, but others do not."

"But no, the couples find happiness with each other."

"Some, not all," he corrected. "Malvolio and Antonio are prevented from having the objects of their desire; Malvolio, because he is unworthy of his mistress Olivia, and Antonio whose love for Sebastian can never be realized. You see, Poppy?" he had asked, a shadow crossing his face, "love cannot conquer all obstacles, and those whose desires go unfulfilled remain in love, but feel the sting of their failures all the more severely."

So, could it be that Sherlock feared love because he was certain he would fail at it? Could I convince him otherwise?

"We're here, Miss," the cabbie said.

I quickly paid him and ran to Uncle's front door. I felt a hand on my shoulder, started and twirled around. It was dark and the fog was dense, but I made out the figure of a little boy in the shadows. He was thin as a scarecrow and almost as frightening in the dark shadows. His hair was raven black and slicked across his forehead, and he wore overalls and a frayed cap. At first I thought he was one of the street sweepers and that I was in his way. But then I recognized him as the little boy that Sherlock had sent to summon me to Bart's to do the autopsy.

"What are you doing, skulking around?"

Pacing restlessly as he spoke, the boy said, "Mr. 'olmes says I'm right good at sleuthing, I am."

Poor little waif, I thought. I contemplated momentarily how it came to pass that London streets were the home to thousands of displaced children like this one before me. What I would give to sweep them all into my arms and keep them safe.

"Your name is Rattle, isn't it?"

He nodded.

"And why do they call you that?"

"Cos I chatter too much."

I laughed. "Well, Rattle, did Mr. Holmes send you here to spy on me then?"

He nodded. "'e sent me to keep yer from goin' inside, Miss."

"But I live there, so why should I stay out here in the dark and

mist?"

"'e says it's dangerous. So jus' come wif me."

"I cannot do that. I am sorry. I'm going in now."

I turned to go inside and he was instantly in front of me. He was lightning quick and agile and found a way to block each step I took, each turn I made. He was so thin and wiry, and filled with the inexorable pertinacity of all children, that I was unsure how to get around him without lifting him by his collar.

"You are the artful dodger, aren't you?"

"I 'as me orders, Miss."

Annoyed, particularly in light of the fact that Sherlock thought I was in danger, yet he had no compunction about putting this child in harm's way, I asked, "Rattle, tell me, are you being compensated commensurate with your duties?"

"'scuse me, Miss?"

"What is Mr. Holmes paying you to keep your eye on me?"

"'e always pays a shillin' per job and a guinea if we does somethin' special. Plus expenses, Miss."

"Well, I shall give you thrice that sum if you will allow me to pass."

After a long silence, Rattle resumed his guarding tactics. His right hand clasped upon my cape, he glared at me. "I 'as me orders, Miss," he repeated.

I withdrew coins from my bag. *Oh, God,* I thought. *I am tempting a child into doing my bidding, just as Sherlock does.* Despite this, I held the coins in my open hand in front of him and cast a tempting little face at him. "Thrice what he promised you, Rattle. Think what you can buy with this. Think, Rattle. Mutton. Sweets. Pudding. And you won't have to steal a lick of it."

He withdrew his hand and shuffled backwards. "I don' like stealin'," he said. "Fat's 'ow yer get lagged ove' t' prison. I know some been quodded no end of times fer i'" He thought a moment. "But what'll I tell Mr. 'olmes?"

"Leave Mr. Holmes to me, won't you?"

"Right." He swiped the coins from my palm and said, "Fen I'll be on my way, Miss."

"Be careful, Rattle!" I called to him as he gave out a shrill cry of joy, ran up the street, and disappeared.

I turned to face the house. I crept up to the window next to the door and peered in. It was completely dark and there was no movement. I opened the door, stepped inside and called out to my aunt. Then I called out Martha's name and Genabee's. A bit panicky now, I called out, "Mum? Are you here? Michael?"

No one answered.

249

47

The house was too quiet, devoid of voices or activity from down below, and neither Sappho nor Little Elihu came to greet me. The trembling in my arms was like ripples on a pond, constant and swelling. My hands shook as I lit the oil lamp in the foyer, and I saw a note leaning against the silver bird perched on the rim of the ornate calling card holder on the marble table. It was where Aunt Susan always left notes for me and Uncle Ormond. She had written that I must join her and my mother at the Langham and that I was not to stay in the house or ask questions. After I read it, I put it back on the table and started to walk through the house. I thought I heard footsteps near the drawing room and headed in that direction. The door was open and I looked inside. There was nothing, no one. I started to amble through the rest of the house.

I called down to the area that contained the kitchen, scullery, the servants' sitting room and the pantry. Again, there was no response. I didn't hear a sound; I didn't see anything out of order. I looked in the sitting room, the drawing room, the dining room, and Uncle's study. This house where I had spent most of my time for a decade suddenly felt unfamiliar, cold, desolate. I continued my journey in silence.

When I got to Aunt Susan's morning room, I opened the door and stared through the darkness at her piano, hearing in my head the last piece she played. I could hear the notes in my head—the 1st movement's agitation and despair and heartache, the violent beginning of the scherzo and its second gentle, reflective section, the mysterious 4th movement with its endless running triplets and the finale . . . the one filled with horror, ending with the victim being killed by his entrapper on the final minor chord. It was that section that pounded in my head as I moved toward the library door.

I stopped and pressed my ear to the door. Hearing nothing, I was about to make my way up to the bedrooms and the garret when a voice came from the shadows. "Eh, yup, Dr. Stamford, we meet again," a man said as he put his hand on my shoulder. I jumped with a start.

He rushed forward and grasped my arm. I nearly dropped the lamp as he jabbed something against my neck. I felt the slightest prick.

"If you do not do as I say, you will be dead in four minutes."

48

"Open the door, Dr. Stamford."

Seeking to place the voice, blinking and trying to focus, I heard my own rasping breaths. "Who are you? What do you want?"

"Open the door."

I took deep breaths and complied. I let my eyes move hurriedly around the room. They found Sherlock slumped in a wing chair near the fireplace. His head drooped and blood dripped down his face. I was certain he was unconscious.

The man gave me a slight push and I moved forward. I started to walk toward the fireplace, hoping I could grab a poker, but he nudged me toward the other chair and said, "Have a seat. You and Mr. Holmes have made a grave error and we are here to rectify it."

I stumbled toward the chair and sat down. That was when I realized that Sherlock's head was bleeding profusely. I turned to look at our captor. When I finally had a chance to see the man's face, I realized it was Zhèng, the Oriental man from the museum. He had a pistol in his hand—Sherlock's. He was pointing it directly at Sherlock.

I stared at Feng Zhèng with a mixture of incredulity and terror. With all that had happened that day, I'd completely forgotten that he was supposed to deliver the Buddha statue. But he was not here to deliver a trinket. The terrible certainty hit me. Mr. Brown was not the British Museum murderer. It was this man and he had come to tie up loose ends.

My hands, my mind were shaking, my blood froze. One fact consumed me with fear. It seemed impossible, but this man had outwitted Sherlock Holmes.

Aware that he was watching my every move, I rose cautiously and took a step toward Sherlock. "Sherlock," I called out. "Sherlock, can you hear me?"

He roused and gave me a vacant stare. Then he mumbled, "I'm afraid that Mr. Henry Chickering refused to surrender."

"Mr. Chickering? Who is—"

Giving me a shove, Zhèng said, "That would be me, Dr. Stamford. Now please sit down. Make yourself comfortable."

I slid into the chair across from Sherlock and asked, "May I please help him? He is bleeding profusely. Please let me apply pressure to the wound."

When he nodded, I slowly and carefully retrieved a hankie from my cuff.

"Hand him the handkerchief, Dr. Stamford. Slowly."

I reached out to Sherlock. He took the fabric and pressed it against the laceration.

"Thank you," he breathed, turning his lips up.

How could he smile at such a time? But his eyes betrayed him. My Sherlock who was always hopeful, who had told me once that the goodness of Providence and hope rested in flowers, was now a bloom caught in a downpour, drooping upon its tired, sagging stem.

"You were caught off guard," I said.

"That shan't happen again," he snarled under his breath. Then he added, "We've come full circle, Poppy."

"What?"

"Isn't this how we met? Me bleeding and you offering medical assistance?"

I nodded.

Zhèng walked over to the fireplace. His back to it, he stood between us.

"You don't sound like—"

"Like the wiry little Chinese man at the museum?" Zhèng laughed. "No, I suppose I do not."

His accent was flavoured with traces of a distinct northern Scottish dialect with its particular mouth postures and sounds, a voice bathed in stone walls, limestone, crags, moors, and waterfalls.

"Mr. Zhèng used his mother's name to gain employment at the museum," Sherlock said, dabbing at the blood that ran down his temple. He turned to Zhèng. "The police will be here shortly. It really is quite pointless to add to the body count. It will only take one noose, you realize."

"They have no idea that I'm here, Mr. Holmes. And I'll be gone—why, we'll all be gone, as it were, by the time they figure it out. They're arresting Mr. Brown, I believe."

I shot a glance at Sherlock. "They think it's Mr. Brown?"

"As did your uncle, Poppy."

Sherlock turned his gaze to Mr. Zhèng. I noticed his expression was quite amiable, his smile constrained but evident. It was as though he were quite enjoying this. But his composure did nothing to soothe the anguish I was feeling.

"May I explain?" Sherlock asked. "It will pass the time until the officers arrive."

"Oh, please do, Mr. Holmes. I'm quite curious myself."

Sherlock continued to put pressure on his wound but returned his eyes to my face. "I visited Mr. Brown on several occasions. You see, your uncle suspected him and advised Mycroft of that. By taking Dr. Sacker to the Yard and then to the prison, Mycroft attempted to kill two birds with one stone. Have Dr. Sacker in protective custody and at the same time, flush out the killer. Mycroft was quite certain the killer would run, as was I at first, which is why I posted my street urchins at every egress out of London. But Mr. Brown did not run because he is quite innocent."

"I don't understand, Sherlock."

"Do go on," Zhèng said.

Still dabbing at his wound, Sherlock looked at Zhèng. "Do give her a bit of background, Mr. Chickering."

"No, no, I would not dream of interrupting. You clearly love the sound of your own voice, Mr. Holmes."

"Very well, then," said Sherlock. "Mr. Chickering's father was from Scotland originally. He was a convict sent to the Australian penal colonies, like our dear friend Victor's father. Van Dieman's Land, I'd wager, since most convicts in the late 1840's were sent there as exiles. They were free to work for pay while under sentence. Mr. Chickering's father escaped, worked the gold rush and then sought passage on a ship to San Francisco, where he disappeared for a time." Sherlock turned back to our captor. "And where he met your mother."

"That's quite correct. Not to detain your intriguing story, Mr. Holmes, but how did you ascertain this information?"

"I shall get to that momentarily," Sherlock replied. "Now, after your parents married, they participated in California's Gold Rush. 1849, was it?"

Zhèng nodded.

"By the following year, your father had accumulated a goodly sum of money and you had come along."

I stared at Zhèng. These dates would make him about twenty-eight years of age. He looked much older.

"The family then returned to Scotland but eventually settled in England. All was well. Until another brother came along who was quite sickly. What was his name?"

Zhèng's face darkened. "Stanley. But his Chinese name was Chongan."

"Appropriate," Sherlock said turning to me again. "It means second brother of peace. But poor Stanley had no peace. He had a neurological disorder. A crippling, debilitating disease. There was no hope. No doctors could cure him." Looking again at Zhèng, he said, "And your father couldn't bear it, could he? He became a drunk, a gambler. He was squandering away your wealth swiftly until he was shot during one such gambling dispute, leaving your

255

mother with a ten-year-old—you—and a toddler who was destined to die.

"But your brother hung on for a bit, his muscles slowly withering, his mind becoming mush. And you watched this, day after day, month after month. Then your mother died. You would call it dying of a broken heart, Poppy.

"However, you had money," Sherlock continued. "You took Stanley to more doctors. You went to medical school yourself for a time shortly before he finally passed away. After he died, you came to London to begin your true mission."

"What mission is that, Mr. Holmes?" Zhèng asked dryly.

"To ease suffering. You were brought up in the tenets of Buddhism by your mother. You believe in the Four Truths, especially in The Truth of the Path That Frees Us from Suffering. And it became your mission to alleviate it."

"Well done, Mr. Holmes," Zhèng said, nodding in approval. "Well done."

49

Pacing now, Zhèng explained. "I sought employment at the British Museum. I showed them my artistic side, how well I could preserve and maintain their ancient Oriental artifacts."

"And then you sought out doctors who concurred with your opinion on euthanasia," Sherlock said. "Doctors you discovered through your association with Mr. Brown and his little Ornithology group."

"Birds? But what do birds have to do with any of this?" I asked.

"Mr. Zhèng—well, he went by his English name on these occasions—has a passionate interest in the study of birds," Sherlock explained. "You might have noticed in his little office several lovely paintings of birds that are indigenous to China, as well as the birdcages containing Chinese finches. He joined Mr. Brown's little bird group, became friendly with him and, quite by accident, stumbled upon several like-minded fellows. Like-minded not only as to the study of birds but of euthanasia. Three such individuals were members not only of this little bird-watching group but of a secret society of euthanasia enthusiasts . . . the physicians who treated the victims. Well, almost all of the victims."

Zhèng's gaze adopted a new degree of interest, perhaps even pleasure and gratitude at hearing his story unfold. It was disarming, disquieting, particularly since his finger rested on the trigger of the pistol.

"How did you come to learn all the facts, Mr. Holmes? About my background? My father—"

"From James Dixon's physician, sir. When I went to speak to him, after talking to Mr. Brown, I told him that he was an accessory to murder, and he became quite talkative. Told me your whole, sad story. Does it give you consolation to know that he has great empathy for you and was most reluctant to give you up? I managed to persuade him, however."

I could only imagine Sherlock's particular art of persuasion with the good doctor.

"But why did Uncle suspect Mr. Brown?" I asked.

"Because Brown is always at the British Museum and because he shared his stories about both societies with Ormond. Ormond discovered that Brown also had developed a very keen interest in Oriental things, thanks to Mr. Zhèng's eloquent yarns and sophist deliveries about Asian artwork.

"When Mr. Zhèng told him that several of his birds had developed some strange disease beneath their feathers, Brown concocted an ointment to alleviate their painful condition, as well as one to, shall we say, relieve them of their suffering altogether if the ointment did not improve the condition. You remember our discussion, Poppy, do you not? Three basic components: benzaldehyde, glycoside amygdalin and hydrogen cyanide. The compound in the bitter almond oil affects nerves and alleviates pain. It induces numbness and anesthetic effects. And poor Mr. Brown, with his very limited intellectual capacity—I do so often wonder how he has not killed a patient himself, considering it his job as an apothecary to concoct medicines—had no idea why Zhèng asked him about the ingredients. And with Zhèng's own medical background and his access to the lab—"

"Wait, Zhèng's access to the lab at St. Bart's?"

Zhèng laughed and shook his head.

"When I went to see Mr. Brown yesterday," Sherlock continued, "because he certainly had not cleared out everything and tried to leave the city nor in any way changed his daily habits—and Mycroft's and your uncle's suspicions simply did not hold water—he was going on and on about how he could not find his keys again. He is always losing his keys. I asked when he had last misplaced them, and it was right around the time that the first murder occurred. Call it intuition, if you will."

If grey clouds started to gather, intuition might deem an umbrella necessary. If a dog whined and then showed the dazzling whiteness of his teeth, one might check the doors and window. But Sherlock Holmes relying upon intuition or a feeling? Impossible.

"Wait. We had this discussion. I thought you said that you do not base any deductions upon intuition."

"Logic then," Sherlock corrected. "Mr. Brown has neither the proclivity nor the intellect to manage this enterprise. It simply is not within the parameters of his character. He is a dolt and also a very amiable and congenial man. Beyond that, there was proof. I compared the prints on one of the Buddhas to prints on one of Brown's beakers. They did not match. Mr. Zhèng does not deliver statues to Mr. Brown. Only his own prints were affixed to the statue.

"Poppy, you remember what I told you about Henry Faulds, don't you? How he first became interested in fingerprints and their use in forensics while on an archeological dig with his friend, an American archaeologist, Edward Morse? He realized that the delicate impressions left by craftsmen could be discerned in the ancient clay fragments. Faulds is, as we speak, working on an article about all his experiments for *Nature* that he believes will be published next year. It's an important breakthrough, although Sir William Herschel, who lives in India has been using fingerprints to identify criminals for two decades, so there is some controversy over whose discovery this really is. But that is unimportant. What is important to the case at hand is that the method exists. And that it proves conclusively that Brown never touched the statues that were left at the murder scenes, but our friend here has."

"But Mr. Zhèng made the replicas," I said. "And Brown could have used gloves," I added, thinking through the exculpatory evidence that Zhèng would offer.

"Brown? Wear gloves?" Sherlock scoffed. "He fails to use them in the lab when he should! And there is something else. I went

259

to Zhèng's little office at the museum. You remember I showed you the pipe with the bamboo stem? The one with the bowl made of yixing clay that comes only from China? I compared the bamboo on Brown's pipe to Zhèng's. Brown's is of quite recent vintage. But the one in Zhèng's office is very old. And the prints on the statues did not match the prints on Brown's pipe either." He turned to look at Zheng. "But your pipe . . . it was handed down from an ancestor, Zhèng? Maternal grandfather, perhaps?"

Zhèng nodded.

"Obviously. I scraped from the inside of Zhèng's pipe, It has a different texture than that of the residue in Mr. Brown's much more contemporary pipe. I'd venture to say that Mr. Zhèng had a quiet smoke while he watched his victims die because some residue from the ancient pipe was left at several crime scenes. You know, Poppy, how zealous Detective Hopkins is about preserving evidence at crime scenes. We have him to thank for the ash residue, the final bit of truth we need to hang Zhèng."

I shifted my gaze to Zhèng. "You unspeakable . . . have you black venom in your veins? How could you—"

"How could I *not?*" he shouted. "And the doctors agreed with me. I told them to have their patients—when they were ready—answer my advertisement. They sent the men to me, advertisement in hand. They came willingly. It was not murder. It was mercy."

"Ah," said Sherlock. "But you also had to leave your little calling cards so the doctors knew it was you. So the game with the police was afoot. You could not resist. And I might applaud your ingenuity, your compassion and your sincerity, sir, but you crossed the line. You killed someone who did not seek your help."

"The reporter," Zhèng retorted.

Sherlock nodded. "The sixth previously unidentified victim," Sherlock explained to me.

"He was the reporter who was sniffing around the police station and the British Museum. He caught Mr. Zhèng coming out of the museum with a statue and a dead raven. Unfortunately, Mr. Zhèng also had with him a syringe filled with his poison."

"Yes, that was a most unfortunate mishap," said Zhèng. "I was on my way to dispose of the physicians and leave London to carry on my work elsewhere. But the newspaper man got in the way."

"I do feel some remorse about that," Sherlock said. "I am the one who fed poor Mr. Porter the information for that article. I was certain it would flush the killer out sooner. Zhèng killed him to try to prevent publication of his article, but I convinced the newspaper to print it anyway, including in the article a little addition about the sixth man's demise . . . the 'unidentified victim.'"

I put my head in my hands. "Oh, my God."

"Well, this has truly been enlightening and entertaining, Mr. Holmes," Zhèng said, "but lest Mr. Brown elucidate the police about our friendship and implicate me, I really must take my leave."

He pointed the pistol straight at Sherlock's head, but Sherlock jumped up and yelled as loud as he could, "Wretched Beast!"

A moment later, I heard a deep growl and the familiar thumping of my dog's feet on the stairs as he came up from his little cubicle near the kitchen down below. He raced into the room and had his jaws around Zhèng's calf in seconds. Zhèng's arm flew up, and the pistol went off, sending a vapor toward the ceiling. Sherlock was upon him immediately, wrested the pistol from his right hand and the syringe from the left. For a moment, I thought Sherlock would jab the syringe into his neck.

Instead, he bashed the butt of the gun against Zhèng's temple and said, "I thought it was time to return the favour."

Zhèng lay helpless and unconscious on the floor.

I rushed to the dog and grabbed his collar but he would not let go of Zhèng's flesh.

"I'll take 'im, Miss," a voice said, and I turned to see Archibald. He gave out a whistle and the dog let go and ran to him. Archie ruffled his neck and showered him with praise.

How did he do that? I wondered briefly, then turned to Sherlock, dumbfounded.

Sherlock had already removed his tie and was tightly winding it around Zhèng's wrists behind his back. He hollered to Archie, "Go tell Ollie to fetch the police."

50

I slumped to the floor, exhausted, spent beyond belief, and stared at Zhèng's limp body.

Sherlock rushed over to me and touched my face and neck and shoulders. "Are you all right?"

I nodded, but I could barely move my legs or feel my limbs at all. I heard water dripping from the oak tree outside. It was raining. It was so strange—the only thing I could form in my mind was the fact that it was raining.

Sherlock helped me back into the chair. "You are certain you are not hurt?"

I looked into his eyes. His decisions were hopeless to foresee, his strategies difficult to foil. He was impossibly brilliant. But just now, I saw only concern.

We did not speak again until the little boy, Ollie, had returned with an entire squadron of police who carted Zhèng away in a Black Maria.

As the gloat of victory returned, Sherlock said, "That should conclude the case, don't you think?" Then he poured two glasses of wine and tried to hand one to me.

"No," I protested. "First, I must tend to your wound."

He touched his forehead, which was still bleeding. "It's nothing."

"It is not nothing. Stay here a moment."

I went to fetch Uncle's medical bag, retrieved medication and bandages, and treated the cut, all the while remembering our first moments together on the lawn at Oxford. He was recalcitrant and ridiculous and unmanageable then. He still was.

When I finished, I gulped down my wine and asked for more. Sherlock poured the lovely, sweet red liquid into my glass and stroked my hair.

"Why don't you ever listen to me, Poppy?"

"Because you were in danger."

"Obviously. And is that not precisely why I've told you I cannot love . . . I cannot . . . I worry about you. And you put yourself in harm's way. It doesn't work."

"How did you get in here?"

Surprised by the change of course, he asked, "What?"

"How did you get into the house?"

He smiled. "Do you remember when you found me flirting with your house servant? What was her name again?"

"Martha."

"Oh, yes. Well, I convinced her that I fancied her and Martha quite obviously fancied me. I asked for a key to the delivery entrance so I could sneak in to see her."

"You didn't."

"I did," he said, smiling again. "Ingenious, don't you think?"

I mentally added that his ruses were equally impossible to predict.

"And wretched beast? Your trumpet call that resounded to fetch Little?"

"I arranged that with Archie in case things did not go quite as planned." He touched his bandage. "Which clearly they did not. I told him to keep the dog downstairs, occupied, until I called that out and then to let him loose. I knew he'd come running. And I suspected he would be more than happy to strike out at Zhèng just as he did at me. He is quite your loyal protector, you know."

"And Zhèng? How did he get in?"

"He picked the lock. You must have your uncle examine his security measures here. I should have been here long before he arrived, but you detained me and Archie was late. His mum abandoned young Billy again and he had to find someone to watch him. I sent one of my young chaps to tell to Mycroft and Lestrade. I suspect they will be rounding up Mr. Chickering's associates now."

"Damn you, Sherlock. Damn you. Archie could have been hurt! He's just a child. He—"

He quieted me with a kiss.

51

We gathered in Uncle's dining room the next morning to enjoy a lavish champagne breakfast. Seated around the table were Sherlock, me, Aunt Susan and Uncle, my mother, Michael, my nephew Alexander, Mycroft, and Oscar Wilde. Archibald "Bill" Wiggins, his baby brother Billy, and Sherlock's other young helpers, Ollie and Rattle, were there as well. Martha was conspicuously absent, having been summarily dismissed by Aunt Susan for her indiscretion, even though it was orchestrated by Sherlock.

As Aunt Susan raised her glass to toast, I said, "Uncle, thank God you are home."

Sherlock gave me a glass of bubbly, pale liquid, and quipped, "God had nothing to do with it." Then he leaned close to my ear and whispered, "What is Oscar doing here?"

"Hush. He is here because we want him here. Don't be unfriendly."

A thought split through my brain like sunlight through the clouds. "Excuse me a moment, will you?" I said to everyone. "I'll be right back."

I ran up to my room and took Effie's journal from the nightstand. I opened it and read the words of her poem again.

For now I scry beyond the rods of sunlight
In the mists, in the haze

I turned to the page where I'd left off. She'd been about to render another warning, but I'd not had a chance to read it.

Another dream—most unusual.

I am in a dim room, surrounded by beauty. It reminds me a bit of your mother's morning room with its birdcages, seashell collections, paintings and Japanese prints. But not the seashells. And the paintings are a bit different. Oriental, definitely, but somehow different. There are many birdcages and the birds are black, black as thunder clouds. And a little Buddha gazes at me from the corner, his arms outstretched. He says 'beware the maker of idols.'

I don't know what it means. I hope you will.

I shuddered. I had not read it and would not have understood even if I had. I did now. I turned ahead a few pages.

Rutted roads, cobbled footpaths, houses made of bamboo and thatch, mangoes and guavas, sweet dates and coconuts. And rosaries made of cowrie shells.

You asked me once about what I saw for your future. You asked:

"Would you tell me if you saw me working a hospital in one of your dreams? If you saw me tending to patients, not as a nurse but as a physician? If you tell me you have, I shall know it will come true. You are never wrong."

And I had said, "Poppy, I do not conjure things or summon dreams. They come or they do not. I have no control. And no, I have not seen you in a hospital."

I told you then about the railway tragedy that was to come. I saw you there. And now I see you not in a surgeon's apron, but in a deep-blue sari. I always told you that blue is your colour.

You will be the hero of that epic, my sweet friend. People will think you work miracles.

She was not describing England, nor America. It sounded a great deal like the excerpts from letters that Victor had sent to Michael from India.

I closed the diary. It made no sense. Victor wanted nothing to do with me. And how could I leave Sherlock? Now? When it was so clear that he did care for me? We were almost there.

I went back to the dining room, sat down next to Oscar and asked, "How does it go with you?"

He wiped his lips daintily and laughed. "Well, not so exciting as things around here! Soon another hanging at Wandsworth Prison—I hope I never see the inside of that place!"

"If you do, I am certain you shall write a poem or ballad about it," Sherlock said.

I shot him a nasty glance.

"Certainly I could. About your uncle's arrest, Poppy," Oscar continued, ignoring Sherlock. "And about this killer who was captured right in your home. Perhaps I should write a drama about all of these events."

"You should just finish your collections of poems," Aunt Susan chided.

"A collection?" I asked. "What is it called?"

"*Poems.*"

"How creative and innovative," Sherlock sniped.

"Be quiet, Sherlock," I snapped. "Tell me more, Oscar. Recite one for us."

"None of them is finished," he said.

This made me think of Rabi, the young man at the museum.

"That's all right. Tell us just a little then."

He puffed out his chest. "I'm not sure if this is the first stanza or the second. But . . . well . . . . " He took a breath and said,

268

"For, sweet, to feel is better than to know/And wisdom is a childless heritage/One pulse of passion—youth's first fiery glow—Are worth the hoarded proverbs of the sage/Vex not thy soul with dead philosophy/Have we not lips to kiss with, hearts to love, and eyes to see!"

I turned my head to look at Sherlock. Was he *listening?*

Then I glanced around the room. Uncle and Sherlock were engaged in a conversation about Hume's philosophical essays on euthanasia, a topic I wished to learn nothing more about. Archibald, wearing the silly suit that Sherlock had purchased for him, was grabbing more food from every plate, and his young cohorts Ollie and Rattle followed suit. Mother spoke to Michael as she bounced my little nephew on her knee. I noticed that Michael's glass of champagne had not been touched. I was glad of it.

And Aunt Susan, what a pretty picture was she, as she rocked little Billy.

Those hands were meant to swaddle babies, I thought. *Those arms to hold them close.*

I had an epiphany. "Archibald," I called. "Would you join me in Dr. Sacker's study for a moment?"

Sherlock disengaged himself from conversation for a moment to stare at me but said nothing.

"'as I done sumfin' wrong, Miss?" Archie asked.

"No, of course not. Just give me a moment of your time. Bring your glass of milk and the muffin."

He grabbed both and followed me.

"Wha' is i', Miss?"

"Archie, I was thinking. My aunt and uncle have always wanted children. Do you think perhaps . . . well, I was just wondering if maybe they could take Billy—and you—in. I have not broached the subject with them yet, but—"

"Take us in? Would yer be meanin' t' be stayin' in fis place? Me and me bruva?" he asked, throwing his arms into the air.

"Well, yes. You would have fine clothes and plenty of food. You could get an education."

"Me? Naw. I's 'appy with me lot."

"Archie, you live on the streets. And Mr. Holmes takes advantage of you."

"Mr. 'olmes keeps us busy, Miss," he admonished. "We likes wha' we does."

"But Billy is just a baby, Archie. A little toddler, like my nephew."

He thought a moment. "Well, yah, Billy's anothe' matta all tageva. 'e's a good boy."

"Yes, yes, that's my point. If he were educated, perhaps he could grow up to have a far easier life than yours. Become a page or even much more. I wanted to speak to you first, of course. Before I consult with Uncle and Aunt Susan."

"Lemme thin' on i'. Can I go back t' eatin' now?"

"Of course," I laughed.

"And Miss, call me Bill. Everybody calls me Bill. Or Wiggins. I's th' li'l one 'ho's Billy now."

"Yes, Master Wiggins. As you wish," I said. "Now, run along."

He ran from the room and before I could rise to leave, Uncle came in and closed the door behind him. His expression spoke volumes and I knew he had much to say. He opened up a folded piece of paper and read from it.

We shall be notes in that great Symphony
Whose cadence circles through the rhythmic spheres,
And all the live World's throbbing heart shall be
One with our heart, the stealthy creeping years
Have lost their terrors now, we shall not die,
The Universe itself shall be our Immortality!

"What is that, Uncle?"

"A few more lines of Oscar's poem. I asked him if I could borrow them for a moment. It's quite good, actually. I rather hope there is some form of immortality. For the sake of those young men we've recently buried. Oscar can be quite profound."

"He can be that . . . sometimes. "

A shadow crossed his face.

"What is it, Uncle?"

"I think we should talk, Poppy. Don't you?"

52

Uncle sat down and folded up the piece of paper. "I just wanted to say I am so very sorry, Poppy."

"I'm the one who should be sorry, Uncle. How I ever could have doubted you . . . entertained such horrible thoughts—"

"No, no," he said cupping my hands with his. "I'm sure when you saw all my little notes in margins and when I wouldn't speak to anyone, you became suspicious."

"And why, Uncle? Why wouldn't you tell us what was going on?"

"As Sherlock told you, it was an elabourate ruse to catch the killer out. We all thought that if I were tossed in gaol and refused to speak, then everyone would think me guilty. And then Sherlock had the article placed in the newspaper . . . well, we thought Mr. Brown would make preparations to flee. It never occurred to me to see if anyone at the museum . . . that this Oriental fellow—"

At that moment, I suppose I was like a frantic writer, filled with a jumble of confused thoughts about Sherlock and Uncle, the mercy killings, the dead men, most especially the young reporter. I did not know how to express myself.

So I simply said, "It's over. That's what counts, Uncle. And I love you."

"But all the time I was in prison, I did think a great deal about euthanasia, about everything that's been written on the subject and how the debate goes on and on."

"And so it shall. But, Uncle, you cannot goad me into a philosophical discussion right now. I am just ever so glad you are home. But I do have a proposition for you."

"A proposition?"

I told him my thoughts about Archie and his little brother Billy. Then I waited.

He sat back, looking a bit stunned. "Children? Here? As if they were our own kith and kindred?"

"I don't know about arrangements, Uncle. Archie does not seem inclined to give up his little brother completely. But perhaps clothing, food, some education. Something to give little Billy a chance—"

"I should like a reliable page one day," Sherlock said as he burst into the room, champagne bottle in hand. "I think it's worthy of consideration, Dr. Sacker."

"Do you now?" Uncle asked, smiling. Then he slapped his palms on his knees, rose and said, "I imagine the two of you should like a bit of privacy."

Sherlock poured some champagne into a glass and gave it to Uncle. They lifted the glasses to one another.

"In all likelihood, you have some totally unlawful and dangerous plotting of another adventure together. Good fun!" Uncle said. Then he left the room, closing the door behind him.

Sherlock sat down and stared at me. "Well?"

"Well, what?"

"I suspect you wish to discuss some things with me. Please, no heart-shaped notes of gratitude."

"Gratitude!" I scoffed. "As if you ever evoke feelings of gratitude!"

I turned to look out the window. I could still hear the thunder rumbling ever closer and the rain dripping from the trees, polishing the leaves that would not stay for much longer. In a short time, it would be autumn and then winter, that ever-so-quiet and still season of diamonds sparkling on the snow.

I had a sweet memory, a clear image of Effie and me, the two of us skating in Norfolk. I could hear in my mind the blades cutting across the icy ponds. Me, dressed in the warm pantaloons she'd made for me and my heavy, blue wool coat; she still wearing her long, cumbersome skirt, made in gold to match her hair. And a white fur hat and muff, and her O'Flahertie tartan scarf trailing behind her in the wind. She was like a healing bouquet of stamens, delicate as the gossamer filaments, like anther, sweet and ready to burst forth, weaving into hearts with her infectious laughter. She skated with such zeal, as she did with every endeavour. As she had lived.

"Poppy, you must know, you *must*, how difficult this is for me," Sherlock said.

"What?"

"It is difficult for me to—"

"To love. To trust. You feel you cannot have your work and have me as well."

"Yes."

"You would trample on such treasures rather than extract them."

"Poppy, I—"

He rose and stood near the fireplace. For a moment, he reminded me of a painting in St. Paul's, a depiction of Jesus preparing to knock on an overgrown and long-unopened door. It illustrated a passage from Revelations: "Behold, I stand at the door and knock; if any man hear My voice, and open the door, I will come in to him, and will sup with him, and he with Me."

The artist said that he painted the picture by what he thought to be Divine command, unworthy though he was. And I sat there now, as if by Divine Command, still hoping that one day Sherlock might knock on my long-unopened door again.

"It's all right, Sherlock. Truly."

"I won't change my mind, Poppy. I cannot. It is too dangerous for you."

And too dangerous for your heart, I thought.

"But you would still like me to be your assistant?"

He grinned broadly. "Well, yes, of course!"

Sherlock's heart was bound by crude blocks of ashlar, and nothing I could do right now would coax the blossoms through such a finely dressed stone wall.

So, for now, I would linger in the vicinity of Sherlock's heart, waiting for him to knock again.

EPILOGUE

"I don' see no elephants," Archie said as I shifted the balance of little Billy's weight against my chest. "You said fere'd be firteen. And clowns. You said fere'd be clowns."

"Ten or more of them," I laughed. "They'll come along, Archie."

"Wiggins," he reminded me and I nodded.

"Yes, Master Wiggins. The elephants and the clowns will come, I promise."

I glanced over at Michael who was similarly trying to distribute Alexander's weight as we waited for the Lord Mayor of London's Show to come around the bend.

It was a dark, dull November morning and a heavy fog hung over the city. I wondered how the gilt coaches, the steel armour and the gay, coloured flags would even be discernible.

"Will we see the Prince, Miss?" Ollie asked, tugging at my skirt. "It's 'is birthday."

"Birthday!" Rattle screamed. "Will there be cake?"

Laughing, Oscar said, "I don't think so, little one. But you never know. Our prince is full of surprises," adding a wink.

"So it's official now, Oscar, is it not?" Michael asked. "You've completed your studies at Oxford?"

"Yes, Michael. Well, almost. My official degree will be registered on the 28th."

"And then?"

"I shall settle here for a while. But I am thinking about going to America."

"America!"

"Poppy," Oscar whispered in my ear. "Come with me."

"Why would I go there?"

"Why would you stay *here*?"

I studied his face a moment. Then he said, "I am almost finished with my poem. You should read it. You should heed it."

"What should I heed?"

"'I am too young to live without desire, too young art thou to waste this summer night.' Do not waste your summer nights on Sherlock, Poppy."

I shook my head and kissed Billy's head, wondering if he and my nephew were the only babies I would ever hold in my arms.

The parade was grand, as it had been since the twelfth century. Young boys sold little books with brightly coloured pictures representing the procession. Little girls dressed in pink stockings and boys in canary breeches watched the parade and begged for sweets, for all the shop windows were filled with them. The yellow coach of the Master of the Company and the carriage of the Worshipful Master of Broderer's passed by. Then came men in uniforms of red and blue and the Worshipful Company of Bakers. Some of them held their banner high, the one that said, "Praise God for All;" others carried large bouquets of flowers. And after them came the Vintners' Company, its commissioners bearing shields, and the Bargemaster in full uniform, followed by the Swan Uppers, those who look after the swans of London and mark the young swans in the spring. They were dressed in dark cloth jackets spliced with white and blue and white striped jersey shirts and white trousers.

The crowed roared with delight when the elephants approached, dressed in their Oriental trappings and howdahs, ridden by boys not much older than Archie. Gorgeous, magnificent, triumphant, I thought, as I glanced at my nephew and saw them through a child's eyes. Several knights in steel armour, bearing lances and pennons and mounted on magnificent chargers, followed and then came the Epping Forest rangers in their green velvet coats and hats with long feathers.

Hats Effie would have loved the hats, I thought, and I saw in Michael's eyes that he had just had the same pinching memory.

Trumpeters, aldermen, a gorgeous coach with hammer-cloth of red and gold and then four fine horses bringing in the Lord Mayor and his household cavalry in their crimson coats atop white horses.

When the parade was almost over, I gave Billy over to his brother and told him I was heading to the museum. There was no point waiting any longer for Sherlock. Clearly, he was not coming.

"Kin I come, too, Miss?"

"No, not this time. I'll see you later back at my uncle's house for lunch."

I walked to the museum and just before I went inside, I heard Sherlock call out my name.
I turned.

Out of breath, he bent over and let out a few puffs into the cold, still air. The sun had finally peeked through and seemed to settle behind him like a halo.

"Well, Mr. Holmes. Nice of you to join us at the parade."

"You know those are not things I wish to attend, Poppy. But I did go. I sought you out; how do you think I knew where to find you? Master Wiggins told me you were on your way here."

"So what was so pressing that you were detained?"

"Mycroft. What else? He is insane because some of the Queen's swans have been slaughtered."

My mind reeled back to my quiet moments in Victoria Park, watching the swans swim. Watching them love.

"But that's criminal."

"Indeed, it is. But not something in which I wish to be involved. Nevertheless, I am on my way to inspect one of the

278

creatures to see if something interesting is afoot. I've had it taken to the morgue at St. Bart's. Will you join me?"

"Yes, I will. But not just yet. Run along. I'll catch up to you."

He kissed me flagrantly, right out there in the open, and I thought for a moment he might clap his hands.

He is elated, I thought. *On to yet another case.*

As he turned and walked swiftly down the street, I went into the museum and visited the room with the Buddha Vairocana, his hands still those of a teacher, telling us that truth ends ignorance. I was staring at him, studying him when I heard a voice.

I twirled in the direction of the sound and saw Rabi, the lovely young man from India.

"Rabi, how wonderful to see you. You are still here."

"Yes. For a bit longer."

"How are you?"

"Longing for home."

Longing. I understood longing.

"And you, Miss Poppy. You are still unhappy. You also long for something. Do you wish to be somewhere else?"

I sighed and paced. "Sometimes, Rabi. Sometimes I do."

"But you are hesitant."

I nodded.

"You cannot cross the sea merely by standing and staring at the water."

I stopped and smiled at him. "No, I suppose not."

"You do look very sad, Miss."

I started to pace again. "I am sad. And frustrated. You see," I added, wringing my hands, "it's just that I have this . . . this friend who is infuriating. He values work and logic above all else and he is going to miss so many things in life."

Rabi's eyes narrowed. "Then I am sad for him as well, for a mind all logic is like a knife all blade. It makes the hand bleed that uses it. One must embrace all of life. One should see each morning for the first time as a newborn that has no name sees it."

I stared at him, wide-eyed. "Yes, yes!" I cried in a tone a bit louder than my 'museum voice.' "You're exactly right. I agree completely."

"We should appreciate the boundless fields, the songs of birds, the shade of the trees and the shadows."

I nodded and felt tears stinging.

"But weeping is wasted, Miss, on one who does not understand why you cry."

"Yes, Rabi. I've thought of that. Often."

"Maybe you should go away. Find a peaceful village with ancient palms and dark green foliage and paths that go on out of sight."

I gulped. He was so right. It did me no good to fantasize if I was not prepared to act. It did no good to long for a man who would not give love, who would not give light, who liked living in danger and darkness. And then I thought of Victor, of India. Who knows how I might feel in a new place?

"But this friend . . . you love him?" Rabi asked.

I nodded again. "God knows why."

He laughed a laugh that was a like a whisper through the trees. "Perhaps only God knows why, Miss. After all, love is an endless mystery, for it has nothing else to explain it."

"A mystery. Yes, Rabi, but I know that if only he would open his heart to me . . . ." I stopped and stared at him. Why, I wondered, was I so open with my feelings to this stranger? Yet this stranger seemed to know me so well. Six months earlier, I had thought I was over Sherlock. I thought I had put a stop to my ridiculous fantasies. But when I saw him again, he had stolen in once more like a thief, stealthily watching, descending into my heart and numbing my blood-thirsty ambition. Even after we had parted, I realized now, he lingered like a drowsy rumble in my ear, then settled in by my side, immovable despite his cold arms and icy heart.

"If you love him, Miss, do not try to possess him. Love should not claim possession, but must give freedom."

How did he know? I wondered. How did he know that I was not prepared to give up on Sherlock just yet?

"Rabi, you are so wise for one so young."

He shrugged. "It is simply that I believe we should not dwell on the past or worry about the future as much as we do. It is better to be like the butterfly. The butterfly counts not months but moments, and has time enough."

I felt the blood drain from my face and swallowed a gasp as I recalled my conversation with Oscar about Effie reincarnating as a Swallowtail. "Oh," was the only word I could croak out as I gazed at him in awe.

After a moment, I looked at his hands, in which he held his notebook. "I see you have your notebook at the ready. Are you writing something new?"

"Yes. Another poem."

"Unfinished?"

"Yes, unfinished."

"May I hear some of it?"

"Let love melt into memory and pain into songs. Let the flight through the sky end in the folding of the wings over the nest."

I felt myself choke back a sob. "That's so beautiful, Rabi. I can't wait to hear the rest."

"Someday, Miss. Someday."

We said adieu—he specifically said, "Til we meet again," and he disappeared down the hallway.

I walked out into the sunlight, brilliant now, shining all over my dark, dangerous city.

"Effie, can I do that someday?" I asked aloud. "Can I let love melt into memory and pain into songs?" I said aloud.

Wondering what new adventure I was getting myself into this time, I turned to start walking to St. Bart's as the new ring of twelve pealed out from St. Paul's.

Also from MX Publishing

MX Publishing is the world's largest specialist Sherlock Holmes publisher, with over a hundred titles and fifty authors creating the latest in Sherlock Holmes fiction and non-fiction.

From traditional short stories and novels to travel guides and quiz books, MX Publishing cater for all Holmes fans.

The collection includes leading titles such as *Benedict Cumberbatch In Transition* and *The Norwood Author* which won the 2011 Howlett Award (Sherlock Holmes Book of the Year).

MX Publishing also has one of the largest communities of Holmes fans on Facebook with regular contributions from dozens of authors.

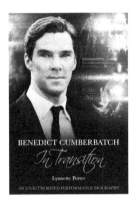

www.mxpublishing.com

Also from MX Publishing

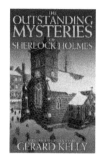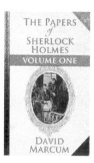

Our bestselling books are our short story collections;

'Lost Stories of Sherlock Holmes' , 'The Outstanding Mysteries of Sherlock Holmes', The Papers of Sherlock Holmes Volume 1 and 2, 'Untold Adventures of Sherlock Holmes' (and the sequel 'Studies in Legacy) and 'Sherlock Holmes in Pursuit', 'The Cotswold Werewolf and Other Stories of Sherlock Holmes' – and many more......

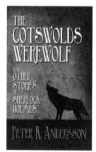

www.mxpublishing.com

Also from MX Publishing

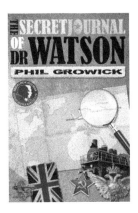

"Phil Growick's, 'The Secret Journal of Dr Watson', is an adventure which takes place in the latter part of Holmes and Watson's lives. They are entrusted by HM Government (although not officially) and the King no less to undertake a rescue mission to save the Romanovs, Russia's Royal family from a grisly end at the hand of the Bolsheviks. There is a wealth of detail in the story but not so much as would detract us from the enjoyment of the story. Espionage, counter-espionage, the ace of spies himself, double-agents, double-crossers...all these flit across the pages in a realistic and exciting way. All the characters are extremely well-drawn and Mr Growick, most importantly, does not falter with a very good ear for Holmesian dialogue indeed. Highly recommended. A five-star effort."

The Baker Street Society

Also from MX Publishing

The Conan Doyle Notes (The Hunt For Jack The Ripper)

"Holmesians have long speculated on the fact that the Ripper murders aren't mentioned in the canon, though the obvious reason is undoubtedly the correct one: even if Conan Doyle had suspected the killer's identity he'd never have considered mentioning it in the context of a fictional entertainment. Ms Madsen's novel equates his silence with that of the dog in the night-time, assuming that Conan Doyle did know who the Ripper was but chose not to say – which, of course, implies that good old stand-by, the government cover-up. It seems unlikely to me that the Ripper was anyone famous or distinguished, but fiction is not fact, and "The Conan Doyle Notes" is a gripping tale, with an intelligent, courageous and very likable protagonist in DD McGil."

The Sherlock Holmes Society of London

www.mxpublishing.com

Also from MX Publishing

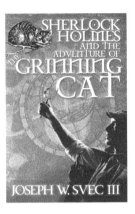

Sherlock Holmes and The Adventure of The Grinning Cat

"Joseph Svec, III is brilliant in entwining two endearing and enduring classics of literature, blending the factual with the fantastical; the playful with the pensive; and the mischievous with the mysterious. We shall, all of us young and old, benefit with a cup of tea, a tranquil afternoon, and a copy of Sherlock Holmes, The Adventure of the Grinning Cat."

Linda Hein, Hein & Co Used Books, and founding officer of the Amador County Holmes Hounds Sherlockian Society

www.ingramcontent.com/pod-product-compliance
Ingram Content Group UK Ltd.
Pitfield, Milton Keynes, MK11 3LW, UK
UKHW021453140125
4105UKWH00017B/86